WAKING THE GODS

THEIR DARK VALKYRIE #4

EVA CHASE

Waking the Gods

Book 4 in the Their Dark Valkyrie series

First Digital Edition, 2018

Cover design: Rebecca Frank

Ebook ISBN: 978-1-989096-26-0

Paperback ISBN: 978-1-989096-27-7

 Created with Vellum

1

Aria

To some people, a bad day was when it was raining, and their heel broke, and then they were late for work. Those people had never had a bloodthirsty giant appear out of nowhere on a flaming bridge ready to slaughter them and everyone they cared about.

Right now, as the giant Surt descended toward me and my gods, swinging his fire-laced sword with a vicious grin, I wished I were one of those people with their blissfully mundane lives.

"Hello, Asgard," he bellowed. "I've finally come to finish what I started."

The flames of his bridge arced down to singe the grass in the field where I'd just been having my first really peaceful day in Asgard. Heat wafted over my skin, and the thin smoke coated my nose and mouth. With a twitch of my shoulders, I urged out my valkyrie wings.

They'd been a part of me for so long now that their weight as they sprouted from my back felt more like a comfort than a burden. I grabbed my old switchblade from my pocket, wishing I had a larger weapon on hand.

Thor and Baldur, who'd been sprawled in the grass enjoying the peace with me, braced themselves at my sides. Thor hefted his magical hammer, his square jaw clenched and his normally warm brown eyes now blazing with fury. Baldur's hands beamed with the supernatural glow he could turn into a weapon of his own. His normally bright boyish face had shadowed.

Loki sped over on his shoes of flight to join us. "Lovely to see you," he hollered to Surt. "You've saved us the trouble of tracking you down. We'll finish this war, all right, but not with the outcome I think you'd prefer."

He'd grabbed a sword of his own. His other lithe hand held a crackling ball of fire, the same pale red as his hair.

Surt chuckled, low and rolling, as he strode down the blazing bridge. The flames shuddered under his brawny form. He was nearly as big as Thor, and his magic made him a formidable foe—but there were a bunch of us and only one of him.

At least, that's what it looked like in that first moment. Then a rush of shambling bodies poured over the peak of the bridge's arc after him.

My heart seized at the sight of their deathly pale faces. The smell of damp rot reached my nose an instant later. They were draugr—the undead figures Surt had been collecting into an army.

But we'd *destroyed* his army. Just yesterday, we'd

smashed his hidden caverns to bury the creatures and then burned them to ash. Where had this mob of soldiers come from?

Something gleamed on their skin and in their hair. Streaks of water, I realized—melted water. Here and there, flecks of ice and snow still clung to their clothes, disintegrating with the bridge's heat as they marched down toward us.

Somewhere behind me, Hod cursed. Even if he couldn't see the threat we faced, the god of darkness must have caught enough from scents and sounds to understand the gist of it.

"Not so confident all of a sudden?" Surt rumbled. "Did you really think I'd keep all my eggs in one basket? Underestimating your enemies has always been your downfall, Asgardians."

"So, you carted most of your army off to Niflheim," Loki said, his tone acidic. "How very clever. You're lucky they thawed."

Niflheim was a frozen realm that the gods had mentioned in passing. I'd never been there. It was the last place we'd have thought to check for the army of a giant who was so keen on fire, that was for sure. Especially when we'd had every reason to believe we'd already decimated that army.

My heart thumped faster. Had our victory yesterday meant anything at all? We must have taken out at least part of his forces. But he might have gathered more draugr than we'd ever suspected.

"We destroyed the army you left behind in Muspelheim, and we'll destroy the one you've brought here," Thor said. "No giant takes Asgard!"

He raised his hammer, and the other three gods converged around me. After all the battles behind us, we moved instinctively, following the sense of connection that had bound us together ever since the four of them had combined their talents to bring me back from the dead as a valkyrie.

As I sprang forward, I saw Freya arrive beside us, her golden hair streaming behind her. She swung her sword with a bolt of magic.

"This will be your end, cur," a sharp voice shouted. Tyr came charging up, swinging a dagger with his remaining hand. I guessed the war god could still put up a good fight even missing part of one limb.

Just like every other time I'd fought beside the four gods I was bound to, my awareness expanded with a sense of their pulses thudding in time with mine, the energy surging through their bodies as they launched their attacks. And just like before, their powers merged as they threw them forward. Flares of light and darkness searing with a fiery intensity swirled around Thor's hurled hammer, straight toward Surt.

At the same moment, the giant jerked his hand, and the bridge lurched. It tossed him in an epic leap over our heads and sent the rest of his army spilling down toward us even faster. Thor's hammer and the blaze of magic around it toppled a dozen draugr, but there were hundreds of them, maybe thousands.

The thunder god spun around as Mjolnir flew back to his hand. Loki, Hod, and Baldur drew closer in a circle around me. We had the giant at one side of us and the draugr behind us now.

Surt left us no time to regroup. He was already lunging at us, fire streaming from his sword. We flung ourselves out of the way of the lashes of fire. Loki toppled the first line of draugr with a wave of his own flames, but others raised shields that propelled the heat back toward us. His scorching magic wasn't much use when these soldiers had been equipped by an enemy with his own affinity for fire.

Odin appeared at the edge of the field, striding toward us with his silver spear. Tyr and Freya darted along the sides of the horde. They were trying to surround the giant in turn, I suspected, but Surt hurtled forward again—toward us and then around us as he whipped his sword through the air.

Thor yanked me to the side, but one of those tongues of flame sliced across my calf, sizzling straight through my jeans and, it felt, down to the bone. A stabbing pain radiated up my leg.

"Little valkyrie," Surt said, not even stopping for breath before he charged again. "So small and frail among the gods. Yet somehow you broke my raven's prison. I don't think you can escape *me*."

Thor squeezed my shoulder, I gave a quick nod, and the five of us moved together to meet the giant's attack. Somewhere to my left, a draug let out a groaning sound as one of the other gods must have crushed the life from it. Thor and Loki pushed ahead of me, Baldur's light blazing over Thor's hammer and Hod's darkness twining around Loki's sword.

But Surt cut his charge short. He planted his feet with a thud that shook the ground and slashed out with his blade. Some of the flames that spilled from it shattered as Loki's sword cut through them. Others smashed into nothingness with the impact of Thor's hammer. One thick hissing current shot straight at me.

I tried to dodge, but my wounded leg wobbled under me with a fresh spear of pain. With a flap of my wings and a hiss through my teeth, I threw myself to the side, but I wasn't fast enough. The streak of fire slammed into my arm and torso, throwing me to the ground.

I really cried out then. A thousand burning needles might as well have jabbed into my skin.

An instant later, a cool blanket of shadow dropped over me, smothering the flames. "Ari!" Hod said hoarsely.

Surt bellowed. I shoved myself upright, stumbled, gasped, and clenched my teeth against the pain. We had to keep fighting. The gods needed me. Even if half my body felt as if it were still on fire.

A thicker smoky scent prickled my nose. Some of the draugr had barreled past us to reach the halls of Asgard. The enchanted weapons they carried had set fire to the thatched roofs and anything flammable inside. Sparks blew from the windows in a flurry like glowing snow.

No. This was my home now, as much a home as I had. I hadn't fought all the battles I'd been through already to lose this place to some asshole giant.

"Keep at him," I choked out. "We can take him."

But the draugr were swarming all around us too. Blazing knives and pikes stabbed at us from every angle, and Surt sprang at us with another roar.

Thor moved to hurl his hammer, and a draug's blade sliced into his forearm deep enough to spill blood. Surt aimed his blast straight at me.

He'd called me out for a reason. That thought hit me with stark clarity in the instant as his fireball whipped toward me. I was his main target. Because I was weaker than the gods, and because I had strengths he didn't understand.

He wanted to destroy *me* more than anyone—or at least to destroy me first.

This time I threw myself upward, into the air as fast as I could sweep my wings. The fireball crashed into my thighs and propelled me several agonizing feet through the air. My wings shuddered with the pain. I dropped to the ground and rolled, barely conscious of anything except the vicious throbbing crackle and the need to make it stop somehow.

I ended up facedown in the grass, smoke penetrating the earthy smell of the field, every muscle in my body knotted. Just the movement of the air against my raw skin made me suck in a sob. I wanted to push myself up, to move, to do *something*, but my limbs refused.

Shouts and the clang of weapons echoed around me. A groan that sounded more godly than zombie reverberated through the air. More thuds. More warbles of magical fire. I flinched at the sound.

Someone crouched down beside me. "Keep going," I said, my voice coming out a rasp. "Keep fighting. Don't worry. I—"

"That's enough talking, pixie," Loki said, wry but

strained at the same time. "We're getting you out of here."

Out of the field? But Surt—the draugr—

He lifted me, even his gentlest embrace turning my body into a maelstrom of pain. Tears trickled down my face and stung my scraped cheeks. I wasn't sure I could feel anything below my ribs anymore. Not anything except that vicious searing.

"Let's go!" Loki called out, and then he started to run, cradling me against him to shelter me from the wind that stirred when he sped across the landscape. I managed to focus on the world around me for long enough to realize that we weren't just heading for shelter in the city. He was racing past Asgard's buildings, past the stone-tiled streets, toward the edge of the realm, where Odin could call out a bridge of his own that shimmered like a rainbow.

He was taking me out of Asgard.

"No," I murmured. If we left, then Surt would have won. We couldn't lose the realm of the gods to him and his zombies.

"It'll be fine, Ari," Loki said in his breezy way. "We'll patch you right up and then put that charcoal-brained kin of mine back in his place. Where is the damned Allfather?"

He wasn't able to keep the urgency completely out of his voice with that last question. It occurred to me then, through the haze of pain, that maybe we weren't letting Surt win by leaving. Maybe he'd already won.

2

Thor

With every fall of my feet as I rushed after Loki past our city, I felt as if I were leaving part of myself behind. My teeth gritted against the rage surging inside me.

We'd been complacent. We'd assumed our victory before it had been truly ours. And now Surt and his army had all but overpowered us. The halls of Asgard were burning. Our *valkyrie* had been burning.

I could barely make out Ari's slim form in the trickster's arms, but a few strands of her blond hair flew out with the breeze. The ends were singed black. I hadn't heard her say a word since Loki had picked her up.

"As soon as we have somewhere to take shelter, I should be able to heal her," Baldur said, racing along on a beam of light beside me. Despite my brother's words, his face was grim. Healing Ari would depend on her still being alive when we made it to somewhere Surt couldn't blast her again.

"He went right at her," Hod muttered from just behind us. "He wanted to take her down first."

"Because he knows how strong she is—how strong she makes us," I said. A burst of pride penetrated the fury in my chest for a second as I remembered how Ari had leapt up to fight the giant and his army without the slightest hesitation.

But her strength had revealed our own weaknesses when we'd lost her. We gods had battled Surt and an army alongside him before, during Ragnarok, but there'd been dozens more in Asgard then. The seven of us remaining hadn't had much hope of pushing back both him and his mass of undead that he'd armed with blazing blades and shields.

Our main hope had been the heightened power the four of us had discovered together—the power that linked us through Ari. Without her, our weapons and magic wouldn't merge and amplify. From the first moment she'd stumbled, I'd felt that connection waver. When Surt's last blast had left her slumped and charred, our attempts to halt him and his draugr had faltered completely.

I'd managed to clip his shoulder with Mjolnir, but he'd barely seemed to feel it. And at the same time, one of his undead soldiers had stabbed a brutal wound just below my ribs. If I'd dodged any slower, I might have lost my liver. The cut made my hasty breaths burn. With the blood that was dripping down my side, I really was leaving part of myself behind here.

We'd be back. We'd be back, and we'd reclaim it *all.*

Freya whipped around us with her falcon cloak and hurled a bolt of her magic toward the attackers on our heels. Her lovely face was tight with pain. A burn streaked across her other forearm all the way to the hand she held her sword with.

I couldn't let her and the others behind me do all the fighting. As we reached the stone tiles of the courtyard that stretched almost all the way to the point where the rainbow bridge would form, I sprang around and landed with a thump of my feet that would have made the clouds thunder over Midgard beneath us.

In a split-second, swift as lightning, I took in the scene we were fleeing. Freya had dipped down to cover Odin as he slashed his spear through the line of draugr that had nearly caught up with him. Hod paused for just long enough to heave a wave of shadow that caught a few of the undead figures before the others sliced it apart with their fiery weapons. Tyr had lost his dagger somewhere in the fray, but he was making use of what he could. His warrior arm flung a stone hard enough to smash a draug's skull.

Hundreds of draugr were still charging toward us, Surt near the fore of their crowd. More were pouring through our city, setting fire to whatever they could reach. My hands clenched at my sides. Smoke coated my mouth and clouded the sky. How *dare* he degrade our home this way?

If we could just topple Surt—if we could take him down, his whole assault would crumble. The draugr had no stake here beyond what he'd ordered them to do.

I flipped my hammer in my hand and pitched it toward the giant with every ounce of strength and fury I had in me.

Mjolnir's shining surface shimmered through the air, but even with the speed I'd given it, Surt saw it coming. He snatched up the body of a hulking draug in front of him and threw it toward my hammer to shield himself while he dodged to the side.

The draug exploded in a hail of undead flesh that its companions barely appeared to notice. Mjolnir whipped onward, fast enough to make Surt's beard twitch—but it smashed through a line of draugr just beside him instead. His harsh laugh ripped through the air as my hammer flew back to my hand. A growl of frustration reverberated in my throat.

Just by stopping for those few seconds, I'd let his army gain several feet on us. I hadn't destroyed enough of them to make any real difference. I caught Mjolnir, meaning to throw myself after Loki toward the edge of the realm. But Surt lunged forward right then with a swipe of his sword.

That eerie fire it carried coursed off its gleaming surface and hissed toward us like a raging forest fire. Hod tossed another wave of shadow at the flames, and Freya cast out a waft of magic that chilled my skin as it rushed past me.

Most of the flames sputtered out. One small lick scorched across the tiles to where Tyr had been standing and heaved him into the air.

Surt had used his fire magic that way at the start of the battle, when he'd made his bridge launch him over us right into Asgard. Now he had it hurl my fellow god all the way to his flaming blade. Tyr tumbled onto the ground in front of the giant. Even as I jerked back my hammer, Surt sliced his sword down on the war god's neck.

The blade severed clean through Tyr's neck, leaving behind a smoking stump. I lost sight of his head in an instant as it rolled into the horde of draugr.

"One god down, just a few more to go," Surt hollered with a vicious grin. He spun his sword in the air. "Your people rose once. Let's see if he will again—or if that blessing ended with his second chance."

My gut lurched. As I hustled backward, away from the draugr's continuing charge, my gaze shot to the field where we'd all risen after Ragnarok—the field that was now a scorched ruin. Surt snatched a spear from one of his soldiers and stabbed it into Tyr's chest. He hefted the limp headless body in the air and brandished it like some kind of trophy.

Our former bodies, mangled by Ragnarok's battle, hadn't lingered when we'd returned. They'd vanished with our resurrection. I watched Surt's display for several thuds of my heart, willing Tyr's form to disappear, to reform whole and well in the distance.

The warrior god's blackened legs dangled lifelessly. His body stayed solid—solid and dead.

Surt left out another bellow of a laugh. He flung the spear with Tyr's body at the nearest hall, so hard the weapon dug into the stone. My comrade's body hung there from the building's wall. Not just a trophy. A warning.

We hadn't known for sure whether Asgard's gift of rebirth could touch us again, whether we were fully immortal or merely graced with endless life as long as we protected that life. Now the question was answered with gruesome certainty.

It wasn't only Ari who could die in this battle. It could be any of us.

Surt picked up speed, running at us with a wave of his arm to urge the draugr faster too. I wrenched my gaze from Tyr's far-too-mortal body and spun on my heel.

Loki had reached the edge of the realm. Odin, just catching up, thumped the end of his spear against the ground. Bifrost arced out through the air and down into the clouds, its rainbow glow the most welcome sight I'd ever seen. Ari's body huddled in Loki's arms looked nearly as limp as Tyr's did. My rage sputtered out beneath the chill of my fear for her.

"That's right," Surt bellowed. "Turn tail like the cowards you really are. Asgard is mine!"

Every particle of my being roared in defiance of that statement, but I couldn't see any way to defeat him now. I dashed for the bridge with the others. Hod's shadows snaked past me over the tiles, helping guide his way.

He and I reached the bridge last. I grabbed his elbow, hurrying him onto the rainbow's gleaming surface. Loki was already racing down into the clouds. As I hustled on after him, Bifrost's surface faded behind me.

"I won't let him follow us," my father said, his low voice sounding even more hollow than usual. One of Surt's attacks had burned part of the broad brim of his hat to a crisp. Ash dappled his shoulder over his dark blue traveling cloak. "Neither he nor his fiends will set foot on my bridge."

I wasn't sure the giant even meant to try. Surt's laughter carried after us as we fled down toward the world of humankind, but it sounded distant now, as if he'd halted his chase.

He *would* follow us down to Midgard before long, though, wouldn't he? From what we'd understood, his plan was to take control over both of the remaining stable realms among the nine. It made sense that he'd started with Asgard—smaller, and easier to catch us in a vulnerable state by surprising us there. But the vast and wonderful realm of humanity would be his next target.

Tension wound around my lungs, sharpened by the still-seeping wound on my side and the other on my arm, and by the sight of Midgard's forests and towns below the clouds. I was meant to be the protector of humanity, more than any of the other gods. This realm was my responsibility. I hadn't managed to protect my own realm from the invader. I had to do better by the mortals here, who were so much less equipped to fight back than we'd been.

First, though, I needed to know that my recently human companion had made it through.

I pushed myself faster, but even my well-muscled legs couldn't beat Loki's enchanted shoes. He'd already reached the ground. Odin had set Bifrost down by a barn that, from its sagging roof, hadn't been used in some time.

The trickster carried Ari into the barn. Baldur flew after him. When I reached the doorway, Loki had lain Ari on the straw-strewn floor. The musty smell that reached my nose must have been why he was wrinkling his, but his amber eyes were fixed on the valkyrie.

Her wings had contracted into her back, making her look as if she were fully human still. Her face had escaped the worst of the damage from Surt's attacks, but her eyes were shut, her lips parted and jaw slack. The rest of her was a mess of charred fabric and skin mottled black and red. My fingers clamped around Mjolnir's handle so tightly my knuckles ached.

Ari wasn't just a fighting companion and a friend. She'd seen parts of me even I'd almost forgotten existed and helped me recover them. She'd shown me tenderness and affection I'd never thought I'd find again.

I'd started to think I'd get to spend the rest of my days with her by my side—and if the trickster and the twins shared her affections too, that didn't diminish what she and I had, only showed the capacity of her heart. She captured *my* heart, with a depth I hadn't entirely known until right now, watching Baldur bend over her ravaged body, feeling that pounding vessel inside me nearly tear itself apart.

"Is there anything I can do?" I asked, every muscle in my body clamoring to be put to use.

The god of light shook his head without glancing up. He rested his hands gently on Ari's chest. A glow began to seep from them through her body.

"Her heart is still beating," he said, his voice ragged with relief. "She's breathing, just barely. It'll take some time, but I can save her."

Loki stood up, his mouth twisting. He'd managed to

pull his lips into one of his usual sly smiles by the time he met my eyes.

"Let's give the healer room to work his magic without distraction, Thunderer."

Reluctantly, I stepped back from the doorway. Hod stayed turned toward his twin, his stance tense, but the blind god couldn't speed up Ari's recovery any more than I could.

Odin had sunk down by the weathered fence along the dirt road that divided the farmland from the forest. Freya was crouched next to him. Where she'd moved aside his cloak, his trousers were darkly damp with blood. One or more of Surt's soldiers had gotten to my father too.

Baldur was going to have his work cut out for him, patching up the lot of us.

A fresh surge of fury gripped me. I stalked toward the road, tossing Mjolnir in my hand. With a satisfying heave, I hurled the hammer at one of the nearest trees.

The trunk burst like the one draug's body had, splinters pattering against the neighboring trees. The top of the pine crashed down into the forest. My momentary pleasure drained away. This wasn't accomplishing anything. It was senseless destruction.

"You're leaking," Loki said lightly, nodding to my wound. "I might not be able to magic it better, but I could cauterize it for the time being."

"I'm fine," I grumbled, which might not have been the most sensible response either, but the thought of dealing with my injuries when Ari was still unconscious from hers made my spine stiffen.

I prowled along the line of the fence all the way around the abandoned farm, telling myself I was keeping guard. As long as I was in motion, my worries and aggravations could only nip at my heels, not gnaw right into me. I'd just finished my eighth circuit when a thin but clear voice carried through the barn doorway.

"Where are we?"

My heart leapt. I barged through the doorway, only managing to make it there ahead of Loki and Hod because I'd been closer to begin with.

Ari was sitting up against the wall. Her cheek was smudged with ash and her clothes still hung in burnt tatters on her small frame, but her limbs were only mottled pink now instead of the raw horror they'd been before.

Baldur was gripping her shoulder as he explained where we'd ended up. His white-blond hair clung to his forehead, damp with sweat from all the energy he'd expended.

Ari's gaze leapt from him to the rest of us as we came in. A smile lit her face all the way to her blue-gray eyes. "All right," she said. "So, how are we getting Asgard back?"

Here she was, just restored from the verge of death and already eager to leap right back into battle. A laugh of joy tickled up my throat. But the sound had hardly fallen from my lips when my chest tightened all over again.

How *were* we getting Asgard back? I didn't have the faintest idea where to start.

3

Aria

The gods set up their little council in the barn, mainly so that I didn't have to try to walk anywhere yet, I suspected. I wasn't keen on being carried around, but my body still throbbed enough just sitting propped against the rough boards of the wall that I didn't trust my legs to hold me up yet. Baldur might have had magic hands, but even divine magic had its limits.

That truth of that thought hit home even harder when I glanced around the circle of figures that had hunkered down around me and noticed we were one short.

"Where's Tyr?" I said, my stomach already clenching with dread in anticipation of the answer. Somehow I had the feeling he hadn't just gone for a stroll.

The gods all glanced at each other as if hoping someone else would take on the task of replying. Odin sighed, adjusting his grip on his spear, which he'd leaned against his shoulder as he sat on an old crate.

"Tyr fell in the battle as we retreated," he said. "A worthy companion lost."

"Lost," I repeated. "So he didn't—he isn't going to— You weren't sure whether any of you *could* really die or not."

"Now we're sure," Loki said, his tone arch but a little subdued by his standards. "No more do-overs. We fall and we're gone."

I sucked in a deep breath full of the dry smells of straw and dust. The possibility that the gods might die had hung over us in every battle we'd found ourselves in, but now, looking at them in the beams of dwindling sunlight that were streaking through the gaps in the barn walls, it felt as real and solid as my hands. Because it was a fact now and not a possibility. Because for the first time we'd faced an enemy strong enough that he'd sent the gods on the run from their home.

Of course, maybe they wouldn't have needed to run at all if they hadn't been trying to save me. My hand dropped to my knee to rub an achy spot there. The outer marks of Surt's attacks were fading, but I could still trace the lines his magical fire had carved into me.

"He took us by surprise," I said. "When we're ready and properly equipped—when we can take *him* by surprise—no one else will have to fall on our side. Right? So what's the plan?"

"I'd imagine the most difficult part will be getting back into Asgard without walking straight into an ambush," Hod said, his dark green eyes instinctively moving over the faces around our circle even though he couldn't see any of us. I knew he had a clear enough picture of where we all were from every small sound of our movements, our breaths. His boyish face had always looked harder than his gentle twin's, but now his expression was outright strained.

"Surt knows where Bifrost connects to Asgard," the dark god went on. "He knows the only other entrance into Asgard is through the paths along Yggdrasil. He'll have both the head of the bridge and the base of the great tree surrounded by his draugr. We won't take him by surprise that way."

"Are there really no other ways in?" I asked. "Surt managed to show up right where he wanted with his fire magic. Aren't there any gods who can do something like that?" I looked to Odin. "Can you make your rainbow touch down in some other spot?"

Odin shook his head, his silvered brown beard swaying. "Bifrost is born from Asgard. I call it forth from the place of its origin. It's only the other end I can aim at my whim." From what the gods had told me, the abandoned farm he'd set us down in today was somewhere in the middle of the French countryside.

"But there might be other ways of creating a bridge," Loki said. "The five of us know we aren't any use for that—we gave it a shot when you were missing, Allfather—but if we could track down one of the gods with a closer affinity." He snapped his fingers. "Heimdall."

"He was the bridge's guardian," Thor said. "Nothing to do with creating it."

Loki waved his hand dismissively. "He rules over

connections and the binding of one thing to another. That sounds bridge-like enough to me."

"It only helps us if we can find Heimdall," Hod put in. "We did spend a good chunk of the last couple weeks searching for the other gods, and Tyr is the only one we turned up."

"We didn't have Muninn with us then," I said. "She might have spotted one of them in her travels around Midgard." My pulse stuttered. "Where's the raven?"

Odin's former raven of memory had become a part of our group so recently and been an enemy of sorts for so long before that, I hadn't immediately been thrown by her absence. Had she been caught or even killed by Surt and his draugr too?

"We don't know," Freya said, with a slight edge. I suspected it was going to take her a while to completely forgive the raven woman for imprisoning her husband and allowing Surt to torment him.

"None of us saw her during the battle," Baldur said, his voice as clear and melodic as ever. "I wouldn't blame her if she fled from the start. She isn't a warrior."

My shoulders tensed. "If Surt catches her, he might kill her. He's got to know by now that she betrayed him to us in the end."

Thor tipped his head toward the doorway. "Baldur laid out a bit of a light display that she should recognize if she's searching for us. If the giant has her, we'll just have to hope we make it back to Asgard before he takes his full revenge."

Back to Asgard. An idea jarred loose in my still pretty muddled head. "I can jump straight back to

Valhalla," I said. "Obviously I can't fight Surt and his army on my own, but I could at least take the lay of the land, see where the guards are..."

Anything else I might have said caught in my throat at the darkening of Hod's face. "No," he said. "We *know* there'll be guards in Valhalla, lots of them, watching the entrance to Yggdrasil, remember? They might even be on guard specifically for you to appear if Surt's aware of that valkyrie skill. He's not going to give you any opening. He'd just take the opportunity to kill *you*."

It was strange to think that a month ago, Hod hadn't even wanted me around. Now, his anguish at the close call I'd already met at Surt's hands threaded through his words. My connection with each of the four gods who'd summoned me had deepened in all sorts of ways, many of them very enjoyable, since I'd found myself with them, but Hod had opened up the most. He'd offered me his heart, his love, whether I could bring myself to say the same to him or not.

I hadn't managed to repeat that sentiment to any of my gods yet. Love wasn't an emotion I had a whole lot of experience with after years of my mother's abuse and worse at the hands of her boyfriends. I tried to show them how much they meant to me in other ways, though. In that moment, I wished I could put my arms around Hod and show him how much I really was still here, alive and unbroken. That might not be a very productive move for getting on with this meeting, though.

"But Surt's guards might *not* be watching for me," I said. "They could be all at the end of the hall by the hearth. I think I can control, at least a little, which part of the room I appear in. If I landed between the tables, they might not even notice me sneaking by."

All of the gods were frowning, even Freya. Loki reached out and squeezed my arm. His touch sent tingling warmth over my skin without any magic involved. "For once in my existence, I agree with Mr. Doom and Gloom. It's not worth the risk. We have time to attempt other strategies."

Not worth the risk. Just like it hadn't been worth the risk of continuing to fight when I'd been wounded? A lump rose in my throat.

"Yggdrasil may be the key, nonetheless," Freya said. "They can guard the entrance, but no one but those of Asgard can open it. If we found one of the gateways from the other realms, and we assembled enough of a force, we could possibly take whatever draugr he's stationed in Valhalla by surprise and slaughter them before they can raise the alarm. We'd just need to be ready to strike directly at him right after that." The goddess of love and war set her mouth in a firm line.

"Do we know where the gateway from Midgard is?" I asked.

"There isn't one," Thor said. "It was closed at this end ages ago, after it became too likely some human would stumble on it and get himself into trouble." He glanced at Hod. "But we do know where at least one gate to Nidavellir is, and the location of their gate to Asgard."

Hod nodded slowly. "I could go and plead our case to the dark elves. I think it would shatter all the good will we've managed to restore with them if we simply demanded the right to barge through their home at our convenience."

Not that long ago, the dark elves had been helping Surt, but for understandable reasons. Nidavellir, their home of underground caves, had started to fall apart after centuries of the gods' unthinking neglect. Surt had promised them a place in one of the realms that was still stable if they helped him claim those realms. Hod had managed to regain their trust by going to help restore their home, but it was a tentative truce so far.

"If we're asking the dirt-eaters for help, perhaps you could put in a request for some of their creative weaponry as well," Loki said with a grin.

I perked up. I hadn't thought of that. The dark elves had constructed most of the gods' greatest weapons, from Thor's hammer to Odin's spear.

"I'll see what I can do," Hod said. "They aren't all that happy with us, remember. Just a few weeks ago, they were trying to *kill* us."

"A grave misunderstanding now rectified. But I take your point."

"In the meantime, the rest of us could set out more messages in places the other gods seem likely to visit," Thor suggested. "That did work to bring Tyr back to us."

Only Tyr, after days of searching. I nibbled at my lower lip. "How long do you think we have before Surt starts his attack on Midgard?"

"He'll wait until he's confident in his defenses around Asgard," Freya said. "That might not take more than a day or two, though. After that... We can hope that he'll enjoy his victory for some time before attempting to extend it, but I don't think we'd be wise to count on a delay. And there's no way of telling where or how he'll even begin his assault on this realm."

"If he arrives in Midgard via that flaming bridge of his, I should sense that magic." Loki wiggled his fingers. "It makes my own turn prickly."

At a fluttering sound outside, all our mouths snapped shut, our gazes jerking to the doorway. A second later, a raven swooped inside. It banked over our heads and dropped to the ground just inside the barn, shifting into the form of a skinny knobby-limbed woman at the same time.

Muninn crossed her arms over her chest and peered at us with her dark eyes. From her stance, she was considering whether she'd need to bolt back out that door.

None of us had exactly been on friendly terms with the raven woman until even more recently than our dark elf alliance. Once Odin's servant as the guardian of memory, she'd let out however many centuries of pent-up rage by agreeing to help Surt capture the Allfather and then tormenting us with awful moments from our personal histories in a prison she'd created.

She'd given us a tip to help us destroy Surt's fortress. Suddenly I couldn't help wondering how much she'd known about his decision to move most of his army to a different realm. Had she still been playing both sides?

"I found you as quickly as I could," she said, with a bird-like cock of her head. "By the time I realized you were leaving Asgard, Bifrost was already retracting."

"How did you end up here, then?" Thor said. His

tone was even enough, but his hand had dropped to his hammer where it rested at his side.

"I flew straight to Yggdrasil, before Surt had time to notice." Muninn shuddered. "He would not be pleased to see me."

My valkyrie senses were designed to read emotion and motivations—to help me decide who lived and died on a battlefield, if I'd been a proper valkyrie with the old guard. Picking up impressions from divine beings was always a trickier business than with mortals, but her horror felt genuine to me. I relaxed against the wall.

"What did you see before you left?" Freya asked.

"Little you wouldn't have, I'd imagine," the raven woman said. "I was only a few minutes behind you. Lots of burning, lots of smoke. Surt shouting about how wonderful he is." She cut her gaze toward Odin. "In case I didn't make it clear enough before, I never *liked* him. Our agreement was a matter of necessity."

Odin dipped his head in acknowledgment. I knew the two of them must have talked more than I'd been a witness to. He didn't look especially troubled, but then, it was hard to tell with the Allfather. You might say he had kind of odd reactions to things. Or you could just say he was batshit crazy.

"We were just talking about looking for the other gods who left Asgard," I said. "I was thinking you might have seen them in the time you spent here. It sounded like you've done a lot more roaming around than these guys did when they visited."

Muninn paused. She shifted her weight from one

foot to the other. "You were thinking I could take you to them, you mean."

"You're under no obligation to help us," Odin said.

Thor let out a guffaw. "I'd say she is. If it wasn't for her helping Surt, the giant might never have raised enough of an army to challenge Asgard in the first place."

Muninn's shoulders twitched in a motion that brought to mind ruffled feathers. "I had my reasons. And I serve no one now." She eased back a step toward the doorway.

"Ah, let's not bicker," Loki said. "We've got plenty of draugr skulls to bash without turning on our own, don't we?"

"And she is our own," Baldur put in quietly. "She's of Asgard, even if she was turned against us for a time."

I caught the raven woman's eye. "Don't go. Everyone's just... riled up, after what happened up there."

Muninn's jaw worked. She didn't move forward again, but she stayed where she was, at least.

"The other gods," she said. "I may have an idea or two."

4

Aria

A gust of snow stung my face as I glided down to land on an icy ledge next to Muninn and Freya. I dug my feet deeper into the fur-lined boots Loki had procured for me and tugged the coat he'd doctored to allow room for my wings even more tightly around me. My valkyrie strength protected me from the cold some, but not completely. And the chill was waking up all the aches that hadn't quite healed after yesterday's encounter with Surt.

I wasn't going to mention that to anyone, though. The gods had fussed enough about me joining in on this undertaking. As if I wanted to sit around cooped up in some dusty barn while a mad giant planned to destroy this entire world. My heightened senses might help us spot the goddess we were searching for if she tried to take off on us. I *had* agreed to getting a night's rest first, and that should be enough for them.

Muninn and Freya seemed impervious to the weather in both their forms. There on the ledge, they transformed from raven and falcon so that we could talk with each other, Muninn wearing her usual loose black dress and Freya in an elegant blouse and slacks with her feathered cloak still slung over her shoulders. I tucked my wings closer to my body, the wind tickling over their silver-white feathers.

"You two should stay here while I fly closer to the usual spots on my own," Muninn said. "She might slip away if she sees a whole brigade approaching before we know exactly where we're going." The corner of her mouth curved up. "The gods are not always as observant as they like to think. They rarely noticed me coasting by."

"Come for us as soon as you've found her," Freya said, tossing back her golden waves. She set her hand on the hilt of her sword and scanned the snowy mountainside as if she expected Surt might appear even here.

Muninn leapt up into her raven form and flapped deeper into the valley we were perched on the edge of. She'd said she'd seen Skadi, the goddess of the hunt and of winter, in this range enough times to think she'd made a home here. A hunter sounded like a decent ally to have on our side.

"How easy do you think it'll be to convince Skadi to come back with us?" I asked.

Freya shrugged. "Skadi was always something of a

loner, but she was loyal to Asgard. She won't want to see it or this realm fall to Surt."

"Do you think she's more likely to listen to you than the others? I have to think..." Suddenly I wondered if I should be bringing up this subject at all. But I'd already started, so I barreled onward. "You must want to keep searching for your daughter."

She'd mentioned her regrets over her falling out with the younger goddess, whom I'd gathered she hadn't seen in at least a couple centuries, after we'd started searching for all the other former inhabitants of Asgard a week ago.

"I wouldn't be sure where else to try with Hnoss," Freya said. "And I know Skadi better than any of the louts we're with. She was married to my father for some time—and she did truly care for him. They just wanted lives that were too different from what suited the other."

A hint of melancholy had crossed her face. How much because she was thinking of Odin, who was constantly wandering off without her on his rambling journeys, and how much for the daughter she hadn't seen in hundreds of years—partly because Hnoss had disliked her new stepfather?

I wasn't any stranger to fucked-up family dynamics. I knew what it was like to hate the new guy your mother had brought around, to know he was up to no good. Of course, at least Odin had thought he was doing the right thing, even if he'd encouraged his realm toward destruction and forced Loki to play the villain for that purpose. My mother's boyfriends—the one of them in particular—

I shoved that thought aside. I wasn't letting Trevor affect me anymore. I'd risen above everything he'd done to me, all the pain he'd caused and the ways he'd torn us apart. *My* mom didn't give a shit what had happened to me—that fact she'd made abundantly clear. There was a lot more hope for Freya and her daughter. Freya cared.

The icy chill was starting to penetrate my boots. I shuffled my feet to encourage the blood flow through them, and a sharp twinge ran through my hip. No, this body was definitely not in fully working order yet.

"Are you all right?" Freya asked, her blue eyes as keen as in her falcon form.

"Just a little cold," I lied.

It didn't matter if I wasn't totally recovered from my wounds. I had to do whatever I could to help finish this war with Surt, not just to support the gods I'd started to consider family but to protect the one part of my original family I still cared about.

My little brother Petey was off with the foster family we'd arranged for him. I'd thought he'd be safe there from everyone who'd threatened him. If Surt claimed Midgard too—or if he found out I had a brother he could use to hurt me—I didn't want to think through what would happen to that sweet kid. He didn't deserve any of this.

Petey deserved better from *me*. Hod had wiped his memories so he couldn't accidentally slip up and give away anything about our real mother. If the agency found out who he was and where he'd come from, they'd have to send him back. Back to her and her latest lover who'd left fingerprints on his neck.

A black shape soared back toward us, stark against the white snow. Muninn dropped to join us. She was smiling when she shifted into a woman.

"She's here," she said. "There's a cabin just over that slope. I think Skadi's been living there. She's farther down the valley, hunting hares. I don't think we can completely surprise her, but if we arrive quickly enough, she'll see it's you and hopefully stay to chat."

Freya nodded and drew her cloak over her head. In an instant, she was a golden falcon, darting up toward the sky.

Before Muninn could transform too, I grasped her arm. I hadn't had much chance to talk to her alone until now.

"Before," I said, "when you were working with Surt... Did you ever tell him about my brother?" I knew she was aware of Petey's existence. She'd used him to torment me in that prison of memories she'd trapped us in.

The raven woman shook her head. "I never had any reason to. You've seen how Surt is. With an 'ally' like that, you're best off keeping everything you can close to your chest in case you need it later."

I guessed that comment was a little comforting, other than the implication that she probably would have told him if she'd thought it would get her out of a jam.

"Did you hear any of the dark elves mention it to him?" I asked. They'd threatened Petey to try to get me to back down too, although Hod had wiped their minds of all memory of my brother as well as he could after. I didn't know how many specifics of their plans they might have shared with Surt.

Muninn's gaze held mine with a gleam that looked almost curious. "To the best of my knowledge, Surt has no information about your brother. He didn't even think much about *you* until you broke out of my prison. Even if one of the dirt-eaters did say something, they couldn't know where your brother is, could they?"

"No." She only did because of the memories she'd peeked at in my head and Hod's. I let out my breath. "Okay. I'm sorry. I just needed to know."

"I'm glad I could help," she said, with a strange note in her voice, as if she were a little surprised by that gladness.

Freya's falcon wheeled in the air overhead, letting out a faint cry of impatience. I waved to her and sprang off the ledge with a flap of my wings.

My knees throbbed for a moment from the jump, but my newest appendages had escaped the worst of Surt's blows. It was a relief to glide through the air with the wind buffeting them, the rest of my body barely needing to move. Freya swept up toward the top of the slope Muninn had indicated, and I pushed myself faster, speeding after her. The raven streaked into view alongside me.

We whipped up over the slope and plunged down the other side. A log cabin, the roof blanketed with snow like everything else around here, stood about a mile down the mountainside. My sharpened valkyrie eyesight picked up a smattering of footsteps between the door and a heap of chopped firewood leaning against the cabin's side. A hint of pine smoke reached my nose from a fire that must have been put out no more than a few hours ago.

More footprints headed off to a small shed a few feet away on the other side. From there, long slivers of tracks sliced through the snow, heading downward. Skadi was on skis, I realized after staring for a moment.

Freya was hurtling down the slope. I caught a gust of wind that propelled me after her. A few seconds later, I spotted a figure with a trim jacket and a white wool hat pulled over her dark brown hair. She was braced on her skis, her arms lifted to pull back a bowstring, the arrow aimed at something I couldn't make out amid the trees across from her.

She let the arrow fly. Freya emerged from her cloak, keeping it unfurled behind her. "Skadi!" she called in her bright but firm voice.

The other goddess's head snapped around, her bow slipping in her hands. I hung back as Freya moved to greet Skadi. Muninn swooped around and flew back toward the cabin. I wondered if she planned to reveal herself to the goddess of the hunt at all.

"Freya," Skadi said, shielding her eyes from the sun as she stared. She shook her head in disbelief. Her smile was tight. "It's been a long time. What are you doing all the way out here?"

"It has been," Freya said, smoothly but quickly. "And I know you've wanted your peace from the politics of Asgard. I wouldn't have disturbed that peace if it weren't an incredibly urgent situation." She sucked in a breath. "Surt has returned. He's taken Asgard—the entire realm."

Skadi's eyebrows shot up, and her eyes flashed. "We can't have that."

"Exactly," Freya said, her own smile relieved.

"Come back to my cabin where we can sit properly,

and you can tell me the whole thing while I pack," Skadi said. Her gaze slid to me. She looked me up and down where I was still hovering in the air. A thread of disdain came into her voice. "What did you bring a valkyrie for?"

Freya hesitated. "We didn't think it wise for any of us to travel alone," she said, which I guessed was the answer she thought Skadi would most easily accept.

"As if you need the protection of one of Odin's warrior dolls. Well, come on."

My mouth refused to stay shut. "I'm not a doll," I said. "And I have very good hearing, by the way."

Skadi rolled her eyes at me. "You're created for the gods' purposes, and you'll break much easier than any of us. Sounds like a doll to me. Just try to keep up, all right."

I bit my tongue against several barbed comments I'd have liked to make in return. Freya gave me a pleading glance and then turned back to Skadi. "Aria has proven herself well. I don't think you've any reason to worry that she'll slow us down."

Of course I'd be able to keep up with them. I had my wings, and Skadi was skiing uphill.

But then, it turned out I'd underestimated the goddess's strength. Skadi whipped up the mountainside with shoves of her powerful thighs, each push carrying her at least a tenth of a mile. I managed to keep pace, but by the time we reached her cabin, the tendons in my wings were starting to throb too.

Skadi shed her skis and stalked into the cabin, leaving Freya to hold the door for me. Muninn stayed perched on the roof.

Inside the single-room home, the pine smoke smell

was sharper, but the goddess of the hunt didn't bother lighting the logs again, as much as I'd have enjoyed a little relief from the constant chill. She opened up a chest at the foot of her simple wood-frame bed.

"Tell me what happened," she said. "Just the important parts."

"Well," Freya said, sinking into the room's single chair, "it seems Surt was planning this invasion for a rather long time. As in, as far as he's concerned, he's wrapping up unfinished business from Ragnarok."

She summed up the events of the last several decades faster than I'd have been able to: How she and the five gods who'd remained in Asgard had come down to Midgard for one of their regular visits, and not long after Odin had set off on his own usual wanderings. How he hadn't returned for tens of years, longer than ever before, until they'd started to worry about him. How the other four gods had summoned me, and how I'd ended up managing to lead them to Odin in Surt's grasp, from which we'd freed him.

Freya breezed over the details of the prison we'd been trapped in, our efforts to make peace with the dark elves, and our attempt at destroying Surt's army. I guessed that made sense. The only thing Skadi really needed to know was that Surt had arrived in Asgard with most of that army and proceeded to batter us.

"We weren't prepared for the attack," Freya finished. "And there were only the seven of us—well, and Ari."

I tried not to tense at being an afterthought. How much had I added to their defense anyway? How much had I held them back with the weaknesses Skadi had pointed out so briskly?

She wasn't completely wrong. The gods had made me, and I was a lot more fragile than their nearly immortal selves were.

"So you're gathering as many of the old guard as you can," Skadi filled in. She'd stuffed a bundle of arrows and a few pieces of armor into a pack she now slung over her shoulders. She hooked another bow, larger and gleaming with a golden sheen, onto its strap. "Of course I'll help. And I can do one better—or maybe two. I know where Njord settled down in this realm."

An amused glint lit in Freya's eyes. "You never could completely stay away from each other, could you?"

Njord must be Freya's father—Skadi's former husband whom she'd mentioned before. A slight flush colored Skadi's cheeks before she shrugged with a jerk of her shoulders. "I know where he is, is all I'm saying. And I think he still meets with your brother from time to time. We may be able to gather them both. It sounds as though time is of the essence. Are you ready for a longer journey?"

She aimed the question at Freya but then shot a pointed look my way. Freya didn't miss it. Before I could bristle, she stood up and rested a soothing hand on my back. "We're ready. You're right—the faster we can gather everyone, the better."

And they weren't leaving me behind. I was starting to wish we could leave *Skadi* behind. But she clearly knew her way around that bow, and she was tough enough to battle Surt. It wasn't as if I'd never met a blunt-talker before in my life.

I'd just usually been stronger than that talker—or in a position to head elsewhere if they annoyed me.

Outside, Skadi strapped on her skis with a few firm jerks of her hands. "Quickest way down the mountain," she said when she caught me watching. There was a challenge in her voice. *There's no way a mere valkyrie could outrace me.*

Freya lifted into the air in her falcon form, and Skadi started to push off. I was already getting left behind. I moved to leap after them, and my foot slipped on the slick snow. My other calf jarred as I caught my balance. A spear of pain pierced through my muscles from ankle to hip, and I couldn't swallow the gasp that flew up my throat.

Skadi swiveled to the side to peer back at me where I'd come to a stop, half-crouched and panting. "Are you coming?" she said.

I clenched my jaw. Squeezing my hands against the pain, I straightened up and rose from the ground with a sweep of my wings. It wasn't a grand departure, but the slow ascent allowed me to avoid putting any more weight on my sore leg.

"I'm right behind you," I said, knowing I hadn't quite erased the strain from my voice. Skadi gave a little sniff and sped off. I'd just proven everything she'd been thinking about valkyries, and we still had who knew how many miles to cross.

There was nothing I could do but flap these wings and hurry after her.

5

Hod

The cold rock trembled against my palms, but as I pushed more shadows into its rough surface, it steadied. With my mind's eye, I could see the miniscule cracks that had been forming all through this underground passage filling in and solidifying.

The effort sent a prickling through the muscles of my shoulder and back. I set my jaw and compelled more of my dark energy into the cave around me.

This rock would never have weakened in the first place if we gods hadn't neglected all the realms except our own and Midgard. The dark elves of Nidavellir had needed us, and we'd ignored them for hundreds of years, too caught up in our preferred pastimes. When the ceilings of their home had started collapsing on them, I wasn't sure we could really blame them for buying into

Surt's promise that he could conquer a new home for them if they helped him gather his army.

If I wanted them to help *us* now, I had to show just how committed we were to making up for those past mistakes. If I'd had the power to seal the stone through the entire realm all at once, I would have. I'd learned that one length of cave was enough to leave me sweating and breathless, though.

When I felt my magic smooth over the end of the passage, I let myself ease back. The space around me was quiet other than the faint rasp of my companion's breaths.

The commander of this clan of dark elves had insisted on staying to watch my work. The gate we knew of into Nidavellir from Midgard was at a different end of their realm from the one I'd mainly been arriving through from Asgard, and I'd never spoken to this man before. Any other inhabitants of this section of cave, he'd told me, had been evacuated a few days ago when a few chunks of the ceiling had started to fall.

"It'll be stable now," I said, turning my face toward him as closely as I could estimate his position. "I can return again soon to work on another passage."

His steps padded past me into the cave. The cool air shifted against my damp skin. I swiped the back of my hand over my forehead, wishing I'd thought to bring a warmer shirt. It was summer where we were staying in Midgard, but nowhere in Nidavellir ever got all that warm.

A rapping echoed from within the cave as the

commander prodded the walls with what sounded like a metal cane. He strode back to me.

"It appears as you say. I'd heard the Blind One of Asgard had been restoring parts of our realm, but it was difficult to believe without seeing it."

"We've stayed apart from your people for too long," I said, with a respectful dip of my head. "I'm doing my best to make amends. We want all the realms to be safe and secure for their people."

I'd gone so far as to swear a blood oath with the local commander near the Asgard gate committing to my continued help. I'd shown this dark elf the scar on my palm when I'd arrived here.

"We appreciate your efforts," the commander said, but his tone still sounded guarded.

I had to broach the other reason for my visit sometime. "I want you to know that what I did here today—what I'll keep doing—is solely part of those amends. I don't expect any repayment for it, and I'll continue doing it regardless of how you respond to what I say next. We—Have you heard of the recent attack on Asgard?"

"Ah." The commander shifted his weight. From that one syllable, I could tell that he had and that he'd already guessed my intent. "Your attempt to eliminate Surt and his army was not as successful as you'd hoped."

That was one way of putting it. "He has taken over Asgard," I said. "That's why I could only reach your realm through the gate from Midgard. We need to regain our realm—and to protect the realm of humans, which he's indicated he means to conquer as well. We won't ask you to fight on our behalf, of course, but if you'd give us permission to reach Asgard through your realm, if we decide that's our best option for launching a return attack, it could make all the difference."

"Yggdrasil's root reaches us many sectors from here," the commander said. "You'd want us to host an army of gods as you travel that distance?"

"It's not likely to be a very large army," I had to admit. "And we'd simply be passing through." But tramping through miles of caves could be plenty of disturbance on its own, especially when the dark elves were already crowded into the more stable areas of their home after so many cave-ins. I wet my lips. "We'd follow whatever requirements you set out."

"And that's all you'd ask?"

I hesitated, but if I didn't ask for the rest, the others would no doubt press for me to pursue the subject next time, and then the dark elf leader would feel I'd lied.

"If you had any weapons to spare, or could forge a few that might assist us in taking back our realm—we would repay you in every way we could."

"If you actually win back Asgard, where all your riches are," the commander said.

"We will," I said firmly. We had other riches, bank accounts and stores of cash in Midgard that we'd used for our visits there, but that wouldn't appeal to the dark elves. They'd want gold. We might be able to buy some bars of the stuff in the realm of humans, though. "And I can see if we can offer some in advance—just a portion of the full reward."

The commander hummed to himself. He still sounded skeptical. My fingers twitched with the urge to ball into my palm, but I forced them to relax. By Asgard, if only I had Loki's quick tongue. He'd always been able to charm just about anything out of the elves, sometimes without any payment at all. Sweet-talking wasn't exactly a skill of mine.

"Surt will know we were involved," the commander said after a moment. "If you fail, he'll punish our people as well as yours."

"We won't fail," I said, as if I could guarantee that. "Having your support will make that even more sure."

"Nevertheless... I will need to discuss it with some of the other sector leaders. I certainly can't make a decision like this for all of us on my own."

"Of course," I said, even though my heart had sunk. I believed he'd bring forward our request, but I had the suspicion he wasn't going to put a positive spin on it. "I'll return within a day or two, as soon as I'm able to, and you can let me know if you happen to have an answer then. Either way, I'll see to another of your caves."

"Then we will welcome you." The commander motioned, and one of his guards approached with heavy footsteps. "Please escort our guest back to the gate."

I'd paid enough attention to the turns and the shifts in the air that I probably could have navigated back to the gate on my own. We hadn't come that far. But having a guide gave me room to confirm my impressions of this area. It seemed I might be venturing down to this part of Nidavellir rather frequently in the next several days.

When I stepped out on the other side of the gate, a hot humid breeze washed over me with tart smells of vegetation. I conjured a sheet of shadow to lift me off the ground and glided up over the treetops where I could soar along freely. I knew from the taste of the wind and the rippling of my strands of dark magic across the ground below which way to go to find my way back to the others.

Last night, we'd moved from the musty barn to the farmhouse down the lane, which was equally abandoned. With a touch of magic, we'd make sure it stayed that way as far as the locals were concerned for as long as we needed it.

And it was a good thing we'd put wards in place to hide our activities from any outsiders, because as soon as I directed my swath of shadow down toward the farm, the sounds of spirited conversation reached my ears, loud enough to draw attention.

Three voices I hadn't heard in quite some time had joined those more familiar.

"My goodness, Thor, I think you've managed to bulk up even more since I last saw you." That slightly husky alto belonged to Skadi.

"Baldur, it's good to see you looking so well." That deep, almost creaky bass was Njord.

"We really mustn't let it take a war to bring us back together next time." That spritely tenor was Freyr.

Freya and Ari's mission had been successful, then, even more so than they'd expected. Muninn hadn't led them astray. The newcomers and our original group had gathered in the yard outside the house. From the comments I'd overheard, I had the impression these three had only just arrived.

I bade my magic to set me down at the edge of the yard.

"Well, and here's Hod," Njord said. My ears were too practiced to miss the flattening of his tone compared to how he'd spoken to my twin. Baldur had always been the popular one. After all, who wouldn't prefer basking in sunny light over a wintry chill?

"So, he managed to escape even your hammer?" Skadi was saying to my left, and Thor let out a self-deprecating chuckle.

Odin stirred by my right with a rustle of his cloak, and everyone went still. "We'll need all of Asgard in this trying time," he said. "I commend you for your swift arrival."

"How could we do anything else, Allfather?" Freyr said, a respectful lilt in his warm voice. Most of our fellow gods had drifted away from Asgard because they hadn't enjoyed living under Odin's watchful eye, but they recognized his authority all the same. "As soon as Freya gave her horrific account of Surt's assault, we knew there should be no delaying. Surt will fall, swift and hard."

"What bright plans have you been coming up with, hmm?" Njord said, with a soft thump as if he'd given Baldur a friendly slap on the back.

"Oh, I think it's best I leave the planning mainly to the gods of war," my twin said with a smile in his voice.

"But you'll be there to light our way. Don't sell yourself short." Skadi tsked her tongue.

They were slipping back into the usual patterns, as if they'd never left. Where had Loki gotten to? Probably slinking around somewhere on the fringes, waiting to see where he could get a jab in. There was a reason most of the gods had never been all that keen to keep his company, even if they'd forgiven him for his role in Ragnarok.

And there was a reason they'd barely given me a greeting. I hadn't really played an active role in Asgard's community when it'd been more full—not beyond furtive favors done in the shadows. The darkness I carried with me had always seemed to put a damper on the joys of those around me. I'd almost forgotten what it was like, hanging back on the fringes myself, taking it all in but rarely putting myself forward.

When it had only been the six of us, the balance had seemed equal enough. I'd been a necessary part of the whole. But that would change as more and more of our former companions joined us.

An ache ran through me for my study full of scientific and philosophical texts in our usual house in Asgard. For the even larger library in my hall above, if Surt hadn't burned every page in it. If this were a normal situation, if I'd had access to either, I'd have holed up with my books and lost myself in their words rather than make an awkward attempt at socializing.

I wet my lips, and the one voice I would always be happy to hear reached me. Unfortunately, it came with the question I was the least looking forward to answering.

"Hod's come back from Nidavellir," Ari said, with a hint of annoyance in her tone. "If we want to stop Surt, let's give him a chance to share what they said."

I felt all the gods' attention turn to me. I shot a quick smile toward our valkyrie, but my stomach had twisted. Sticking to the sidelines had been my choice as much as anyone else's. What did I have to offer even now other than more gloom?

"The dark elves were unwilling to commit to allowing us to move through their realm or to supplying us with any equipment for our attack," I had to admit. "The commander I spoke to said he'd discuss it with some of the others, but... I think we'd do best not to count on them."

6

Aria

The big table in the farmhouse's dining room didn't have any chairs, but that didn't stop the gods from using it for their conference. With the nine of them squeezed around the worn oak surface someone had wiped the dust from yesterday, there wasn't much room for me. Loki had caught my eye and motioned me over when we'd first come in, but I'd waved him off. The truth was I only trusted my legs to hold me up when I had a wall to lean against.

I could hear just fine from where I was standing anyway. And the truth was there wasn't a whole lot I could add to the discussion they were having right now.

"I haven't spoken with Heimdall in at least a hundred years, maybe more," said Njord, the sea god with a long weathered face and twinkling blue eyes that matched his daughter's. "I got the sense he roamed around quite a bit."

"Yes, I agree it'd be useful to have him on board, but I'm not sure where we're likely to find him," agreed Freyr, Freya's brother and Njord's son. His golden waves fell only to the tops of his ears, and a golden sheen of a beard colored his narrow jaw as well. "I'd imagine you'll have already looked anywhere I'd have thought of."

"Frigg would be useful in a battle with that magic of hers," Skadi said. "But you'd know her inclinations better than any of us, Allfather."

Odin frowned at the mention of the goddess I'd gathered was his first wife. "I can think of a place or two we may not have investigated yet," he allowed. "I doubt she'll be eager to see this face at her door, though."

"I can go speak to her if we find her," Baldur offered, and everyone around the table nodded. The story of the bright god's death came back to me. Frigg was his mother—she was the one who'd gotten every object in the world to swear it would never hurt him... except the mistletoe.

I didn't want to linger in the memories that thought brought back. Muninn had re-enacted Baldur's death for us in agonizing detail. I'd had to watch him fall, speared through by a throw from Hod's hand, with Loki's guidance and Odin's implicit approval.

The three newer gods didn't know about that last part. Which was probably why they were saving their wary glances for the god of darkness and the trickster while hanging off the Allfather's every word.

Skadi cut a glance toward Loki right now, her eyes

narrowing for a second before she said, "What about Vidar? He could nearly rival Thor in a fight."

"Hey, now," the thunder god said in mock dismay.

The goddess of the hunt rolled her eyes at him. "I did say *nearly*. But he proved himself well during Ragnarok."

Everyone's eyes seemed to twitch toward Loki then. I wasn't sure if it was just because of the role he'd played there or if there was something more about this Vidar guy. From the bits and pieces I'd heard about Ragnarok since joining the gods, I knew it was Heimdall who'd killed Loki during that battle, so it couldn't be that. But there'd been plenty of anguish going around, clearly.

Loki raised his chin, but Odin spoke before he might have. "Yes. It would be good to see another of my sons again, as well."

"You know," Freyr said, tapping his chin, "I think I can guess the general area where he might be. We crossed paths once a few decades ago, near the coast of Tanzania, and he said he was headed inward to the savanna. That sort of terrain does seem to suit his temperament. Whether he's stayed there, who can say, but it would be worth a try."

"A few of us should head over there to check at once," Freya said, straightening up.

I pushed myself off the wall, drawing myself up straight too. I might not have any clue about the temperaments of the rest of the gods we could be looking for, but once I got pointed in the right direction, I could pitch in with my valkyrie eyes and ears. "I'll go."

Njord gave me a quizzical look. "The valkyrie? I

expect he'll react better to a familiar face. The right familiar face."

He wasn't as disdainful as Skadi had been, but his dismissal pricked at me anyway. "I've got supernaturally sharp eyesight and hearing," I said. "I'd be useful for covering more ground, for looking for signs of where he might have been. I'm happy to let someone else do the talking."

"Ari has been a great help many times before," Thor put in, with a slightly threatening rumble that dared anyone to argue.

"Should she really be flying off around the world when she's not even recovered from that first battle?" Skadi said. "She took a bit of a tumble when Freya came for me."

"What?" Hod swiveled toward me. "You didn't say anything."

"I'm *fine*," I insisted, but when I moved to demonstrate my fully functional body, my traitor leg chose that moment to twitch with another jab of pain. My balance wavered, and my jaw clenched. "My legs are just a little sore still," I added quickly. "I can fly perfectly fine."

Hod had already moved to my side. He touched the side of my face. "Baldur should look at you again," he said, and lowered his voice. "Surt hit you harder than any of us. It's nothing to be ashamed of."

Had the giant hit me harder, though, or had I simply taken the hit harder than the gods would have? I grimaced.

Loki spoke up in his flippant way. "We really

wouldn't want any additional harm to come to those lovely legs of yours."

I glowered at him, and the trickster grinned back at me. Hod grasped my arm, bending closer. Baldur had already stepped back from the table.

"I'd be okay," I told the dark god.

"Of course you would," he said, his blind eyes aimed straight at mine. "But you'll be more okay if Baldur heals you wherever the pain is lingering. Don't make me carry you out of the room, valkyrie."

I made a face, which didn't do me any good because he couldn't see that either, but I knew he'd do it. And maybe I should see if a little more healing would help, so I'd be able to defend myself when I really needed to.

"All right," I grumbled. Then, because I could, because I knew it'd stop him from looking so worried, and maybe a little because it was the only other way I could think of to show the new gods that I had a place here beyond just "the valkyrie," I tipped my head up to catch his lips for a quick kiss.

Hod returned the kiss with a brush of eager warmth. His mouth curved into a soft smile when I eased away. I'd probably left him with a bunch of questions to answer from the others, but he didn't look as if he minded at all.

Baldur rested his hand on my back as he walked with me into the hall. A sitting room a couple doors down held a few armchairs and a sofa. Baldur sent a gust of light through it that washed the dust from the furniture. He motioned for me to sit on the sofa with my legs sprawled out, closed the door behind us, and tugged over one of the chairs so he could sit next to me.

"Where does it hurt?" he asked.

"It's just my right leg. Sometimes in my hip, and sometimes my knee, and sometimes my ankle... Kind of everywhere," I admitted. "But the pain will probably get better on its own. It's only been a day."

"It won't heal on its own if you're running all over the place," Baldur said, raising his eyebrows at me with a pointed look. He set his hand on my calf, and the heat of his hand seeped straight through my jeans. "There may be new tears in the muscles I can heal."

"Fine, if it'll make you and Hod feel better."

Baldur smiled, with a clarity in his bright blue eyes that I hadn't seen until a couple weeks ago. Back when I'd first met him, he'd hardly seemed to ever totally focus on me through his dreamy haze. He definitely wouldn't have been alert enough to tease me. "I think the point is to make *you* feel better."

He started at my right ankle, his fingers circling the joint. A glowing sensation tingled through my skin and down to the muscles and tendons. I let myself relax against the cushioned arm of the sofa.

"You light him up, you know," Baldur said after a moment.

I blinked. "What? Who?"

"Hod." His hand slid up to my calf, trailing his shimmering warmth in its wake. "I've known him my whole life—and his, obviously—and I don't think I've ever seen anyone bring that much joy out in him. He worries about you because he doesn't want to lose you." He paused, his thumb tracing a gentle arc over my shinbone, and raised his gaze to meet mine again. "None of us do. You're one of us now, Aria."

None of the four—my four—who'd brought me into their world wanted to lose me, he meant. "I'm planning on sticking around," I said, but his words had sent a flutter through my chest. I'd spent a lot of my life not caring about anyone other than Petey, but I *wanted* to matter to them now. I wanted to be someone who made their lives better, in every possible way.

"If I bring out the light in him, do I bring out the darkness in you?" I had to ask. "How... How have you been coping?" Shadows had seeped inside the light god while he'd been trapped in his temporary death. As he'd woken from his peaceful daze, the darkness that had lodged inside him had seemed to wake up too. He'd found it hard to control, at least at first.

"You help me accept the darkness in me, Aria," Baldur said, his voice softening in a way that had me tingling all the way up my leg. "I've been releasing it, here and there, as I can. But I know it doesn't have to diminish my light."

"A little darkness can be very useful," I said, unable to stop myself from thinking of when we'd come together in Valhalla—the way he'd mingled heat and cold in his touch to spark all kinds of sensations through my body. As his hand moved to my knee now, fresh heat pooled between my thighs.

If I'd changed the gods, they'd changed me at least as much in turn. Before them, I hadn't realized I had the capacity to care this much for anyone other than my brother and myself. They'd given me a second chance at living, offered me new strengths and led me to uncover others I'd buried deep, made me want to brave and move beyond the horrors of my past.

The gods might have resurrected me for their own goals, but because of them this life was fully *mine* now, in a way my first one hadn't really been, not from the first moment that asshole boyfriend of my mother's had crept into my childhood bedroom.

These four gods were mine, and I was theirs, no matter what any of their cohorts thought about it.

Baldur's fingers skimmed up my thigh. The remaining tension in the muscle there melted away—and a bolt of longing shot straight through my core. My breath hitched.

Baldur stopped, peering into my eyes. "Did I hurt you?"

"No," I said, my cheeks flushing. "Um. The opposite."

He looked confused for a second before understanding dawned on his face. It brought with it the slightly wicked smile I loved so much. Oh yes, a little darkness mixed with Baldur's light extremely well.

"I'd take advantage of that fact," he said. "But I do have a whole other leg I should check over just in case, don't I?"

He reached for my left ankle. This time, as he eased his hand over my limb, he stroked me through my jeans in a way his healing efforts hadn't required before. Each graze of his fingertips stoked the heat inside me higher.

The longing that had risen up inside me earlier knotted into need.

Baldur leaned forward as his hand caressed my thigh. His natural glow washed over me with an even headier tingle, leaving me a little breathless. His thumb worked along the inside of my leg, closer and closer to the spot that was throbbing in a pleasurably torturous way for his touch.

"All healed up," he murmured. "If you're not in any hurry to get back to the others..."

"Fuck them. No, better idea—fuck *me*." I tangled my fingers in his soft hair to yank his mouth to mine.

Baldur's kiss was as bright as the rest of him, like a beam of sunlight racing through my nerves. He met my urgency with equal passion. His tongue parted my lips and swept past them to tease over mine. He slid off the chair, bracing his knees against the edge of the sofa.

His hand slipped up my body, skipping over the place where I'd wanted it most, but it was hard to regret that omission when a moment later his fingers grazed my breast. I arched into his touch with a whimper. A shimmer shot over my skin, chased by a flicker of cooler darkness that licked over my nipple. I nearly bit his lip trying to hold in a moan. If we got too loud, if the other gods left their conference, someone might hear us.

But then, why should I care what they thought? Three of them could join in if they wanted. The others would judge us however they decided to no matter what I did.

I wanted to absorb Baldur's brilliance, to be lit up

from the inside out with a shine so stark no one could ever get close enough to hurt me—not Surt, not snarky remarks, not any of it.

The god of light nudged up my shirt so he could caress me skin to skin, and I raised my arms so he could strip the top right off me. He tugged his own shirt off in turn.

"I want to feel you," he murmured. "All of you, right against me."

My pulse skipped a beat. Baldur didn't often talk about what *he* wanted, he was so busy trying to keep the rest of us in harmony. If he was asking something of me, I'd do whatever I could to give it. I expected I'd enjoy this request as much as he did.

He knelt over me on the sofa. My heart stuttered again, with a jolt of anxiety this time, but I focused on the brilliance and the warmth and the flecks of darkness that brought a gasp to my lips with their giddy contrast. This was Baldur, the kindest gentlest man—the kindest gentlest *being*—I'd ever met. If I could trust Loki, trusting the bright god was nothing. Not a single particle in me doubted that he'd sooner sacrifice his own life than do me harm.

Baldur lowered his head to my breast. I sucked in a breath as he slicked his mouth over the tip, heat and cold twining together with the swivel of his tongue. His hand dropped to the waist of my jeans, and I arched to meet him, offering myself up to him. With a careful tug, he undid the fly.

When he tilted forward to claim my lips again, I

fumbled with his slacks. A moment later, we were both groping and kicking our way out of our pants and underwear. My body trembled with need everywhere his fingertips so much as grazed. But I remembered what he'd said about wanting to feel me against him.

I looped one arm around his back, the other across his shoulders, and drew him to me. Baldur let me pull him close with a faint groan. He kissed me harder as our bodies fit together, our legs intertwining, his heart beating over mine through his chest.

I was engulfed. I was embraced. Every movement of his mouth told me I was treasured.

The firm length of his cock by my hip confirmed he was definitely interested in more than just cuddling. I squirmed to bring his hardness right against my core and couldn't bite back a moan. Baldur nuzzled my cheek and nibbled along my jaw.

"What do you want now?" I asked, my voice thick.

He flicked his tongue against the crook of my neck, provoking another shiver of pleasure. "To be inside you. To feel you in every possible way. To make love to you like a fucking symphony."

Hearing a swear word drop from his lips always got me twice as turned on. I clutched his shoulder, my hips already starting to rock in encouragement. "I'm ready when you are."

He chuckled softly and tucked his hand under my ass to find the right angle. A little cry broke from my throat as he eased his cock inside me. He filled me with heat, but it wasn't the same as Loki's fire or Thor's crackles of lightning. Baldur's heat was a steady beaming glow that radiated through every nerve, leaving them somehow soothed yet quivering with bliss at the same time.

He adjusted his position again, stroking my hair with the hand he'd braced near my head to carry some of his weight. His next kiss was sweet as melted caramel. He pulled a little back and then thrust deeper, and deeper.

A little pulse started to beat over my breasts in time with his rhythm—a patter of bright warmth and a lick of cool shadow, teasing my nipples even harder with a melody of pleasure. I gasped and arched into the sensation. The song he was playing on my body and the smooth hot skin of his chest made me giddy with bliss.

As he increased his tempo, the pulsing slipped down over my belly, flowing and condensing, until it reached my clit. It hummed against that sensitive spot over and over, faster and faster in harmony with his movements. With each flutter of warmth and cold, my nerves sparked from my core all through the rest of my body, brighter and brighter.

"Do you like that?" Baldur asked, almost shyly.

"Oh, God, yes," I said, and then I was lost. Lost in the pulsing glow against my clit and the sweetness of his mouth and the gleaming heft of each thrust inside me.

Light started to glitter at the edges of my vision. It whirled around me, surrounding me with pleasure. Bliss flooded every inch of me and Baldur was everywhere, and I let go of any last shred of hesitation inside me. Just let go and let the ecstasy of the moment carry me wherever it and he wanted to take me.

My orgasm rushed through me like a solar flare. My head tipped back with a sob of pleasure. For a few seconds, I lost track of my limbs, of the beginnings and ends of my skin, of everything except that bliss and the choked breath as my lover joined me in it.

7

Aria

I dozed for a while with Baldur tucked against me on the sofa. There wasn't really a whole lot of room for both of us, though, which is probably why when I woke up some hours later from what must have turned into a deeper sleep, he was gone. He'd left a blanket wrapped around me, imbued with his sunny warmth. I snuggled deeper into it for a few minutes before I convinced myself to go back out and see where the gods' discussion had taken us.

When I stepped into the hall, voices reached me from the dining room. It sounded like the conference was still in progress. Maybe I hadn't slept as long as I'd thought.

My stomach grumbled, announcing that it had been at least long enough for me to have missed a meal. I ambled into the kitchen at the back of the house to sort through the groceries someone had picked up while Freya and I were off in the snowy mountains. Mostly for my benefit, since the gods didn't require food quite the same way, as much as Thor enjoyed sating his expansive appetite.

The farmhouse had no electricity, so the offerings were all non-perishable stuff that required no cooking. My nose wrinkled as I poked through the bags. I was about to rip open a bag of sour-cream-and-onion potato chips—not the healthiest meal I'd ever eaten, but not the worst either, to be fair—when a shape passing by the kitchen window caught my eye.

It was Odin's broad-brimmed hat, a little less broad after some of Surt's fiery magic must have caught it. And it was sitting where it usually did, on Odin's head.

The Allfather strode by the window and out into the backyard, his spear in hand like a walking stick and his cloak wafting out behind him, giving no indication at all that he planned on stopping any time soon.

I craned my neck toward the window, but I couldn't see anyone else out there with him. Why was he heading off alone while the others were still deep in conversation?

There were plenty of possibilities, but something about his silent departure sent a prickle down my spine. I dropped the bag of chips and went to the back door.

The hinges squealed as I opened it. Odin had already reached the broken chain-link fence that surrounded the yard. He swung his leg over the crumpled metal, and I darted down the back steps.

"Hey!" I said. "Where are you going?"

Odin paused and peered over his shoulder at me. For

a second, I thought he might decide I wasn't worth the effort of an answer. His single eye was as inscrutable as always, and the ridged scar where its partner had been told me even less.

I loosed my wings, both because I thought I might need them and as a sort of threat—if he kept going, I planned on following. The Allfather studied me a moment longer and then turned to face me. I tucked my wings close to my back as I hurried across the patchy grass of the yard, but I didn't retract them. If I'd learned anything since we'd retrieved Odin, it was not to trust the king of the gods any farther than I could throw him, even if he had made a few amends recently.

A cloud had passed over the summer sun, cutting the worst of its glare, but the muggy air stuck to my skin. At least my legs held me up without even a twinge as I hustled over, thanks to Baldur's ministrations. The additional sleep had probably helped too.

I stopped a few paces from Odin and folded my arms over my chest. "Where are you going?" I repeated.

"I mean to wander in search of a vision," the Allfather said in his measured voice.

Sure, that sounded like a typically Odin thing to do. And also an answer typically short on the details. "For how long?" I asked.

"Until the vision I need finds me."

My back prickled again. The last time he'd gone wandering, hadn't the gods lost track of him for *decades*?

"You're leaving," I said. "You're taking off on us. Did you even tell the others that you're going? You look like you're sneaking away."

Odin's expression didn't shift. "They know my ways. It is best, when I am seeking answers, that I am not distracted by the concerns of the rest of the world."

The slight sharpening of his tone suggested that he didn't appreciate the distraction I was creating here either. Well, he could bite me. Maybe slinking off into the unknown without a word was what his wife, sons, and friends were used to, but it was time *someone* put their foot down. It'd also become very clear in the last couple weeks that Odin had gotten away with an awful lot of bullshit for way too long.

"What the hell good is a vision going to do us if you're not here when we have to get everyone together to take on Surt?" I said. "You're needed *here*."

He blinked slowly. "There was a time when you appeared not to appreciate my guidance."

I shook my head. "No, you're not getting away with playing that card. Just because I don't want you calling *all* the shots without listening to anyone else doesn't mean I think it's perfectly fine for you to abandon us to fight your battles for you. You know how to use that spear as more than a walking stick."

"Seeking visions is the best advantage I can lend to those battles," Odin said. "They bring insight from beyond the nine realms. They may lead us to the gods we need to turn the tide or to some other course of action we might not otherwise have considered."

Wasn't it those craptastic visions that had convinced him to prop Loki up as a villain and speed on the end of the world way back when? Maybe it was better if we left the courses of action they prompted unconsidered.

I didn't think Odin would see it that way, though. He might have made apologies for a few of his past acts, but he hadn't shown any sign of doubt over Ragnarok. I guessed you had to be pretty committed when you were planning for the destruction of your home and everyone in it.

"Are you sure that's the best you can do?" I said instead. "Or is it just the advantage you can offer that lets you not be around when the flames are flying? What makes you think a vision is going to come soon enough to help? Surt could start his invasion in five minutes."

"The giant waited centuries before he made his first attack," Odin said evenly. "I expect he'll take his time carrying out his intentions."

"You can't *know* that."

Odin thumped the end of his spear against the ground. "You have been part of this world for barely a heartbeat compared to our lifetimes, valkyrie. I can judge what is right. And I will find no visions standing here discussing the matter with you."

With a whirl of his cloak, he swung back toward the fence. He stepped over the sagging part and marched off, his steps even brisker than before.

I wavered on my feet, wanting to fly after him, unsure it'd do me any good. If he got frustrated enough, would he stab me with that spear? I wouldn't put it past him.

In his mind, as in Skadi's and, it seemed, Njord's, "valkyrie" didn't mean much at all. If some of the other gods would have been upset about my death, there was no reason to think that mattered to Odin. He hadn't seemed to care much about their feelings when he'd let Loki guide Hod into killing Baldur.

A small dark form swooped down beside me. Muninn transformed from raven to woman as she landed. I held back a flinch. I hadn't been sure she'd stuck around after she'd guided us to Skadi. She must have been hanging around outside the house in her bird form.

She'd obviously overheard my conversation with the Allfather. She glanced toward Odin's swiftly retreating back and then at me.

"He knows what paths to travel," she said.

I stared at her. "Are you okay with this? Shouldn't you be more upset than anyone that he's leaving us in the lurch?"

She gave a twitch of a shrug. "I didn't like that he ordered me around, sent me to do his bidding without concern. I had no problem with him choosing what he did with himself. Why shouldn't he follow his own will?"

"Because his visions are a load of crap and the real planning is happening in there?" I gestured toward the house.

"He has seen a great deal," Muninn said. "Some of it more telling than you could imagine. He'll return with knowledge of value—he always has."

It was hard to stay angry when the woman who'd raged at Odin in the past was taking his departure so calmly. "So, we just stand around and wait for him, then?" I said.

She gave me a piercing look. "I believe there's more

the rest of you are capable of than that. Why are you out here instead of in there helping to make those plans?"

"Well, I— He—" I let my protest go with a sputter of frustration. She wasn't completely wrong. "Are *you* going to come in and join the conversation?"

She shuddered beneath her loose dress. "Too many fraught memories crowded into one space," she said. "I'll join the fray as I'm needed."

She hopped up into the air again, shifting into her raven form in a blink. A few flaps of her wings carried her to the house's chimney, where she dropped down to perch.

Fine. I guessed I'd go inside and see if the gods had figured out any way *I* could be needed. They must be discussing something interesting if they still hadn't noticed Odin's disappearance.

Thor's deep voice rang down the hall as I approached the room. "We shouldn't part ways for more than a day at a time. We already know we have trouble tackling Surt with smaller numbers."

"Which is why it's more important that we take all the time we can to search for our comrades, isn't it?" Freyr answered. "How much could the giant possibly manage to destroy in a few days? Midgard's a large realm."

My hackles rose automatically. The thunder god obviously didn't like that answer either. His normally ruddy face was flushed an even deeper red than usual when I peeked into the room.

"And the people of this realm depend on us to protect them from threats like that. There may be thousands of cities, but that doesn't make it all right for the giant to level ten of them."

"Brother," Baldur said from the spot where he'd rejoined them around the table. "Freyr. I'm sure we can reach a compromise that accomplishes all our goals."

"Or we could just go and stop with all the talking about it," Skadi put in, but her voice sounded more weary than anything else.

Freya was rubbing her forehead as if she had a headache. Loki had stepped back from the table completely to lean against the wall, his arms crossed and his eyes narrowed. I might not be able to read the gods' emotions very clearly, but I didn't need any special sensitivity to pick up on the vibe in the room. Everyone was worried and worn down by uncertainty.

The gods had never really lost Asgard before, had they? Even during Ragnarok, they'd simply been reborn right back into their home. They were on unfamiliar ground as much as I was. And they were a whole lot less used to having to cope with situations they couldn't simply overpower.

My stomach grumbled again. Loki glanced over with an arch of an eyebrow, but I wondered if my body's signals might be a sign of what everyone here needed.

"Maybe before any more talk or traveling, we should all have a proper dinner," I said, pitching my voice loud enough to fill the room. "I know you don't *need* three meals a day, but we haven't had much since yesterday morning—it can't hurt, anyway, right?"

Loki pushed off the wall with a clap of his hands. I wasn't sure if he actually thought eating was a good idea or he was just happy for an excuse to end the conversation. "Excellent thought, pixie." He made a grabby motion toward Thor. "Come on, Thunderer. I know where we can find ourselves some decent food, but if you want enough to fill that gut, you'd better be the one to carry it."

Thor guffawed, but he followed him. Baldur aimed one of his brilliant smiles at me.

"We could make a bonfire in the yard," he said. "Skadi, if I remember right, you'd be the best of us to set up a spit."

The aloof goddess couldn't seem to resist a compliment to her skills. Soon we'd all tramped out into the backyard. Skadi sent Freya and Freyr into the nearby forest to gather some firewood with strict instructions and set to work constructing a roasting platform. By the time Loki and Thor made it back carrying several skinned chickens, fresh cobs of corn, and apples from a farmers market, flames were dancing against the growing dark.

Hod came to stand beside me as the smell of roasting chicken filled the air. "Better?" he asked softly.

"Yes," I said. In more ways than one. Baldur's second round of healing had erased the last of my body's aches, and our encounter afterward had soothed some of the ache in my heart. No matter what the new gods thought of me, my four saw me as an equal.

I reached out and slipped my hand around Hod's. He twined his fingers with mine, a smile curving his lips. Then Njord looked around.

"Where's Odin gotten to?" the older god asked.

My back tensed. The worst part of having seen him leave was that now I had to deliver the news.

"He took off," I said. "I saw him going. He said he was going to look for a vision that would give us some more ideas of what to do."

I'd been braced for raised tempers, but the closest I got was the tightening of Hod's hand around mine. Loki rolled his eyes. Njord simply chuckled and said, "Well, that's the Allfather's way, isn't it?" and everyone went back to debating whether the first chickens were totally done, as if the Allfather's absence really mattered that little. Well, they had to be a lot more used to Odin's wanderings that I was. Who was I to point out that this might not have been the best time for it?

The tense vibe I'd sensed in the dining room faded away as the gods dug into their meal. I had to admit the fire-roasted chicken leg I devoured was just about the best thing I'd ever tasted.

As I licked the last bits of grease from my fingers, wondering if I had room for another cob of corn, Loki's head jerked up on the other side of the fire.

"Quiet!" he snapped.

We all stared, the other gods' voices falling away. The trickster closed his eyes and drew in a slow breath through his mouth. His shoulders had gone rigid.

"What is it, Sly One?" Skadi asked after a moment, managing to sound both skeptical and nervous.

Loki's eyes opened. The amber in them glowed with the firelight. His mouth twisted for a second before he said, "I can taste his fire. Surt has arrived in Midgard."

8

Aria

In the first moment after Loki's declaration, we all stood frozen in shocked silence. Then Freya blurted out, "Where?"

The trickster's head swiveled to the right. He opened his mouth again, drinking in the air. I couldn't taste anything except the chicken juices going sour on my tongue, couldn't smell anything except the thin smoke of our own fire, but I'd gotten my honed senses from Loki. His were even sharper than mine—and he was tied to Surt by both his giant ancestry and his fiery talents.

"East," he said. "I'll be able to narrow it down as we get closer."

"Are we ready to challenge him?" Njord said.

He wasn't really suggesting we just stayed here enjoying the rest of our dinner while Surt ravaged communities some other place, was he?

Hod squeezed my hand. "We'd better be," he said. "We'll have the advantage of being prepared to get into a fight this time."

Thor already had his hammer in hand. "That giant will regret ever setting foot on this realm or ours," he said in a growl.

Freya held out her hands. The fierceness of her war goddess nature shone through her beautiful face. "We can't just rush in. If we want to defeat him, or at least push him back, we need strategy as well as strength. Gather whatever weapons you brought with you, and Loki will lead us to him. We'll hang back and take a lay of the land before we plan our defense."

Whether she had enough authority as Odin's wife or as a warrior in her own right, the new gods nodded at her words. They hustled into the house where they'd left their belongings, Freya alongside them. Loki hadn't removed his sword from his belt since we'd left Asgard, and the twins fought with magic rather than weapons.

My hand dropped to the pocket of my jeans where I kept the switchblade my older brother had given me a couple years before his death. It'd gotten me through plenty of mundane jams in my first life, and I always felt a little more secure carrying it, but it wasn't going to get me far against a giant.

"I still don't have a proper weapon," I said.

"Don't worry yourself about that, pixie," Loki said, his voice still taut despite his light tone. "Considering the grudge Surt appears to have against you, I expect you're better off not trying to engage in any hand-to-hand combat. You move with us, create that connection, and then let us tackle the brute."

That was mostly how we'd fought as a unit before. Even with a sword and my valkyrie powers, I couldn't pack anywhere near as much punch as a god. But I'd always put up at least a bit of a real fight before rather than simply going through the motions. My stomach knotted.

"I could at least— Do you think the draugr have life energy I could tear away?" As a valkyrie, I had the ability to snuff out lives with a touch—the shadowy power Hod had contributed to my formation—but I'd never tried it on a creature that wasn't exactly alive anymore to begin with.

Hod frowned. He should know better than anyone else. "It's magic that animates the draugr, not any natural energy," he said. "No true life there for you to claim. The only way to stop them is to destroy them or destroy the one controlling them."

Great. Well, at least if I had something bigger than a pocketknife, I could behead a few or something.

The other gods were already hustling back from the house, Freya with her sword, Freyr with one of his own, Skadi with her golden bow and a bulging sheath of arrows, and Njord with a trident in his hand and a hooked blade dangling at his side. My gaze caught on a glint of metal in the shed beside the house. I dashed over, snatched up the hatchet the farm's former owners had left behind there, and ran back to join the others feeling a little more confident with its weight in my hand.

Loki took off into the sky. His shoes of flight could carry him miles with every stride if he didn't hold himself in check. The rest of us couldn't manage to soar quite that fast by our various means. I swept my wings through the cooling summer air, grateful for the nap I'd taken. My nerves buzzed, and my pulse thumped with anticipation, my mind starkly alert.

I didn't know if there was any chance we could end this war now, but we could at the very least prevent Surt from taking any more ground. Maybe we could wound him enough to make the battle to regain Asgard easier.

We were flying away from the sinking sun, into total night. Within a few minutes, we'd left the last glow of dusk behind completely. The lights of human civilization gleamed by beneath us: cars and trucks weaving along winding highways, little towns and vast cities glittering with their lesser and greater nightlife.

Loki paused and swerved to the left once, then again, and then a tad to the right as he must have been orienting himself with his awareness of Surt's magic. I still couldn't sense it at all. Then I didn't need his fiery affinity to track the giant's location, because a streak of flames came into view over the distant horizon, streaking down from the sky into the center of a sprawling city. A hint of acrid smoke prickled in my nose.

My heart lurched. Lights dotted skyscrapers and shorter buildings for what looked like several miles in every direction. There had to be millions of people living in that city. Millions that Surt and his army were probably slaughtering without hesitation right now.

I flapped my wings harder. A fresh strain spread through the muscles in my shoulders, but every second until we reached the city could mean dozens more lives lost. The people who lived there were just ordinary human beings who'd never had any idea that gods and giants might fight over their home. Ordinary men and women, innocent kids...

My fingers clenched around the handle of the hatchet. I'd take *Surt's* head off if I could. Let's see how he liked the same treatment he'd given Tyr.

The flaming bridge arced down into what appeared to be the downtown core, in the middle of some of the tallest buildings. Even as we soared over the suburbs, we couldn't make out what might be happening on the ground. The hiss of the flames reached my ears first. Then a distant booming like a series of sharp explosions.

We swooped between the skyscrapers. Freya darted into the lead and held out her hand to slow us. Take the lay of the land first, she'd said. I guessed that made sense, even if every muscle in my body was itching to dive in there and chop up any draug or giant I could.

At the goddess's gestures, we glided down onto the edge one of the lower rooftops and walked along it in silence to the far end that overlooked the foot of Surt's bridge. There was no need to worry about the locals noticing us, because our natural magic kept us invisible to humans unless we consciously decided to reveal ourselves, but one glance told me they wouldn't have been paying attention anyway.

The flaming arc touched down in the middle of a

wide road. A car unlucky enough to have been driving past that spot at exactly the wrong moment was now a mass of melting metal. The asphalt bubbled with a liquid gleam.

Draugr lumbered all across the road, hacking at the other cars that had pulled off at awkward angles, breaking down the doors of the shops and restaurants that lined the street. Bleeding bodies scattered the sidewalks. Shrieks and gasps carried up to us as more locals fled down the side-streets. Fire was crawling up the faces of several of the buildings the draugr had already trashed.

Surt stood in the center of it all on the top of an abandoned SUV, brandishing his sword and letting flames leap from its polished surface. "You see what I can do," he roared. "Obey me! Bring your leaders to me, or I'll raze this city to the ground."

"What does he want with their leaders?" I asked with a shudder. I didn't think any mayor would be in a hurry to offer himself up to that sword.

"It'd hardly be efficient for Surt to take over all of Midgard one city at a time," Loki said, his tone as sharp as it was wry. "He must think he can negotiate control over the entire country."

Oh. Maybe he could manage that. Anyone here who wasn't already desperate to end the carnage would be soon. These people didn't know how to fend off a monster like him.

But we did.

"There'll be no negotiation tonight," Thor rumbled,

swinging his hammer. "Let's take him. If we go at him now and fast, we might get a fatal strike in before he even realizes we've arrived."

That sounded like a perfectly good plan to me. Freya hesitated and then nodded. "You four and the valkyrie work your special connection. The rest of us will slip around to the other side to surround him. Wait until you see the flash of my cloak."

The other three gods followed her as she darted across the roof and vanished over the side. Thor leaned his brawny arms against the railing at the edge of the roof, studying the scene below us with a grim expression.

"Loki, since you can't bring your fire to bear directly against Surt, perhaps you should switch positions in our usual formation with Baldur," he said. "And Ari... You can stay behind all of us instead of in the center. That'll give Surt a harder time if he tries to target you again."

I wasn't going to use my gods like a shield. "I'll be fine," I started. "I'll be even more on guard this time."

Hod turned his head toward me with a pained grimace, and I realized I didn't really want to have this argument. I didn't want them worrying about me because I'd insisted on being closer to the front lines than I had to be. That would only distract them from the important thing here, which was pummeling Surt into a pulp.

"But I'll be fine at the back of the formation too," I amended. "You focus on Surt, and I'll be there to cover you if the draugr get feisty."

Loki snorted at the same time as he tousled my hair affectionately. "They'll be sorry they ever met you, pixie."

"Get ready," Thor said. "We need to move the moment we see Freya's signal."

We gathered around him at the edge of the roof. Doing my best to ignore the bloodbath on the street, I searched the shadows around the building across from us, a bank office with mirrored windows.

I'd just caught a flash of golden feathers when Loki, who must have spotted it a split-second sooner, said, "Let's go!"

We moved together so well now that we didn't need any more cue than that. The gods sprang over the railing straight into our formation as they swooped down toward Surt; I fell in behind them with a flap of my wings. I braced my legs and raised my axe, and that common pulse flowed through us all as the gods launched their attacks.

Unfortunately, as soon as we'd left the shelter of the building, the element of surprise was gone. Surt's head snapped around at the motion from above or maybe the sound of Mjolnir whipping toward him. With a gnash of his teeth, he threw himself down and to the side of the SUV.

Thor's hammer clipped him across the shoulder all the same, making him lurch. He still slashed his sword up to deflect the bolt of scorching darkness Hod and Loki must have produced in tandem. Then he ripped the blade through the air, sending out a roaring wave of flames.

He'd marked my presence, even here at the back. The flames dipped and leapt and twisted, a few streaks of them racing around the magical shields the gods threw up. Those streaks raced straight toward me.

My body flinched in memory of yesterday's pain. My wings heaved me upward, but the rippling lines of magical fire shot after me. I dodged to the side, and hands grasped my shoulders, yanking me down.

I hit the street cushioned by a swath of shadow. Hod braced himself over me, Surt's flames sizzling against the dark shell he'd called up around us. The blind god's chest pinned me to the ground, his breath spilling with a rasp against my cheek. I might have been able to enjoy the feeling of him lying over me now if I hadn't known we had a battle to get back to.

"I was getting out of the way," I said.

"Ari," Hod said, his voice ragged, "I could hear the fire. You were almost cinders."

He shoved himself onto his feet and offered his hand to help me up. I didn't even have time to thank him before Thor let out a war cry. We dashed back into the chaos.

Freya's contingent had launched an attack from the other side of the street and then scattered in the wake of Surt's flames. Our group came at him again, but the gods shifted closer together, their movements more defensive than offensive. Trying to protect me.

Guilt jabbed at my gut. I'd been the one who'd deepened their connection with each other, and now I was holding them back.

We swiveled around Surt as one, searching for an opening. The crackle of gunfire echoed down the street. My gaze jerked up.

A mass of human soldiers in army fatigues was pouring onto the road, rifles raised. The gods lurched out of the way as the squadron opened fire on Surt. The giant whirled his sword in the air, sending the bullets ricocheting away with a wheel of fire. He laughed and waved his draugr army forward.

One of the soldiers hollered. With an eerie whine, a land missile hurtled toward the giant.

I thought I saw Surt's eyes widen. He lurched backward, but the projectile came too fast. It tore through the side of his thigh, shredding the flesh almost to the bone.

His draugr gouged open the chests of several of the soldiers, but the human army smashed a whole bunch of their skulls in turn. Surt scrambled around the SUV, blood gushing down his leg. He slapped his sword against the wound to seal the flesh with a stomach-turning hiss. He looked as if he were gnashing his teeth.

"It'll have been a long time since he tangoed with any humans who weren't already dead," Loki murmured beside me. "I do believe our fiery giant has underestimated their resilience. And their weaponry." He motioned to the other three. "I can fend off the bullets with my fire. We can take him down while he's dealing with the bazookas."

But before the trickster had even finished speaking, Surt had heaved himself onto the base of his flaming bridge. "You'll all die!" he roared. "Gods, humans, all of you pathetic things."

He jabbed his sword into the bridge. The flames flooded the street, bowling over the nearest soldiers, licking under the horde of draugr. Then, carrying Surt's army and the giant himself, it retracted back into the sky toward Asgard like an elastic band recoiling.

Thor grasped my arm with one hand and Hod's with the other, dragging us away from the road. "He's not doing any more damage here tonight. We'd better regroup before he does."

9

Loki

"Surt was stronger than I expected," Freyr admitted with a dramatic shake of his head. The god of plenty had always enjoyed making much of his opinions. "And the draugr, with the weapons he's given them—they were formidable too."

"The *humans* were the ones that forced him back in the end, not us," Skadi said with a note of disgust. Her lip curled disdainfully.

We were gathered around the farmhouse's dining room table again, a little fresher after a night's rest but far from at ease. Ari was pacing along the edges of the room around us, her eyes bright with what looked like an equal mix of panic and ferocity. Her shoulders twitched at the huntress's remark.

"There were a few hundred more of those human soldiers than there were of us," I pointed out. "And I think we can claim a partial victory. If Surt hadn't needed to contend with us as well as the humans with guns, he might very well have managed to level them—and then the rest of the city."

"But we need to be moving into offense efforts, not constantly defending against him," Freya said. "He's still dictating the battlegrounds."

"If we're going to have any hope of confronting him in Asgard now that he's entrenched there, we'll need greater numbers of our own," Skadi said. "There has to be a faster way of tracking down the rest of the gods."

"Whoever's still left," Hod said quietly. The blind god had seen a few of the lesser Aesir off to their final ends. I didn't think those petulant souls would have contributed much to our cause anyway.

"Vidar may have seen some of the others," Njord suggested. "If his brothers manage to bring him back, Freyr and I could search the coastal lands with Freyr's boat. We'd cover a lot of ground that way."

"But that would leave us without the two of you for several days at least, through any other attacks Surt launches on Midgard," I said. "I'd imagine Thor would have my head if I approved of that plan in his absence." Our valkyrie wouldn't be terribly pleased about it either.

Njord scowled at me, but he couldn't exactly argue with my statement. The Thunderer had made his feelings about prioritizing the safety of Midgard very clear yesterday. I doubted the sea god would have mentioned the idea at all if Thor and Baldur hadn't set off on Freyr's directions to see if they could bring their hard-hitting brother back to us.

Freyr raised his head at a haughty angle. "Do you have a plan, Trickster? Isn't plotting supposed to be your area of expertise? Or have you lost your touch for scheming?"

It was hard to tell from his tone whether he'd have preferred I'd gone dull over the centuries or not. I offered him a sharp smile. "I do have a thought, actually. In consideration of... How many of the gods we haven't yet collected are even warriors? There's little point in gathering those with no relevant skills to offer. We ought to accept that we're not going to build up an entire army of our own—not one large enough to simply barge into Asgard and toss Surt and all his undead minions out."

"You're not saying we should leave the realm of the gods to a *giant*," Skadi said, with just enough edge to her horrified voice to tell me she remembered very well that I had been born kin to Surt myself.

Through an epic effort of self-restraint that I wouldn't get any credit for, I managed not to glower in her direction. "Of course not," I said. "I'm simply suggesting that *we* choose the grounds of our final battle. We can't do that in Asgard where he's already laid claim to all the ground. We already know he's prepared to act on Midgard. *He* knows we're here and doing our best to get in his way. It shouldn't be too difficult a thing to lure him into an ambush."

"An ambush," Njord repeated, as if it were the first time that word had entered his vocabulary.

"Yes. We lead him to believe we'll be up to something—gathering weapons for the battle, meeting with potential allies, something else he wouldn't like—in a specific spot. He'll charge down to slaughter us, but we'll be waiting for his arrival. Before he can get his bearings, we end him."

"Do you think he's really worried enough about our interference to bother?" Freya asked.

That was a reasonable question. "Perhaps we need to offer more incentive than that," I said. "We could use a human city as part of the lure, make him think it'd be an ideal target because of worldly influence or what have you. Two birds with one stone—very tempting."

Ari halted in her pacing. "Then you'd be tempting him to come down and kill a whole bunch of defenseless people."

I offered her a mollifying look. "The intent would be that we'd kill him before he had the chance. I don't want to see more bleeding bodies in the streets if I don't have to either."

Njord muttered something under his breath even my excellent hearing didn't quite catch—something along the lines of he'd have thought I'd have enjoyed a scene like that. I kept my hands braced against the table, my smile in place.

There was nothing strange about his attitude toward me—or Skadi's or Freyr's. Not long ago, any of my usual companions might have made the same sorts of remarks. If Hod was expressing himself more moderately now, it was only because of how his eyes had been opened, figuratively speaking, to the fuller truth of our shared history. After those revelations about their own father's insistence on my supposed duplicities and after discovering the connection we'd forged through our valkyrie, I thought he and Baldur and Thor might be finally setting the old wariness and prejudices aside.

But now we were calling the rest of Asgard back to us, and I could hardly replicate the exact same experiences to transform their opinions of me. I wasn't certain I'd even want to go through all that turmoil again.

No, the truth was that if we settled back into Asgard as a larger community again, it would be as it always was before. I would be the interloping traitorous giant only allowed a place thanks to Odin's possibly misguided good will, every comment I made would be viewed by nearly everyone around me with suspicion, and every tragedy would immediately result in at least a few fingers pointed my way.

Perhaps the last several weeks had changed *me* more than I'd realized too, because even as that realization settled over me, my usual ire didn't stir. What of it? I'd lived that way for centuries before. *I* knew who I was, possibly better than I ever had. This time, at least, I had a few companions I might hope would speak up in my defense without prodding. The opinions of those four were the only ones that mattered to me.

It really would have been too much to hope we'd all live together in Baldur's dream of perfect harmony for more than a few hours, hadn't it? I was more practical than that. If I felt a pinch of loss, surely it wasn't for that hogwash. It was for the frown that crossed Ari's face as her gaze jerked toward Njord too.

She might very well have heard him. The newly returned gods would do their best to make her regret her associations with me, no doubt. And what happened to her... that mattered to me more than nearly anything else I could think of.

I had faith in her affections. After the way she'd gazed into my eyes and told me she trusted me with her in every possible way, how could I not trust her? She wasn't the type to waver because of someone else's snarky remarks. But she shouldn't have needed to bear those remarks in the first place.

She deserved to take pride in every man or god she chose to stand beside.

"How would we pass on word to Surt without him realizing we wanted him to arrive?" Freya asked, drawing my mind back to the current topic of debate.

"Perhaps Muninn could go to him as if to make amends," I started.

Ari shook her head. "She expects him to try to kill her if he sees her again. She might not have the chance to say anything if we sent her to Asgard—if she'd even agree to take the risk."

I couldn't fault the raven for looking after her own feathered hide. I tapped my lips, considering our alternatives, and the house's front door thumped open.

"Look who we dredged up," Thor called in a jovial tone. He and Baldur ushered our newest arrival into the dining room.

Vidar might as well have been created by throwing those two of his brothers into a blender. He stood just an inch or two shy of Thor's massive height, his shoulders and chest nearly as broad. His short-trimmed hair and neat beard gleamed a reddish gold. His expression, though, was almost as solemn as Hod's so often was. So perhaps all three of his brothers had ended up in that blender.

I wondered if that was the face he'd made when he'd kicked open my wolfish son's jaws and stabbed a sword down Fenrir's throat. It was hard to say, since whenever I'd seen him speak of that moment during Ragnarok, he'd always smiled with the telling.

"Brother," he said, with a tip of his head to Hod. "It is unfortunate that these are the circumstances under which all of us have come back together. I understand we have a rampaging giant to put down."

"We were just discussing our next steps," Skadi said. "The trickster, naturally, thinks we should trick Surt into an ambush. Laying a whole city out as bait."

She hadn't seemed to care all that much about human cities when she was complaining about the effectiveness of their soldiers.

Vidar's gaze slid to me. "Surely there is a more honorable tactic we can employ?"

I managed not to roll my eyes. I didn't even hold any particular animosity against Vidar—he had killed my son avenging my son's devouring of his father, so really, who was I to criticize?—but his strengths were clearly not in his head.

"Surt has shown no indication of honor," I said. "We can't expect him to comply with any rules we lay down for fair combat. It seems to me the most honorable thing is to prevent him for destroying any more innocent lives as swiftly as we can by whatever means necessary. Any other definition of honor may give him room to destroy dozens more cities while we dress up our war in silks."

"I agree with Loki," Ari said, catching my gaze for a second before meeting Vidar's eyes. "I don't like putting more people in Midgard at risk, but it does seem like they're in more danger otherwise. And that's speaking as the only person here who was ever human herself."

Even as I saw a few pairs of eyes narrow at her, I couldn't completely suppress my smile. Our valkyrie certainly provided plenty of reasons to be proud of *her*. She wasn't going to be cowed by any god.

Hod shifted by the corner of the table. "I agree with Loki too," he said, and I was still capable of being a little surprised he'd admit as much. "Surt has been preparing for this war for decades, maybe centuries. How can we compete with that unless we find some way to even the odds in our favor?"

"He's certainly made use of everything and everyone he could," Freya muttered, and my mind lit on just the idea.

"Not just Muninn," I said. "The dark elves as well. One of *them* could manage to pass on word of some city we're especially trying to preserve. Send someone injured by one of their cave-ins—he'll believe they'd still want to claim Midgard alongside him. Can you get them to agree to that, Dark One?"

Hod's mouth tightened. "I'm not sure. It would be a much smaller act than giving all of us permission to carry on our war efforts through their caves or handing over weaponry..." He hesitated as if he weren't sure of his next words. "Maybe they'd be more easily persuaded if you came along to lay out how well this plan of yours ought to work."

The god who was recently my most obstinate critic was inviting me along to meddle with his alliance? I blinked as I recovered my tongue. We really had come a long way, hadn't we?

"If you think it would make the proposal go down more smoothly, I am entirely at your disposal," I said with a mock bow. The corner of Hod's lips curled with what might have been a hint of a smile.

"Hold on," Vidar said, as if he'd been leading this discussion rather than arriving toward the end of it. "We'd better hammer out the details of that proposal first before we go setting the pieces in motion."

"I completely agree," I said, and snapped my fingers to call up a tracing of flames on the tabletop in the shape of Midgard's continents. "First let us pick a city."

As the other gods leaned forward in consideration, a small spark of satisfaction leapt in my chest. Whatever they thought of me, they couldn't deny the worth of my insight. But all the same, the victory rang a bit hollow.

This plan was more trickery, as Skadi had said. Sly schemes were how I worked best. Would there ever be more than that I could offer and have accepted?

10

Aria

"He may be reluctant to show himself," Vidar said in his knowing voice as Muninn and I prepared to leave. He'd insisted on walking us to the front door and then out, adding a few last-minute bits of advice that just rehashed what he'd already told us. "I'm lucky I saw Heimdall recently at all. The second I moved toward him and he noticed me, he pushed me backward with his magic and had already hurried off when I recovered myself."

"Got it," I said. We'd heard all about that encounter before we'd started making plans. Heimdall's apparent hesitation to deal with any of the gods was the whole reason Muninn and I were making the trip alone. But I wouldn't be surprised to find out Vidar had forgotten I'd even been in the room when that discussion had taken place. He wasn't overtly condescending like some of the newer gods, but every now and then he shot a puzzled glance my way as if he couldn't figure out why I was in the room.

Muninn tugged impatiently at her dress. The wind rippled over the long grass in the yard outside the country home we'd managed to find not far from Beijing, the city the gods had chosen for their lure and ambush. We had a long flight ahead of us, much of it over the Pacific Ocean. Vidar had spotted Heimdall in a town on the outskirts of the Canadian north, dressed like an outdoorsman.

Vidar sucked in a breath as if he were about to give us some other repeated insight, and I jumped in before he could. "Ready?" I said to Muninn. She gave me a brisk nod, I offered Vidar a quick wave, and the raven and I leapt into the air together.

Muninn's wings might have been smaller, but with only her compact bird body to propel forward, she could match my speed no problem. We soared over the great sprawling city Loki expected would tempt Surt into appearing and across the plains beyond, dotted with innumerable towns. The Yellow Sea glittered up ahead.

With our supernatural speed, we hoped to be back within a day. The ambush was planned for the day after tomorrow—a supposed meeting at noon with representatives of the Chinese government to form a god-human alliance. Skadi had snorted at the idea and Freyr had chuckled, but it seemed like something Surt might believe and want to prevent. What we'd actually do was gather around the park where the fake negotiations were meant to take place an hour early, poised to spring on Surt before his flaming bridge even touched the ground.

Flying with Muninn was a lonely business, I discovered. Not that I wanted to be constantly chattering, but she couldn't say anything at all in her bird form. At least Freya could shrug her cloak back and still fly with it just covering her arms if she wanted to. For a while, there was nothing but salty wind whipping my hair, warbling waves below me, and that small black form flapping steadily on just a few feet away. The sun peaked over us and then started to dip behind us.

Well, at least I was doing something useful. Loki thought Heimdall's magic might give us the advantage we needed to take back Asgard. If the ambush plan failed, he might be our only hope.

My wings were just starting to prickle with fatigue when the coastline came into view up ahead. Muninn glanced over at me, her beady eyes gleaming. I thought I could read the same thing I was thinking in the tilt of her head.

"We'll take a moment to catch our breath?" I said.

Her head bobbed. When we reached the land, we dipped down onto a wild stretch that was all wet rock and brambly bushes. I sank onto a boulder and massaged the base of my wings where they met my shoulder blades.

Muninn shifted into human form and leaned over, touching her toes and stretching her back. The knobs of her spine pressed against her thin dress. We were still on the summer side of the hemisphere, but the evening breeze off the ocean had a cool edge to it that she didn't appear to feel.

I couldn't help glancing toward the dimming sky to the southeast. If my sense of direction was right, we weren't that far from Petey's new home. The idea tugged at my gut. I could have made a small detour and checked in on him... but what if Surt or a lackey we didn't know about managed to track my movements there somehow?

Every part of me ached to see my little brother again, but that was a selfish longing. The right thing to do was to stay far away for as long as I might still put him in danger.

"You're thinking about him," Muninn said. "The little boy."

My gaze jerked back to her. "My brother," I said.

She nodded as if it were all the same to her. "What you're thinking of affects the memories that drift off you," she said, which I guessed was how she'd known. She paused. "He means a lot to you."

"He's the most important thing in the world to me. Can't you see that from my memories?"

"There's not much sense of relative emotion... Caring about someone in that sort of way, as a child, isn't something I have much personal experience with to compare."

She didn't have siblings, presumably. Could the raven woman even *have* kids, in either of her forms? It seemed rude to ask something that private. I shuffled my feet, and then said, "You cared a lot about those three guys Odin brought back for you."

"Yes." Her voice dropped to a murmur. "They're the

only beings I've ever really cared about. Loved. They woke up something in me I hadn't known I was capable of feeling. Serving Odin meant something to me, but as a matter of pride, not..." She shook herself. "But that is in the past now."

She hadn't quite managed to dislodge the haunted look that had come over her face. My chest tightened. How long ago had she lost her three lovers? And all the time since then, she'd been tangled up in mourning them and raging at Odin.

After we ended this war, she'd have a chance to find some kind of love again. Not that it seemed at all polite to mention that either.

"I'm sorry he couldn't bring them back for longer," I said instead. Odin had summoned the spirits of Muninn's three lovers as a sort of apology—to show he understood what she was mourning, I guessed—but they were so long dead he hadn't been able to sustain that magic for much time.

Muninn gave me a small tight smile. "As am I. Are you rested enough? Shall we track down our watchful god? We may need to cover a lot more ground."

Heimdall might not even still be in this part of the world. But the sooner we figured that out, the better. "Let's go," I said.

We flew across thick evergreen forests and rolling green hills that led up to snow-topped mountains. I stayed high so I could scan as much ground as possible, peering through the thinning daylight and then dipping closer to reach out my senses for any hint of the warmly radiant godly energy all of the Aesir gave off. I wasn't sure even straining my hardest if I'd be able to pick it up at any kind of distance, but that talent had helped us find the dark elves before. It couldn't hurt to try.

In the end, it wasn't any supernatural vibe that caught my attention. It was a path of flat stones just above the rushing surface of a wide river. They wove slightly as they marked a course across the water, but they were too close together and too consistent for me to believe they'd ended up there by chance. But we'd seen no sign of anyone living nearby for miles.

Maybe the god who'd once guarded the world's greatest bridge had found himself making new ones?

I swooped along the forested slope beside the river, my search focused on the water now. Several miles farther along the river's course, another line of stones had been set out. Were they for his own use? Just out of habit? I couldn't imagine any god *needed* stepping stones to cross a river.

A thin stream of smoke trickled up against the purpling sky to the north. I slowed, and Muninn did the same. If Heimdall was living out here, we had to go cautiously as we came close. I might not be a god, but he'd know I'd come from Asgard easily enough. He might even recognize Muninn as more than a simple raven. The gods had said his vision was even sharper than Loki's.

Of course, he'd only know I was from Asgard if he saw my wings. The rest of me looked human enough. Human enough that plenty of the gods couldn't seem to forget that I was more than that now.

When the first hint of the smoky smell reached my nose, I decided it was time to switch to walking. I glided down between the pines and drew my wings into my body. The ache of their muscles melted into my back.

Muninn flew on between the trees as I picked my way over logs and past low needley branches out to the riverbank. The pebbles there rattled under my sneakers. Hiking boots would be more appropriate for this terrain, but I hadn't needed to think about footwear too much lately. They'd have to do.

I still had my valkyrie reflexes, which let me set my feet down quietly when I wanted to. With careful control over my balance, I marched silently along the rough slabs of rock that bordered the river. Here and there, the uneven surface had gathered pockets of dirt where grass and little wildflowers sprouted. The river rushed on with a steady warbling.

We must have traveled at least a few miles more when I caught a brief movement up ahead. I froze, training my eyes on that spot farther up the river.

A tall man with shaggy sandy-brown hair was crouched next to the bank. He dipped his hands into the water, and the deer standing next to him lowered her head to drink. A fawn stood on wobbly legs next to her.

The man raised a slow hand, and a stone like the ones I'd seen before rose to the surface of the water. Then another, then another. When they formed a line all the way across the river, he eased upright and swept his arm as if to say to the deer, *There you go.*

The deer and her fawn gambled across the rocks with hesitant steps and then darted into the brush on the other side. The man I had to assume was Heimdall waved his hand, and the stones sank. I guessed he didn't think that bridge would get much use. But he'd raised it with his powers just so those two animals could reach new ground.

He was the god of connections, and he liked to help creatures weaker than himself. It might be a good thing I'd arrived in my sneakers after all.

I let my feet come down carelessly as I walked on, not minding if the pebbles rattled. The breeze tousled my hair, and I let the dark blond strands hang tangled beside my face. The air was mild but not especially warm—a regular human would have been cold in this shirt. I rubbed my arms for effect. A rock rolled under my heel, and I even let myself stumble.

When I looked up again, I was close enough that even regular human eyes could have made out Heimdall. He was standing where I'd seen him before, watching me. I stopped, hugging myself as if scared by the sight. This gambit would work even better if I could get him to come to me.

And he did. With even strides just a smidgen too quick to be of this realm, he came up to me.

"Are you all right?" he said in a brisk voice. "What are you doing all the way out here dressed like that?"

I gazed up at him, opening my eyes wide. "I was looking for you," I said. "Are you Heimdall?"

His shoulders stiffened under his sheepskin jacket. His foot shifted as if to back up, and my hand shot out pleadingly.

"Don't go! You have no idea how far I've come... Don't make me go back with nothing."

"Go back where?" he asked, outright brusque now.

I ignored that question. He was listening well enough that I could get the important part out now. "Surt has taken over Asgard and driven out everyone who was living there. He's trying to destroy all of Midgard too so he can use it for him and his allies. He's already killed so many people."

Heimdall stared at me. "Who are you?" he demanded. "*What* are you?"

"A messenger," I said. "Someone who used to belong to this world and doesn't want to see it going up in flames. You care about this place, don't you? I don't know what problems you have with any of the gods, but you know what Surt is capable of."

"Odin wouldn't want *me*," Heimdall said, his face hardening. "You've come for the wrong god."

He turned, and Muninn landed where he was now looking, transforming while he watched.

"I wouldn't be here if that were true," she said.

"The powers you have might be the key to saving this realm and Asgard," I said. "Even if they're not, we need all the help we can get against Surt's army. You'll have to face him eventually, even if you try to hide away."

"Why would he bother with the wilderness up here?" Heimdall said.

"Why would he let you keep roaming around? He wants to destroy you all. He's going to bring the giants and the dark elves and who knows who else to take over this place. They're not going to care about preserving the forests or the deer." I gestured toward the river.

"I was angry at Odin once," Muninn added. She raised his chin. "I helped Surt capture him and keep him in a cage—I was *that* angry. But I realized, after a time... He truly doesn't intend cruelty, even when that is the result he produces. Whatever he did to wound you, he did it because he thought it was right for Asgard. That's always what he thinks of first. It's a little sad, really. It's his loss, not ours."

Heimdall grimaced at her. "Why are you telling me that?"

"Because letting your anger direct you is like holding a grudge against the river for flowing downstream. Because the Heimdall I knew who watched me come and go so often wouldn't have been able to bear to see the realms shattered by war."

Heimdall's jaw worked. I grasped onto one last appeal I could make.

"Please," I said. "I'm not asking you for them or even for me. I have a little brother. If Surt carries out his plan, he'll end up dead or worse. He's six years old. This realm should be his."

Tension squeezed around my heart as I waited. Heimdall sighed and shoved his hands in the pockets of his jacket.

"You drive a hard bargain," he said, sounding not at all happy about it. "All right. I'll talk with them. That's the most I can promise."

11

Aria

The dining room in our new residence was a little larger than the last one, which was a good thing, because even this one was getting crowded. A couple delegations of gods had managed to turn up three more former Asgardians who'd joined the conversation along with Heimdall. There was constant shifting around the table as one or another made room for someone else to speak.

I hung back in the corner. No one asked what I thought about anything, and maybe I didn't have as much to contribute as the actual gods, but I wanted to at least keep track of what was going on.

Other than a jovial "Good work!" from Thor when I'd walked in with Heimdall a few hours ago, no one had even acknowledged what I *had* contributed. As if they figured it'd been as easy as walking over to the watchful god and just asking him to take a trip with me. Or maybe the newer ones figured it'd been all Muninn.

"That first step is done," Hod was saying, at the head of the table for now. He'd just returned from another visit to Nidavellir. "One of the dark elves will pass on the supposedly secret information about our meeting in the park tomorrow. Their leaders are still hesitating to help us in any more concrete ways, though."

"Do the dirt-eaters really want that giant ruling over them?" Skadi muttered.

"Easy for them to ignore destruction that hasn't yet touched their realm," Vidar said.

Hadn't anyone told him that destruction *had* touched the dark elves—because of the gods' neglect? Why would they jump to put their necks that far on the line when they'd already been burned? From the tensing of Hod's mouth, I suspected he was thinking the same thing.

Before the dark god could say anything like that, Njord pushed up to the table, bumping Hod to the side. "We should expect Surt to arrive tomorrow, then," he said. "What do we still need to get in place for this ambush?"

Several gazes turned toward Loki, I guessed since he was the one who'd come up with the plan. He snapped his fingers. "Who has that map? We'll want to pick our positions carefully."

"Force from all sides," Freya said, squeezing over beside him. When one of the others tossed the map of the park we'd gotten onto the table, she grasped it and took charge of the discussion. "We can't give Surt enough time to deflect all of us. In that first charge, one of us must strike a fatal blow. We won't get half as good a chance once we've lost the element of surprise."

All sides. I perked up with a spark of an idea. "Could we cut straight through the bridge with magic and attack him through it too?" I said, pitching my voice loud enough to carry through the room. "Maybe Hod's shadows could snuff some of the flames?"

"Is that the valkyrie?" one of the newest arrivals asked, craning her neck.

Freyr waved his hand dismissively. "Save the strategizing to those with the experience. For an attack this important, we can't be depending on an unpracticed skill." He turned back to the table, leaning in beside his sister, as if his godly talents had anything to do with war. "Now, it seems to me—"

I stepped back to the wall, my jaw tight, but apparently I wasn't the only one irked by the god of plenty's brisk brush-off. Thor set his heavy hand down on the table.

"Hold on," he said in his rumble of a voice. "Ari has had *more* recent experience with Surt and his minions than most of the rest of you. Her ideas have gotten us far before. We shouldn't ignore them out of hand."

"You have nearly three times as many godly minds at your disposal than you did in recent weeks," Freyr said. "And little time to spare for exploring wild imaginings."

"Aria's suggestion didn't sound all that wild to me," Baldur put in, gentle but firm. "It's not as if we couldn't generate fire of our own to practice with."

"But we don't know exactly how Surt's magic works,"

one of the other new arrivals said. "If we want to end him quickly, we should stick to what we know."

Njord nodded. "I agree. Valkyries have their place—in Valhalla. This is a totally different matter."

"You wouldn't say that if you'd been around for half of the battles we've already fought," Loki said with an edge in his lilting voice. "Perhaps it's been too long since you fought any battles."

"Perhaps we've already fought too many of them, thanks to you and your kind," Heimdall snapped from where he'd been standing stiffly by the far corner of the table.

Thor's hand clenched against the table. Loki grinned with a baring of teeth, a hard glint in his eyes that I didn't think would lead anywhere good. My stomach knotted. I stepped forward, touching their arms.

"It's okay," I said. "I don't have the same kind of experience. I don't have the knowledge. Whatever the rest of you decide, I'll pitch in wherever you need me."

We weren't going to win any battles if we started fighting each other. Up until now, I'd been the one who bound the gods together. The last thing I wanted was to be the cause of some kind of schism between my gods and those we'd managed to gather. Stopping Surt was more important than what any of them thought of me.

I could decide how to earn their respect, if I even bothered to, when there wasn't a mad giant trying to end the world as we knew it.

"Pixie," Loki said, with a look that suggested he'd been looking forward to roasting a few of his companions.

I squeezed his forearm. “No. Keep working out the plan. I need to stretch my legs a bit.”

Hod turned his head my way as I slipped out of the room, but I didn’t wait to see if anyone would follow. I didn’t want them to. I hurried along the tiled floor and ducked out onto the covered porch.

The stretch of my wings as I unfolded them over my head was a sort of relief. After the hard flight yesterday and overnight, the muscles were starting to cramp staying compressed inside my human body. I gave them a few tentative flaps, stretching them out with an enjoyable burn, and then lifted off into the air.

I’d thought maybe Muninn would like some company. We could commiserate about not being entirely welcome among the gods or something. But when I glided up to the house’s curved tiled rooftop, there was no sign of the raven. She must have gone off to patrol or to chase down some other lead.

I ended up circling in wider and wider sweeps over the house’s grounds. A little stream ran through the property at the north end by a wrought-iron fence. To the west, in a small clearing inside a clump of forest, a gazebo stood, its faded blue paint flaking off the wood. South was the narrow road that led into the nearest town, and east was the rise of a hill dotted with little purple flowers. Their delicate scent reached my nose even from high above.

The warm wind caught my wings and let me coast for a while. I didn’t really want to go back down. What the hell *did* I know about fighting giants? I’d developed my chops in minor skirmishes on Philly’s streets, with guys who only stayed tough until you kneed them in the balls—and the guys too tough for that, I'd kept my head low around and skipped any need to fight.

I'd drifted out past the gazebo again when Thor's voice reached me. "Ari?"

He was standing by the structure's narrow steps. I wheeled and dropped down into the clearing to meet him.

It was amazing how the fierce warrior who battered our enemies without restraint could also look at me with a gaze so soft and set his broad hand on my shoulder with a touch so careful. "Are you okay?" he asked.

"Sure," I said. "Are the plans all worked out? What's our position for tomorrow?" The one thing I knew for sure was that my four gods and I would be coming at Surt together, even if they kept me at the back again.

"We worked out a solid strategy," the thunder god said. "But that's not what I wanted to talk about. I want you to know I'd have liked to bowl over most of those knuckleheads with Mjolnir, the way they were talking about you."

The corner of my mouth twitched upward. "I appreciate the sentiment," I said, "but I've got a pretty thick skin by now. I've heard a hell of a lot worse from people who owed me a hell of a lot more." My mother, my supposed father figures, teachers and kids I'd grown up with...

Thor made a growling sound. "Which is exactly why you shouldn't have to put up with that from anyone here. The other gods... We Asgardians can become somewhat stuck in our ways. You shook up our little group, jostled loose some new ideas, but the others are still wrapping their heads around the fact that we've lost our entire realm. They're not looking deeply enough to see everything you have to offer right now, but they will. Even if it requires a hammer to the head to make sure of it."

His vehemence tugged at my heart. Not that long ago, he'd been struggling with the feeling that the other gods in our little group were dismissing *his* ideas, seeing him as nothing more than the brawn with no brains worth listening to. I'd encouraged him to believe he could be more than they saw. Now he was returning the favor.

Our situations weren't quite the same, though. "Hopefully that won't be necessary," I said. "Especially since in some ways they're right. I might be stronger than the average human, but I'm weaker than any of you, by a lot. Both physically and when it comes to any kind of magical powers. It's not like I came into the strength I have on my own either. I'm basically something the four of you made—a human turned into a patchwork valkyrie, powers borrowed and wings pasted on."

I waggled my wingtips and started to retract them into my back. Thor's hand shot out, but his fingers were gentle when they brushed the feathered surface.

"No," he said, his voice so thick and his body so close that I tingled right down to my toes. "Leave them out."

I let them completely open again. Thor skimmed his hand over the bony frame that arced from my shoulder blades through their length and then teased his fingertips down over the thinner flesh that made up most of their surface. Everywhere he touched, a quiver of electricity shot through my nerves.

I'd rarely had anyone touch my wings at all except to slash at them in combat. Definitely no one had ever explored that new part of my body anywhere near this tenderly.

"You're so much more than a patchwork valkyrie, Ari," Thor said. His head bowed next to mine as he traced the arc of my wing again, and my pulse kicked up a notch in anticipation. "You were *you* before we ever found you. All we did was build on the strength you already had so much of. That's why you're here and not the other valkyries we summoned."

"Or maybe I just got lucky?"

He snorted. His warm breath caressed the side of my face. "Not a chance. I've watched you in action. I've fought alongside you. I've seen how fierce you can be. Ask any of the gods in there who the strongest of us is, and they'd point to me. You can bring me to my knees."

A tendril of desire unfurled through my belly, trailing lower. "Oh, really?" I murmured. "You seem to be standing just fine right now."

Thor's hand fell to my side. He tipped his head to tease his lips across my cheek. He kissed the corner of my jaw, the side of my neck, with a more literal electricity, slipping from his caress in blissful little sparks. My breath caught as he started to sink in front of me.

His kisses crossed my collarbone and marked a heated path down the front of my shirt. My nipples pebbled as his head dipped between them, but his stubbled jaw only brushed my breasts briefly. His knees hit the grassy ground, as promised. He pressed his lips just above my bellybutton. His thumbs hooked over the waist of my jeans. He looked up at me, his brown eyes dark with wanting, waiting for my permission.

A tremor ran through me, but it was all eagerness. "Please," I breathed, resting my hand on his dark auburn hair. A few thick strands slipped loose of his short ponytail as he leaned even closer.

He kissed my belly where my shirt rode up just slightly over my jeans. Then the line of my fly, until the pressure of his mouth settled right over my core. Even with two layers of fabric between us, a whimper escaped me.

"Not good enough," he muttered. With a yank of his hands, he wrenched my jeans and panties to my knees. In an instant, his hot lips pressed against me skin to skin.

I whimpered as his tongue flicked over my clit and then delved lower. More sparks raced over my core. My legs wobbled with the rush of pleasure. Thor gripped my thighs firmly, holding me up while he devoured me. My fingers tangled in his hair. I held on tight, riding each wave of sensation as the strokes of his mouth and the wash of his breath sent me higher and higher.

He teased his tongue over my opening over and over, curling up inside so I gasped, before returning to my clit. The edges of his teeth just barely grazed it. He swiveled the tip of his tongue around that nub, making me cry out. I rocked into his mouth, so close, so close.

He suckled me even harder with a blissfully sharp jolt of his powers, and pleasure burst through my body. I came shaking against his lips, drooping over him as my body turned to jelly. He kept working me over, holding me up with those big hands, until the aftershock subsided.

When he started to get up, I'd recovered my wits enough to push him back down. "Oh, no. We're not finished here."

Thor grinned as I nudged him back so he could lean against the base of the gazebo. The old wood creaked faintly at his weight. I trailed my hand down his torso to the hard hot length of his cock. He groaned when I palmed him.

We were *definitely* not finished. I kicked my jeans all the way off and tugged his down in turn. As I climbed onto his lap, our mouths met for the first time. I could taste my own tang on his lips and the thicker salty essence that was all him.

Thor pulled me right up against his chest, cupping my breast, claiming my lips even more thoroughly. I rubbed my core against his erection from head to base and back again.

"Fucking hell, Ari," he said hoarsely. "When I've got you like this, I could stay on my knees for the rest of my life."

"No need for that," I said by his ear. "I like variety."

His chuckle was lost in my mouth as I kissed him again, hard. I sank lower, taking his thick length inside me, and another groan reverberated in his chest. I moaned in turn as he stretched me like no one else ever could.

His hands slid down to my ass. We set a rhythm together, bucking into each other as our mouths mashed and parted with gasps and collided again. His godly strength rippled through his muscles all around me, but right then, I didn't feel weak at all. I matched him pulse for pulse, a fresh surge of pleasure racing through my body with every breathtaking shiver of his electric magic.

He nudged me a little forward, and his cock impaled me even more deeply. Bliss burned through my core. If I split apart, it would be the most beautiful breaking of my life. The wall of the gazebo shuddered as if it might break from the power of our fucking too.

"Ari," Thor said, his voice so ragged with need that it tipped me over the edge. My second orgasm knocked the breath from my lungs and the voice from my throat with a punch of ecstasy. My thighs clenched around Thor's hips, and he surged up into me with a rough sound. The heat of his release filled me even more than I already had been.

I sagged into his embrace, my nerves humming with pleasure. Thor hugged me to him with his chin beside my forehead. The power and the gentleness twined together through his body brought an ache into my chest. I swallowed hard.

How was it that every time I thought my heart couldn't get fuller, it expanded even more? And how could it still feel so impossible to tell this god who'd given me new life and held me up like something sacred even half of what he meant to me?

12

Baldur

The near-noon sun beamed down from a brilliantly blue sky, and the wizened red pines that were giving the five of us some cover gave off a delicate woody perfume. Birds twittered as they jumped from one branch to another. It might have been a lovely day to stroll through the park if we hadn't been waiting for a murderous giant to descend from high above.

No voices disturbed the peace, because Skadi had set down a magical aura to discourage any humans from venturing close to this spot. "It'll make them feel like prey evading a hunter," she'd said, looking more amused than was comforting. At least she hadn't argued about the need to protect the innocent lives of any mortals who passed by.

Aria shifted her weight, peering between the pine branches toward the pagoda where we were supposedly meeting with the government officials to plan our alliance. She'd been more relaxed when she'd returned to the house with Thor yesterday afternoon, for reasons I could guess with a bright hot ripple of memory, but uneasiness prickled all through her aura now.

"I guess there's no way to be sure which direction he'll bring the bridge down from, right?" she murmured. Her silver-white wings were already released, folded close to her back but tensed in anticipation.

"Surt isn't much for preambles," Loki said, propping himself against the trunk of a taller tree with his arms folded over his chest. The trickster could manage to look relaxed in almost any scenario, but we'd fought together enough times in just the last few weeks that I could recognize from the alertness in his eyes and the coiled strength in his stance that he was braced just as much as Aria was. "We can assume he'll touch down close to the pagoda. We won't have far to dash in any case."

Thor tested the flat of his hammer against his palm with a faint thump. One wouldn't need to have spent any time with him at all to notice the fierce light of a battle fury dancing in his eyes. "I still say we should be the ones going for the kill. The Vanir are skilled and all, but..."

"But you'd rather *you* were the one who got to bash that villain's head in," Loki said. "I don't think it'll diminish your status as official giant killer if you let this one pass, Thunderer. Freya *is* a war goddess—I expect she'll handle herself."

"And the others were right," Hod said. My dark twin didn't sound particularly happy about that fact, but then, a certain amount of gloominess was just his nature.

"Surt's powers can at least partly deflect our magic, and your hammer isn't the most accurate weapon, no matter how powerful it is. We have a better chance this way, throwing everything at him for him to dodge while Freya and Freyr slip in there with their swords. One or the other of them has to reach him."

He was frowning, though, his head cocked to one side as he took in the sounds of the park. It wouldn't be the blazing light of Surt's bridge but the crackle of those flames that told him when it was time to act.

"I suppose," Thor muttered, but his grumbling was half-hearted.

Loki grinned. "The entire plan was my idea, let's remember. If we topple Surt today, I'll happily share that victory with the rest of you."

"So generous of you, Sly One," my twin said, but I thought his mouth might have twitched with a start of a smile.

"We are a team now, aren't we?" the trickster said with a sweep of his hand.

Sometimes I'd felt as if that bond were slipping away as more and more of our fellow gods joined our semblance of an army, contrasting personalities and energies bumping up against each other and turning the harmonious vibe I'd gotten used to off-key. But here with the four of them, the connection hummed between us just as strong as before. We might have been an odd team, but I couldn't deny that we were one. I wouldn't have wanted to.

That bond was the only thing that kept me certain we *would* see Surt fall, now or another day.

"I don't need any glory," Aria said. "I just want him gone. Those five or so minutes when we thought we could chill out in Asgard for a while were really nice."

The day she was talking about had been clear and sunny just like this one. With a pang in my chest, I remembered lying sprawled in the field with her and the others. It had been the first day since Ragnarok when I'd been able to sit back and simply enjoying being present with my mind unclouded. I'd spent far too long hiding away from darkness inside and out behind the bright haze I'd wrapped around myself.

"They were nice," I agreed. Aria shot me a smile, warm as the sun. What would it be like to have not just minutes but days, weeks, years to soak up her company?

I was looking forward to finding out.

But even thoughts as pleasant as those didn't ease the unsettled sensation in my own stomach. When I looked back toward the pagoda, my nerves crawled under my skin. Something here was off-kilter.

Maybe it was only Surt's destructive intentions preceding him, marring the natural harmony of this space. Just the thought of him destroying the carefully crafted structure before us nagged at me. The pagoda was three stories of curved slate-tiled roofs with intricate carvings all along the edges and around the windows. Every surface was painted in rich greens and reds. It was a work of art, an aria of architecture.

Well, if we moved quickly enough, he might not even touch it.

I directed a soft calming glow over us and around the pagoda to where our companions were staked out for their part in the ambush. Stay sure, stay focused, let no worries distract us. We of Asgard might have drifted apart over the centuries, but we all still had that one common tie of the realm we'd once shared. We could unite to save our home.

The sun hit its peak overhead. It was noon now, the time Surt had expected our meeting. Hod's frown came back as we waited. I supposed it made sense that the giant would wait at least a few minutes to be sure everyone who'd meant to gather here had arrived. He'd want to catch us absorbed in our negotiations.

Another tremor of discord rippled down my spine. Had I sensed it from Surt? My gaze scanned the sky, but no fiery red glinted against the blue yet.

Loki pushed himself off his tree with a jerk. He stood there, his amber eyes turned oddly vacant, his tall slim body still and stiff. Then he bit out a curse.

"He isn't here," he snapped. "He isn't coming. He's brought his bridge down—somewhere. That way. Nowhere near here. Norns only know what he's doing while he thinks we're too distracted to come. Bloody giant. Come on! Whatever he's up to, it can't be good."

A jolt of panic raced through my chest. I hadn't been wrong to worry, then.

"Asgardians!" Thor bellowed as we rushed out of the shelter of the trees. "Surt has arrived elsewhere. The ambush is off. Loki will help us find the giant—follow as quickly as you can."

Murmurs of confusion and indignation reached my ears, but my heart was thumping too quickly for me to focus on them. The uneasiness I'd felt before niggled right down to my bones. Something in this realm was *very* wrong. We had to reach Surt before he saw his current mission through.

A flick of my hand summoned a bolt of light to carry me up over the landscape. Loki was already sprinting off to the east, Aria flying after him as fast as her wings could flap.

"What do you think happened?" she said, her voice taut and breathless. "Why didn't Surt take the bait about the meeting?"

"He might not have trusted the tip from the dark elf," Hod said, soaring up beside me on his swath of shadow. "He's a lot of things, but he's proven he isn't stupid. He was cautious enough to move his army before."

"Or he may have believed the tip but figured that whatever he's trying to accomplish now would get him closer to his goals than stopping our meeting," I said.

"Or he didn't really think he could take on all of us now that we're on guard and growing our numbers," Thor muttered behind us. "I've never met a giant that didn't turn coward when the odds seemed against him."

Loki made a sputtered sound of protest, and the thunder god coughed. "Ah, present company excluded, I should say."

"In that case, I agree with you," the trickster said archly. "But let's save our breath for this flight. I suspect reaching Surt quickly matters more than debating the exact reasons he ignored the lure."

"Right." Aria's hands balled into fists. The sun shone over her silvery wings and the mussed waves of her blond hair as she pushed herself faster.

I rested my hands against the streak of light that was carrying me, urging more energy down into it. It quivered against my palms. A glance behind me showed that our whole host was rushing after us by their various means.

We raced over the foaming waters of the ocean, a faint salt tang tickling my nose. The sun sank toward the horizon behind us as we left it behind. Surt had come to do his dirty business on the other side of the world under the cover of night.

By the time we approached the far coast, it was merely a glittering of electric lights against a darkened shore. Loki adjusted his direction more to the south. We swept past cities and towns and streams of lamps winding along the roads in between. The jitter of nervous energy that had disturbed me before reached a higher peak. We were close, and Surt was wreaking more havoc than ever before.

He really had picked a spot almost exactly half the world away. My energy wasn't close to spent, but Aria's wings were starting to falter. I cast a wash of soothing light toward her and heard her suck in a grateful breath.

The first flicker of fire against the darkness caught my eye, and my heart thudded even faster. All of us hurtled toward it, the wind licking over our clothes.

Flames were dancing on the ground beside the spot where the bridge had touched down. An eerie glow shifted across the walls and roof of a boxy building, long and squat with two stout towers jutting beside it. A broad river flowed by beyond its concrete yard. The glow caught on several shuffling draugr bodies there, but nowhere near the swarm Surt had brought down before.

There was no sign of Surt himself, but a shock of energy hit me as we descended, rattling my nerves. Something was shifting inside those buildings. Building, colliding...

"Shit!" Ari said, peering down at a sign on the compound's fence with her sharp valkyrie vision. "It's a nuclear power plant."

Loki's face turned even paler than its usual tone. "He must be trying to make it explode. He'll be inside. We've got to stop him before—"

Another wave of shuddering energy washed over us, streaked with a burning heat that felt like a condensed echo of the sunlight we'd been basking in just a few hours ago. My gut lurched. The giant had already done it. The bright hot energy inside that building was quaking and erupting, a chain reaction swelling in every direction faster than we could fly, faster than we could speak.

Instinctively, I raised my hands in front of me. Unstable or not, the energy stirring was the same radiant power as daylight. The same power that thrummed through my body when I called on it. That power gave life all over the realms. It shouldn't sear and destroy. If I could just fold it back into the shape it should have kept—

I sent a surge of my own light toward the building with a flash like a thunderclap. The surge had barely left my palms when I felt my mistake.

My light burst against the energy flaring inside the

building and sent it shooting even higher, even faster. In that instant, I could already feel how the chaotic heat would flay flesh down to the bone and scorch those bones to dust. That light, that twisted twin to the light in me, was the most vicious threat I'd ever sensed.

And I couldn't stop it. I could only hasten its destruction of everything around it.

13

Aria

The air shook with an ear-splitting *boom*. Loki dove at me. He yanked me to the side and spun me around so his body shielded me, hollering over his shoulder in a voice so hoarse and frantic it barely sounded like him at all.

"Stop the explosion! Hold it all in—however you can —just *do* something!"

More shouts whipped past my ringing ears. Clutching me to him, Loki started to race away, the wind whistling as he leaned into the full power of his shoes of flight.

"Loki!" I gripped his shoulders and shoved myself back far enough that I could look into his eyes. "Stop. We can't just leave."

"My fire and my sword aren't going to do a damned

thing against a nuclear explosion, pixie," he said. "And neither will your powers. Getting you out of range is the only thing I *can* do."

I shook my head and pushed at him again. "No. Surt's still there—we could still catch him before he goes back to Asgard. If we don't, he'll just do something like this again."

The trickster sighed, but his steps slowed. He glanced behind us. The warbling echo of the explosion had faded, but I didn't know how much that was due to the distance. Surt's bridge still blazed against the night sky. A sharp metallic-smelling smoke prickled in my nose.

"Well," Loki said, "it looks like they managed to pull a solution out of their asses after all. For now. If we start to lose control over the situation, I'm hauling you out of there again."

I made a face at him. "Shouldn't I get some say about when I get hauled?"

He gave me a crooked smile. "You're my valkyrie, Ari. I picked you; I helped bring you into our world. I'm not watching you get killed all over again barely a month later."

"I'm sure your reputation would survive the failure," I grumbled as he swiveled around and darted back the way we'd come.

"My dear pixie, when have you ever seen me give a damn about my reputation?"

His arm around my waist loosened as we reached the ring of gods gathered around the power plant. At least, the spot where I assumed the power plant had been. I couldn't see it anymore—couldn't see anything on the ground below us now. An area at least half a mile across was cloaked in a thick layer of shadow, darker even than the night.

My pulse stuttered. My gaze darted across the assembled gods and caught on the one I'd been searching for, a head of black hair over a pale face tipped forward.

Hod had dropped down to the road outside the plant. His arms were braced ahead of him, his hands set as if they were resting on that shadowy dome.

They weren't resting, though. It was the opposite. He was conjuring up that massive shell of magic to contain all the radioactive light and heat that had been going to sear through us and half the countryside.

His muscles stood out like chords in his lean arms. The tendons in his hands bulged. As I watched, a quiver ran through his shoulders. It was taking all his strength to hold that shield in place.

The other gods were all hovering above with bewildered expressions. I slipped out of Loki's hold and whirled around.

"Why isn't anyone helping him?" I demanded. "He can't do this on his own."

"I think he's going to have to," Freya said in a thin voice. "The darkness and the cold he can generate are the only things that can push back the energy from that explosion."

Baldur's head jerked up. He blinked as if snapping out of a daze. "I can try to help keep him going. Soothe his body as it tires out." He dropped down to join his twin on the road.

What about Hod's mind? His spirit? I knew what it felt like using the small bit of dark magic I had in me. Those shadows affected a lot more than just my body.

Thor glanced down at his hammer dangling useless in his hand. His mouth twisted. Mjolnir could destroy all kinds of things, but not nuclear fallout.

Before my eyes, the dome of shadow contracted about a foot. I flinched in surprise, but then my breath caught as I understood. Hod wasn't just holding back the explosion. He was defusing it—cooling its heat, darkening its radiance—and shrinking it bit by bit.

"Some of us can at least help solidify the barrier," one of the newest goddesses said. "We may not be able to generate the same kind of darkness, but we can help hold what's there together."

Freya nodded, her eyes and her golden waves wild. Another few seconds, and every god here might have died.

Maybe this was the first time some of them had really believed that might happen.

The surface of the shadowy shield twitched again, but this time the movement came with a shudder and a hiss from Hod below. At the same instant, a figure burst through the shield at the far side near the flaming bridge.

It was Surt. With a gasp, Hod heaved more shadow up to seal the hole where the giant had broken through. A few of the gods leapt to propel the darkness faster over the breach.

Our enemy sprang straight for his bridge. An unsettling glow wavered over his skin, as if he'd absorbed some of the explosion's toxins. But it didn't look as if they were hurting him. Before any of us even had time to charge after him, he'd already landed on the bridge and started up.

"Surt!" Loki yelled, darting over the top of the shield toward the giant. Thor followed at his heels. "A realm's no good to you if you poison the place into a wasteland."

Surt chuckled as the fiery arc of his bridge retracted, whipping him up toward the sky. "I get along with all sorts of fire," he said, his voice fading as he ascended. "Humans are too much hassle to rule. Better to wipe them out. My comrades can have this place when the poison fades."

His last words barely reached my ears before he disappeared, heading back to the realm of the gods. I shuddered. *Better to wipe them out.*

He saw every living being in Midgard as some kind of vermin rather than as people—and, hell, animals and plants—that had as much right to life as he did. It shouldn't have surprised me after the way he'd built his army of murdered people magicked into zombies, but I'd never imagined he'd go this far. That we'd be defending every inhabitant of my former home not just from attacks but outright annihilation.

I wheeled in the air. The ache in my chest was almost as sharp as the one spreading through my wings after so long in flight. I didn't think the darkness in me could add to Hod's shield—I'd never been able to compel it to do anything other than swallow lives in the middle of a fight—and Surt was out of reach. What the hell was I even here for if I didn't offer something? Maybe there was some way I could pitch in that I hadn't thought of.

I glided down onto the grassy shoulder of the road. My wings twinged with gratitude when I folded them against my back.

Hod was just pushing another step closer to the power plant, contracting his dome of shadow a little tighter. Baldur stood next to him, a thin glow emanating from his hands into his twin's chest. I wavered on my feet, abruptly uncertain.

"Is there anything I can do to help?" I asked, looking at Baldur. "If there's something I could bring, or ask the others to do, or—"

"Ari," Hod snapped in a ragged voice, interrupting me. Of course, he couldn't see who I'd been directing the question at—in that moment, I wasn't even sure he was aware of Baldur there helping him. "I've got this. Get out of here."

Baldur winced, but he tipped his head to me with a quick glance as if to say he agreed with the gist, if not the tone, of Hod's request.

The ache around my heart squeezed tighter. I backed up a step, and another, and then launched myself up into the air, because I couldn't think of where else to go.

Hod had this situation under control, but he was barely holding all that explosive power in. If Surt set off another meltdown before the dark god managed to recover—if he set off more than one—

Could the giant even manage that much destruction all at once? How much had it taken out of Surt to set off the explosion here?

There was no way to know, but if he found a way, Midgard was doomed.

The other gods had split apart, the few of them with magic that could support Hod's shield circling the dome, shoring it up as well as they could, and the others hovering in a cluster looking about as bewildered as before. Bewildered and weary. Seeing the fatigue on their faces brought my own exhaustion rushing to the front of my mind.

Loki obviously saw the same thing. He clapped his hands, his voice brisk. "All right. All of us who are useless here, we'd better find some new accommodations. Those who *are* working are going to need somewhere to recover afterward."

Beside him, Thor nodded. "After that journey, we all need rest and something to eat. And we should start planning our next course of action right away."

Skadi set off in the lead, using her huntress skills to seek out a building where we wouldn't be disturbed. We ended up at a sprawling structure that looked like it might once have been a school, with grass overtaking the parking lot around the side and collapsed rusted goal posts on the overgrown field beyond the lot.

A few of the gods rushed off again to get supplies. At Thor and Loki's urging, I found myself bundled in a sleeping bag on the linoleum floor of a small room that must have once been a teacher's office.

The gods' voices echoed faintly down the wide hall outside, but I couldn't summon the energy to strain my ears to listen, let alone join in the conversation. Three cross-Pacific flights in the same number of days was obviously my limit. My eyelids dropped shut like they had weights attached to them, and a second later I was out cold.

When I woke up, the whole building was quiet. Sun streaked through the room's grimy window, filling the space with a faint warmth. It didn't look as if the world had ended just yet. I sat up and rested my head in my hands. A renewed pang filled my chest.

I'd flown all this way, crossed continents and oceans —for what? To be a distraction again, to stand by helplessly while Midgard almost burned?

I had to be better than this. I'd tackled dark elves and draugr and a prison of memories. And this new fight was mine more than any of the others had been. Hell, based on the sign outside the power plant, we weren't more than a few hours by human speeds from the city where I'd grown up. A city that could have been leveled in the explosion or fried with radiation if Hod hadn't acted fast enough.

Not that there were a whole lot of people I'd known in that city who I cared that much about saving. Other than my acid-tongued mother and her string of asshole boyfriends, there were the wannabe and actual gangsters I'd worked as a courier for, the jerks from my schools who'd turned their nose up at my dirty clothes and hacked haircuts when I'd had to rely on Mom's parental skills...

But there were plenty of totally decent people there,

too, I was sure. The kind of people I might have watched enviously while grabbing a cup of coffee or jetting through a park. Once or twice I'd wondered what it was like to have a life where you had people you could just relax and have a laugh with, enjoying each other's company without needing to be on your guard.

That was the kind of life I might actually have been experiencing right now with my gods, in a weird sort of way, if Surt hadn't decided to crash into Asgard.

My mind slipped from those memories to the ones of when he'd blasted into that first human city afterward. All at once, my breath caught.

It hadn't even been the gods who'd pushed Surt back there, at least not alone. The human soldiers with their guns and missiles had helped send him running. With the right weapons, the people here could kick plenty of giant ass.

We'd spent all this time searching out one or two gods at a time when I could have recruited us an entire squadron of fighters in one go.

I didn't give myself a chance to second-guess the burst of inspiration. I couldn't imagine more desperate times than these, so desperate measures it was. No way were the gods—the new ones, anyway—going to approve of this plan, so I'd just have to go get it done, and when I had the results, I didn't think they'd reject them.

I scrambled to my feet and eased open the door. The dim hallway was empty. A snore I recognized as Thor's drifted from somewhere farther down. Hoping Loki and his excellent hearing were similarly out of commission, I dashed for the front entrance.

The door squeaked when I pushed it open, but no one stirred behind me. With a ragged breath, I leapt up into the air and set off toward Philadelphia.

I had some old colleagues to catch up with. Let's hope they were happy to see me.

14

Aria

It might have felt as if I'd left Philly a lifetime ago, but the truth was it'd only been a matter of weeks. The crooks I'd worked for wouldn't have changed their ways particularly.

Back then, most of our business had been done with someone from one gang or another texting me a pick-up spot and a time, followed by a hand-off at that spot that included my delivery instructions. But I'd worked for the city's underworld long enough that I had a decent idea of where to find the second in command of the largest criminal network that operated here.

I landed in an alley beside the pub and pulled in my wings. It was going to take a concentrated effort to make my body visible to mortal eyes. I dragged in a breath, willing energy over my skin. Then I strode out of the alley and into the pub.

The place was pretty dead at this time of day, just a few particularly devoted regulars picking at the sparse brunch offerings around the varnished wooden tables that filled one side of the room and a couple of guys playing pool on the other side of the bar who looked like they probably should have been in school. The balls clattered after one of them took a break shot.

Even before anyone had started much drinking for the day, the whole place smelled like malt whiskey. I marched straight across the thin green carpet. The bartender, an older guy with slicked-back gray hair who'd been the one to pass me a payment several times, glanced up. His whole body went rigid, his eyes widening.

I guessed word had gotten around about my death by junkie jeep. I smiled and gave him a little wave as I stopped by the bar counter. "Hey, Steve. I need to talk to Harrison."

The bartender stared at me for another beat before he recovered himself. "Ari? I thought—we all heard—"

"Funny how these rumors can get out of hand, isn't it?" I said. I was counting on Mom not having bothered with a funeral or anything similarly public. There couldn't have been many eye witnesses. "I get knocked over by some asshole and decide to take a break while I'm recovering, and suddenly everyone's talking like I've passed over to the great beyond."

He laughed, a little hoarsely at first, but then his stance loosened. "That Gene," he said. "The dope. I'm surprised he manages to get his shirt on right way around most days."

"No kidding," I said with a grin. Just like old times. I

almost could slip right back into my old life, couldn't I? Maybe I wouldn't be stuck living out the rest of my days in Asgard when this was over after all. Not that I wanted to pick up exactly where I'd left off or spend that much time with this bunch, but it could be nice change to play human with the old crowd now and then.

"What do you need to see Harrison about?" Steve asked.

That was the complicated part of this pitch. "There's a big deal on offer that I thought he and the boss would want to hear about right away. Kind of confidential, though, so I didn't want to just pass the message on."

Steve nodded and set aside the washcloth he'd been holding. "I'll check with him. We don't usually see a lot of action this early in the day, so I'd imagine he can give you a few minutes."

I was hoping he'd give us a whole lot more than that, but a few minutes would do for a start.

The bartender ducked into the back room. I rubbed my finger on the counter, which was so polished my skin squeaked against it. Steve emerged a moment later.

"Go on back," he said with a jerk of his thumb.

If I'd been one of the guys, Harrison would probably have sent out a tough to pat me down, but I'd never taken sides in the various intra-gang squabbles before, and it wasn't as if there were many places I could have been hiding a weapon while I was wearing fitted jeans and a light tank top. These guys had no idea that I could now do more damage with a brush of my hand than any gun could.

The doorway to the back room had just a heavy

curtain over it, so Harrison could hear if any trouble started in the main bar area. The rings clinked as I eased it aside to step past it.

Harrison Malloy's office-slash-meeting room was nothing fancy. The card table and the chairs around it were a metal folding set, the black paint on them worn down around the edges. Cabinets and shelving units of similar construction and in an assortment of muted colors stood along the walls. The desk he was currently leaning against was a table that had been scavenged from the bar after some idiot had scorched a line in the varnish with a cigar, based on the width of the mark. The liveliest thing in the room was the tall broad-leaved rubber plant that loomed nearly as high as the doorframe.

The whiskey smell faded in here, replaced by a whiff of pot. Not Harrison's, I had to guess. I'd never seen him anything but totally sober.

The man himself wouldn't have turned any heads, in interest or in fear. He had sort of a faded hipster look: his pale gray-streaked hair floppy, his eyes shielded by rectangular glasses, and a thick moustache adorning his narrow and kind of lumpy face. But the eyes behind those glasses were sharp as a steel edge, and the forearms he often rolled the sleeves of his checkered shirt up over were roped with muscle.

You didn't have to be around him much to figure out he wasn't someone to mess with.

"Ari," he said, with a smile that was the business version of warm. "I'm glad to see the stories of your untimely demise were greatly exaggerated."

I returned the smile. "If I'd known I was supposed to

be a ghost, maybe I'd have had a little more fun with the visit."

"A missed opportunity. But not the opportunity you came to see me about." He motioned to the chairs in case I wanted to sit down. "Tell me about this deal."

I stayed standing, wetting my lips. "You and your people have weapons connections, right? You could collect some pretty heavy firepower if you wanted to?"

Harrison's eyebrows jumped up. "Have you got a line to a customer looking to stock up their arsenal?"

"Not exactly," I said. I was going to have to feel this part out carefully. "They'd need your people handling those weapons. They'd pay well—really well." Loki had mentioned the extensive financial resources the gods had set up on Midgard. They had to be able to afford to hire a squad of mercenaries at a very good wage.

The gang commander's eyebrows rose even higher. "And who would we be aiming those weapons at? We wouldn't be interested in inserting ourselves into someone else's turf war."

"It's nothing like that," I said quickly, even though on a broad scale it kind of was. "It's—look, you must have heard about the disaster overseas? Fire and destruction and all kinds of people killed?"

The amusement in Harrison's face dimmed. "They're saying some guy basically dropped out of the sky and started whipping fire around. I've heard people mention *zombies*. Whoever the hell staged that terrorist attack, they had way too much time on their hands setting up their special effects. What does that have to do with your deal?"

I decided I could let the special effects assumption slide. His people would see how real Surt's magic was when they confronted him. No point in trying to argue about it when I couldn't prove it anyway.

"The asshole who did that, he's who my people are trying to take down," I said. "But there aren't enough of us. We want to hire help—help that can supply their own firepower. Ten, twenty, thirty—however many you can get together and arm who are willing to take the job. The more people who join in, the more you get paid. Simple."

Harrison looked as if he had no idea what to make of this story. "Why would you have hooked up with some people fighting terrorists?" he said. "What the hell is this really about, Ari?"

"It's a long story," I said. "But it's about exactly what I said. The guy who brought down all that fire, who ordered all those people killed, plans on hurting people here too. Just last night—look up the Peach Bottom power plant. He destroyed it. Tried to nuke the whole country."

"What!?"

"Look it up," I said again, pointing to the laptop lying on his desk.

The expression Harrison gave me was completely disbelieving, but he grabbed his laptop anyway. There had to be something in the news about the plant by now.

He typed and scrolled, and the color drained from his face. "Shit," he said. "They leveled the place."

Were there photographs, then? That meant Hod must have finished defusing the explosive surge. Otherwise the news stories would be talking about a big shadowy dome.

The urge tugged at my gut to get back to my dark god, to confirm he was okay, even though I wasn't sure he wanted a whole lot of company immediately after that ordeal.

"You're saying this meltdown was caused by the same people who orchestrated the attack in Moscow?" Harrison said. "How do you even know? There's nothing in the news—it sounds like they have no idea what happened."

"I know it was the same people," I said, "because I was there. Trying to stop the guy. We didn't manage it, and he's going to strike again. Maybe next time we won't even manage to prevent the destruction he's trying to cause. That's why I'm coming to you. I thought of all the people I've worked with, and I figured if anyone had the means to turn the tide, it was you."

Flattery could be a very effective tool. I saw Harrison waver for a second with a hint of pride glinting in his eyes. Then he shut the laptop with a snap, and his expression shuttered too.

"No," he said. "This whole thing sounds too crazy. I don't know what you've gotten yourself mixed up in, Ari, but I think we're better off keeping out of it."

Fuck. I scrambled for some other way to persuade him. "You could at least come out and meet with the rest of my, ah, colleagues, or send someone out. Hear everything they have to say."

Harrison was already shaking his head. "This isn't

our area. We can't go jumping into some arena we know nothing about."

"If you don't, this whole city could be leveled tomorrow," I said with a sweep of my arm. My voice was rising, but I couldn't rein it in. "This isn't just about business, Harrison, even if we would throw a lot of money at you. It's about saving the fucking world."

"Okay, okay," he said, holding up his hands. "Obviously you're very caught up in this mess. I'm sorry, Ari. Go to the FBI or the army or whoever. I don't know exactly what's real here, but either way it's a hell of a lot bigger than us."

"I can't go to the FBI or the army," I said. "I don't know them." They wouldn't listen to me. I couldn't simply offer their agents or soldiers a wad of cash to do whatever the gods told them to do. And by the time Surt struck somewhere and we could call the authorities in with evidence, it'd be too late when they got there.

But Harrison wasn't listening either. He'd already shut the conversation down. He was pushing himself off his desk now, ready to show me out.

My stomach twisted. He didn't believe me because he thought it all sounded too crazy. Maybe I shouldn't have been downplaying the craziness. Maybe I should prove to him just how real all that stuff was.

My heart thumped hard at the thought. I'd never shown what I'd become to anyone who hadn't already understood what I was, anyone from my old life. If I did this, there was no coming back again. No pretending normal. No slipping back into the life that'd once been mine.

How much had I really wanted that life anymore? I wouldn't have thought it was that big a sacrifice, but cutting the cord completely suddenly made my lungs clench up in resistance.

I didn't have any choice. It was make the last move I had, or I slunk back to the gods with nothing to show for my gamble.

"Harrison," I said, "we need you because we need people who know how to change the rules and make up their own, because this *is* a completely new arena, and we can't take on our enemies with the usual methods. There's nothing usual about this at all."

I flexed the muscles in my back, and my wings sprang from my flesh. Harrison stumbled to a stop halfway across the room. He gaped at me as I spread my wings to their full span, the tips brushing the walls on either side of me. His mouth closed and opened and closed again.

"The people I'm with now are gods," I said, with a dramatic flutter of my feathers. "They'll pay you a divine amount of cash. But we need people who can get a job done, fast and right, to make sure the entire world doesn't end. Which, as far as I can tell, benefits you as much as anyone. Am I getting through to you yet?"

He walked from one side of the room to the other and then edged a little closer. I turned obligingly so he could see the spot where the wings met my back.

"How..." he muttered. "They couldn't have just come from—where the hell could you have been hiding them?"

"It's called magic," I said. "You start to get used to it when you've been hanging out with a bunch of gods."

He shook his head as if to clear it. "It can't be—this has got to be some kind of stunt—"

Oh, for fuck's sake. I tucked my wings closer to my body and held out my hand. "What do you need for me to prove it to you? Give me something there's no way I could possibly bend or break—if I'm just a regular human being. Come on. Let's get this over with."

Harrison started at me and then groped around. He shoved one of the metal folding chairs toward me.

Well, fine, if he didn't care whether this survived...

I picked it up by one of the metal bars, gripped it with both hands, and bent the back and then the seat at the middle. Then I snapped one of the legs in half, through the solid steel, with a heave of my valkyrie strength. Thor could have crumpled the thing into a ball, but this display would have to do.

Harrison still didn't appear to know how to respond. I let out a huff of breath and stalked to the rubber plant. "I can do more than that. Do you want to see my freakiest power?"

I rested my hand on one of the waxy leaves. A tickle of the plant's living energy grazed my palm. With a silent apology, I unlocked the dark rippling in my chest that was drawn to that light like a shark to blood.

The shadows inside me latched on to the plant's energy and sucked it down. The leaf shriveled, and then its neighbors did too, the stem sagging over—

"Stop!" Harrison said raggedly.

I jerked my hand back. The gang commander took off his glasses, rubbed them on the hem of his shirt, and replaced them. I didn't imagine the cleaning had changed the view very much. His face wasn't just pale but a faint sickly green now.

"What are you?" he said finally, in a quiet voice that was equal parts awed and horrified.

I guessed it couldn't hurt to tell him that after everything I'd already shown him. "They say I'm a valkyrie," I said. "I really did die, and then I got resurrected. It's been interesting."

"Interesting," he repeated with a rough chuckle. He walked up to his withered plant and touched one of the leaves I'd drained. Only the top half had crumpled. "Can you bring it back?"

I swallowed hard. "No," I said. "Not a plant. Not like that. I'm sorry." Maybe some beings I could have blessed as worthy and sent them up to Asgard to claim a new life there, but I was pretty sure plants couldn't be warriors. And also that a plant resurrected in Asgard wasn't what Harrison was hoping for. Besides the fact that I had no idea if a patchwork valkyrie like me was even capable of that kind of resurrection for anyone. I hadn't had any opportunities to try.

"Well, you did make your point." Harrison stared at the rubber plant for a few seconds longer. His gaze slid to me. His jaw worked. "You're serious. These 'enemies' you were talking about—they're trying to destroy the whole world."

"The main one wants to exterminate all humankind," I said. "He nearly got a good start on that last night. We were just in time. I don't want us cutting it that close again. I think we can stop him the next time if we've got your strength to add to ours. There aren't that many of us—and the gods aren't going to pick up guns."

Harrison let out another chuckle, but this one sounded almost exhilarated. My spirits started to life.

"All right," he said. "I'll come out and speak to your gods. I can't promise anything, but I can't just walk away from a deal like that."

15

Thor

Loki had scrounged up a computer somewhere, and now, to my astonishment, Bragi, our god of poetry, was typing away at it as if he'd been using one of those human contraptions his entire expansive life.

"You have to understand the internet as a writer in this realm these days," he said when he noticed the many stares he was getting. "I may appreciate classic styling, but I keep up with the times as well."

"We're not composing verses right now," Vidar said tersely, peering down at the large world map we'd spread on the hard packed dirt of the yard. It was easier to see out here in the sunlight compared to the shadowy halls inside the old building, where the electricity appeared to have been off for quite some time. "Tell us where the other nuclear power plants are."

"Well, it appears there are rather a lot of them..."

Bragi frowned with a purse of his lips. "Let's start with the largest ones, shall we? There's a sensibility to that."

Heimdall, who was standing just behind me, muttered something under his breath that Loki probably would have been able to hear. I could at least make out that it didn't sound complimentary of Bragi's sensibilities. I supposed it would be easier to appreciate the poet after the catastrophe was over when we could bask in his finely worded accounts of our glorious victories.

The trouble was we had to accomplish that victory first.

"All right," Bragi went on. "Simply going by plants still operational... There's one in Canada, near a town called Kincardine, in Bruce County, Ontario. Is that on the map?"

"Canada, Ontario..." Vidar bent down, and everyone else gathered around as he cast about with his hand holding a red pen.

I raised my head at the rumble of an engine. It shouldn't matter if any humans drove past this abandoned place, since they wouldn't see us unless we let them anyway, but I'd only heard a couple of vehicles pass by on that little highway since we'd gotten here. The place Skadi had found was certainly out of the way, even if I couldn't say a whole lot else in its favor.

The SUV that was driving toward us didn't simply cruise by like the other two vehicles had, though. It slowed—and then it pulled into the lane to the building's parking lot. Everyone else's heads jerked up then too.

"What in Hel's name do these people think they're —" Freyr started.

Before he could finish his sentence, the SUV jerked to a halt and the passenger door popped open. A familiar slight figure with a head of mussed blond waves jumped out.

For a second, I could only stare dumbly at Ari. I'd assumed she was still sleeping off the strain of the previous day in the room we'd found her for some privacy. Apparently she'd been up before any of us. Up and off on some quest I couldn't quite comprehend.

Three more people got out of the SUV: two men, one middle-aged with a bushy moustache and the other younger with a crewcut, and a well-muscled woman who looked a little older than Ari. All of them were regular humans. They aimed blank looks across the yard before giving Ari a puzzled glance. She was allowing the mortals to see her, but they couldn't see us any more than the previous passersby had.

"What in the nine realms is going on?" Heimdall demanded, pitching his voice to carry across the yard. He wasn't the tallest of the gods or the broadest—both of those honors belonged to me—but he could have a very imposing presence when he chose to. It was a gatekeeper thing, presumably.

"Wait here for a minute," Ari said to her companions. She jogged over to meet us and stopped at the edge of the yard, setting her hands on her hips.

"I brought help," she said simply, her defiant gaze daring us to complain.

"Those *humans* are your 'help'?" Skadi said before our valkyrie could go on. "What have you told them?

What were you thinking?" She turned toward the rest of us. "I knew we shouldn't have kept her along."

Ari's eyes flashed at that aside, and suddenly I understood why she'd struck out on her own. She'd gone to her former people like I'd gone to the giants not long ago, determined to use the advantages I had even if my comrades had been skeptical.

We'd tried to defend our valkyrie's worth to the gods who'd more recently joined us, but the valkyries in the past had never been more than servants to the gods and attendants to the risen warriors. This bunch hadn't known Ari long enough to understand how much more than that she was. And it wasn't as if she hadn't heard all their dismissive remarks.

"I was *thinking*," she said in a tart voice, "about how quickly Surt turned tail and ran when those human soldiers opened fire on him during his first attack on Midgard. I know these people. They can get us weapons as good as those. We can double or even triple our firepower just like that."

"You expect us to fight with guns?" Vidar said with a note of disgust, his hand coming to rest on the sword hanging from his belt.

Ari looked as if she'd just barely restrained an eye roll. "No," she said. "You've got your ways of fighting already. Why mess with that? They've got people who'll fight alongside us, their way. An extra little army for us. If we pay them."

"Pay them?" Freyr sputtered. "A rabble of humans with—"

"We have plenty of money," Loki broke in before the

other god could say anything more insulting. "That's no issue. Why shouldn't we make use of them if they're willing? It is their realm they'd be fighting for."

"As far as the money goes, we'd be asking them to risk their lives going up against Surt," Ari said. "We owe them something for that, considering it's mainly *your* fault he's here at all. Now can you make yourselves visible to them already? Without all the grumbling about humans? They're going to decide I'm batshit insane and leave in another minute."

Most of the gods looked as though they were absolutely fine with that possibility.

"We can't show ourselves to humans without proper precautions," Njord said. "These days, the way they think—"

"It's just not wise," Heimdall filled in. "They're too unpredictable."

"Oh, for Asgard's sake," Loki said, and stepped away from the group of us toward the figures waiting by the SUV. A brief flaring of light ran over his body.

The humans' jaws dropped as to their eyes he must have appeared as if out of nowhere. Grinning, he sauntered on over to them.

Why had I been waiting around for permission? Ari wouldn't have brought these people here if she hadn't believed this was a good idea, and I trusted her judgment. I focused for a second on the texture of the air, the dusty scent of the yard, willing my body to be fully present in the realm. There. I wiped my hands together and gave our guests a grin of my own.

They appeared to be having some trouble forming

words. Baldur ambled over to join Loki with a faint smile, the sun shimmering off his skin. I skirted the cluster of gods around the map to stand beside the two of them. The humans glanced from one of us to the other.

The older man, the one with the moustache, swiped a hand across his chin. "Well," he said. "Look at that."

"I did mention my colleagues were *gods*, right?" Ari said, her tone amused now that her sanity was no longer in question. "There's more of them here. They're just being shy. Apparently you're very scary."

Loki chuckled at that. The remark must have niggled at a few of my comrades' pride, because a moment later Vidar, Skadi, and Freyr came up beside us.

"We understand you can bring weapons, and you're willing to fight on our behalf," Vidar said, folding his arms over his chest. "What exactly can you provide?"

"Hold on a second," the older guy said. "I told Ari we'd come out here to talk. I'm not committing to anything until I'm clear about the whole situation. What we're fighting. What you need from us. And what you're providing to us in return."

"Payment will be no issue," Loki said with a wave of his hand. "Weapons—covered. You want a hundred thousand a day to be on our retainer, each? We can do that. Is the money your only hesitation?"

"There is the whole thing about fighting some kind of war with gods," the woman piped up. Her stance was still rigid.

"You wouldn't be fighting gods," Baldur said in his mild voice. "We're all on the same side." Loki seemed to cover a snort at that remark, but he let it stand. My brother went on. "It's a giant we need to stop—a giant and the army he's raised of the undead."

"Zombies," the younger guy said. "Holy hell. They weren't just making that shit up."

"Yeah," the older guy said. "That's the stuff I'm talking about. I'm going to need to hear some more about how we go about fighting these... giants and undead and so on before I'm on board with bringing any of my people into this conflict."

Skadi grimaced. "Or you could just—"

"Come with me," I said quickly, before she could suggest they take off. I hadn't been planning on making the offer, but as soon as the words came out of my mouth, they felt right.

I was the champion of this realm, the protector of humankind. When was the last time I'd really talked to a human—someone fully human, not our summoned valkyries?

In the olden days, when I'd often adventured across this realm, sometimes with Loki at my side, I'd taken a human assistant more than once. There'd been something satisfying about watching them rise to the occasion. Humans had so much resilience in their short mortal lives.

I'd been a decent judge of human character back then. These three wanted to evaluate us, and I could evaluate them in turn. And if it looked like an alliance would work in both our favor, then who better to add to our forces?

The humans balked at my beckoning gesture, but after a moment's hesitation, the older guy, who seemed to be the leader of the three, headed toward me. The others fell into step behind him.

"Thor," Vidar said like a warning.

I shot him a look. "I can handle this. Midgard is my domain."

They couldn't argue with that fact. Ari hung back as I led the humans around to the field behind the building, probably figuring she needed to do a little more smoothing over and explaining before she had everyone's agreement. I suspected those instincts were right. At least I could take these three through the paces without constant skeptical commentary.

I stopped amid the overgrown grass where we couldn't see or hear the other gods anymore. The younger man and woman looked around, the guy toeing the rusted post that had fallen over. The older guy fixed his gaze on my face.

"Thor?" he said, half disbelieving, half... hopeful?

"That's me," I said with a smile, and offered him my hand, which dwarfed his lean one. He managed a firm enough shake all the same. "Pleased to make your acquaintance."

"Harrison," he said in return.

"You're *the* Thor?" the younger guy said, outright gawking now. "Like..."

"Thunder god, very strong, fond of bashing giants' skulls," I supplied. "Sorry you haven't seen much of me in a while. I've been distracted with other concerns—and, well, you've all seemed pretty caught up in your new modern world."

Harrison let out a sputter of a laugh. "I can't believe

this," he said, shaking his head. "First Ari's got wings, and now I'm talking to a fucking Norse god."

"You are," I said. "And I've got my hammer and only a certain amount of patience." I lifted Mjolnir from its spot at my side, flipped it in my hand, and tossed it without even that much vigor toward the goal post still standing at the opposite end of the field.

The hammer gleamed through the air and smacked into the post with a metallic *thunk* that buckled the steel. The structure toppled over as my weapon flew back into my hand. I brushed its end against my pant leg and hung it back on my belt. "So let's be straight-forward with each other, all right?"

The younger guy's eyes had lit up. "I want to see what else you can do with that thing."

Harrison waved him quiet. There was something new in his expression now, guarded but peeking through his internal defenses. I thought it was respect.

This might be one of the criminals from Ari's past, but I could see why she'd picked him to go to. I could already tell he wasn't a man who'd give his word lightly. If he signed on to our war, he'd see his end of the deal through all the way to the end.

"Tell me more about this giant and these zombies," he said.

I tipped my head. "The giant is the main problem—Surt. He uses fire magic, and he's strong. He's equipped his undead army with enhanced weapons and shields too. So, basically, a lot of trouble. But if we take him down, his army will fall apart." Possibly in a literal bodily way.

"And he's trying to destroy the whole world."

"He wants to claim Midgard—your realm here—for himself and anyone he likes," I said. "And he doesn't like humans particularly. After that first skirmish with some of your soldiers, he decided he'd rather annihilate the entire species than try to push you under his thumb. He'd have made quite a start of that effort if we hadn't caught him in time last night."

Harrison's jaw tightened, but he didn't look surprised. No matter how Ari had pitched his involvement to the other gods, he wasn't here just for the money. She must have made it clear to him it was about his very survival and that of the rest of the human race as well.

"Well, thank you for that save," he said. "Now, what exactly kind of weaponry would you be needing us to bring to the mix?"

I rubbed my hands together. Now we were talking.

"I'm not sure your average gun would do us a lot of good, but Surt really didn't like those—what are they called?—missiles that got launched at him..."

16

Aria

"This should get you off to a good start," Loki said, handing the wad of cash he'd retrieved to Harrison.

The gang commander made a show of rifling through the bills to confirm the amount, but his expression told me he was already sold. Whatever Thor had said to him and his lackeys, it had gotten through.

"I'll report back within twenty-four hours," he said, with a nod to me. I'd picked up a prepaid cell phone while I was in the city, since my old one had gone kaput with the rest of my former body. It felt weird carrying it on me now, but I needed some way to communicate with my former associates.

"I'll be waiting," I said.

The three of them got into their car and drove off. The second the SUV disappeared from view amid the trees down the road, Vidar swung his brawny body toward me. "Just to be clear, I still say you shouldn't have gone running off—especially to *humans*—without putting the plan to us first. Exposing ourselves to mortals is a serious matter."

"Oh, please," I said. I'd already heard enough criticism in the last hour to last me a few centuries. "Without them, we all might be nothing more than nuclear waste in another day or two. What will it matter what they know then?"

"I'm not convinced a bunch of humans is going to make that much difference."

"It's not the humans so much as what they'll be carrying. You weren't there in Moscow." I motioned to the gods who had been there for that first battle in Midgard. "The missile really hurt Surt, didn't it? That's what sent him running."

"It's true," Thor said.

Even Skadi was nodding for once. "These advanced human weapons can have some impact. On the level of some elf-made contraptions." She cut her gaze toward me, just in case I'd thought she was letting me off easy. "But I agree with Vidar that you had no business arranging this without our input."

I gritted my teeth. "I had an idea. You were all sleeping. I went and got it done. We don't know how much time we have before Surt makes his next attempt."

"You can't make decisions for all of us as if you're in charge," Freyr said haughtily.

"Who *is* in charge?" I said, throwing my hands in the air. "Odin's been gone for days now. He didn't appoint anyone in his place, as far as I can tell. So we're muddling along together. I didn't make any decisions for you. I barely told them anything—nothing more than I had to for them to listen to me. You all had a chance to talk with them and discuss the idea. Can we move on?"

Freyr looked as if he were going to snap something back at me, but Freya caught her brother's arm. "Is this arguing really necessary?" she said, her voice sweet but firm. "Don't we have enough enemies right now without turning each other into them too?"

Freyr's gaze flicked briefly toward Loki. Baldur cleared his throat. He'd stood up with the others to greet Harrison and his people, but something in his face made my stomach knot. He looked as if he hadn't gotten enough sleep or as if something unpleasant were lingering in the back of his mind—a hint of shadow dimming his usual light.

He'd probably just worn himself out supporting Hod. His voice sounded clear and steady enough.

"Isn't the most important thing determining what Surt's next target might be?" he said. "We'd gotten started on that question when our visitors arrived."

Vidar grimaced, but he turned back to the map. "Bragi, you were going over that list you found on the... computer contraption. The largest power stations?"

As the other god mentioned the location of a nuclear plant, I stepped closer to Baldur. "How are you doing after last night?" I asked quietly.

He rested his hand on my shoulder and gave it a gentle squeeze. "I'm fine now that I've rested. Hod is still recovering. We set him up in one of the rooms inside where he wouldn't be disturbed. Containing and cooling that blast took a lot out of him."

"I could see that." I hoped the dark god hadn't strained himself too much. The thought of Hod in pain made my stomach clench even tighter. None of the other gods seemed all that concerned about him even though he'd just saved all our hides.

A black shape wheeled against the sky over our heads. I peered up at it. "It looks like the raven managed to find us again. I wonder what she's been up to." I hadn't seen Muninn since our mad dash from the park in Beijing to the nuclear plant.

"She might have observed something useful." Baldur raised his hand to beckon her down.

Muninn glided in another slow circle as if deciding whether to take that invitation and then swooped down to land beside us. A couple of the newer gods gave her a curious glance, but most of them were focused on Vidar and his marking of the map.

"You came a long way from where you'd planned," the raven said. "I couldn't find you until I saw a report about the disaster on the front of a newspaper."

"Well, if you weren't flying off to do your own thing all the time, you'd have been with us when we left," I reminded her. "Where did you go?"

"I was checking the other gates I'm aware of between Midgard and the other realms." The corners of her mouth creased with a frown. "Surt must realize we can sense when he's brought down his bridge. I worried he might start to diversify his strategies."

I hadn't thought of that. "Did you see anything that looked like a problem?" I asked.

"Not exactly. There were a couple of jotun who had come through their gate into Midgard, but they weren't disturbing anyone. They were acting more like tourists. I didn't like that they'd come here at all, though. The fewer giants, the better."

"Absolutely." A chill trickled through me. "One giant is more than enough."

"I'd prefer none," Muninn muttered, with a ruffle of her dress.

Vidar stepped back from the map, dropping the pen beside it. He rubbed his jaw. "All right," he said. "These are all the largest nuclear power stations in Midgard." His marks were spread out across the map. "I'm not sure how we can predict which one Surt will target. Has there been any pattern to his targets so far?"

"I can't think of any," Thor said. "But we've got no reason to think he'll stay near here."

"He attacked a large city the first time," Freya put in. "And the plant last night isn't far from another one. He appears to be aiming for maximum destruction. Does that help narrow it down?"

Vidar squinted at the map. "We could eliminate a few possibilities, but not many."

"Who's to say he'll follow the same logic that we are at all?" one of the other goddesses put in. "Would Surt even know how to find out which sites are the most powerful? He might be going by some other measure completely."

That was true. It'd hardly looked as if Surt's fortress

in Muspelheim had been set up with internet access. Even the gods who'd been living here among humans for the better part of a few centuries looked at Bragi's laptop as if it were some kind of alien device. Where would the giant be getting his information—and how skewed would it be?

"Wherever he decides to attack next, it took him a long time to get the meltdown going yesterday," I said. "And he can't make us fly much farther than we had to then, considering we crossed half the world to get here."

Njord crossed his arms with a dark expression. "He'll have learned from that first attempt. We can't count on having anywhere near as much time when he strikes again."

Muninn eased forward to peer at the map. "And if he succeeds with this nuclear detonation he wants, what will be the result?" she asked me.

"Millions dead," I said. "Maybe more, depending on how big he can amp the explosion up. Not even bodies left, anyone who's close by—just ash. It'd be awful."

Her chin set. She stepped right into the middle of the crowd.

"I can go," she said. "To Asgard. I should be able to make it from here to Muspelheim and from there to Yggdrasil. I'm small and quick. I'll make sure the guards don't see me, and I'll listen in on Surt's planning."

The tension coiled through her body showed she wasn't making this offer lightly. She was putting her own life on the line.

Skadi gave the raven woman a narrow look. "Weren't

you involved in helping Surt capture Odin in the first place?"

"That's right," Njord said. "How do we know you won't fall in with him again or lead *us* into a trap?"

"I made my peace with Odin," Muninn said. "That should be good enough for any of you. If I'd known Surt was going to carry out a plan like this, I wouldn't have helped him in the first place, no matter how angry I was."

"Easy to say that now," Freyr muttered.

"Hey," I said. "I've got as much or more reason to be wary of Muninn as anyone here. I had to live through her torture. But I believe she wants to help now. We could be so much better prepared if she can spy on Surt."

Vidar gave me a look that seemed to say my opinion wasn't worth any more than Muninn's was, but Thor spoke up then. "I'd say the same. Muninn has proven her allegiances. She made her original contract with Surt to save her life, not because she agreed with him. As I understand it, Odin was the one who forced her to put her life at risk in the first place. We can't judge from that situation."

"The wrongdoings of others are not always as they seem," Loki said with a crooked smile. "I say we let her go and see what comes of it."

The others glanced around at each other. I sensed another argument on the horizon. Then a low dry voice swept into our midst.

"I'll support the raven's suggestion."

We all jerked around. Odin had arrived in the yard as we'd been talking. His head was bowed a little lower than usual, his charred hat looking particularly depressed. Grit clung to his traveling cloak. But his grip on his spear was firm and his single eye glinted at us from beneath his hat's brim.

"Father!" Baldur said, rushing to Odin's side.

"I'm all right," the Allfather said, briskly but not unkindly. "I went looking, and pieces have come to me, but it seemed time to rejoin you all." His gaze slid over the assembled gods. "There are more of you here than there were before. It has been too long. I wish we were having a less fraught reunion."

Heimdall let out a rough chuckle but didn't say anything. Some of the other gods bobbed their heads in acknowledgment. Odin turned his attention to Muninn.

"Fly, dear raven," he said. "Be our eyes and ears where we cannot see or hear. And thank you."

Muninn gave him a flicker of a smile and contracted into her bird form. In an instant, she was flitting off through the air.

"You said you found 'pieces'," Thor said, approaching his father. "Pieces of the answer? What came to you?"

Odin sighed, planting the end of his spear on the ground in front of him. "The visions never come easily. I must see what I can and make what I can of that. What I sensed, from my walking..." He closed his eye. "The light of day can burn before a fire. But only the highest water can put out all the flames."

Ah. So, super useful advice then. I managed not to sputter a giggle, but it was a near thing.

"Excellent," Loki said. "Let us hope the rest of the

pieces to make sense of that foresight find us sooner rather than later."

No one else seemed to know what to say about Odin's prophesying. Maybe that was for the best. With a sharp breath, Vidar turned back to the map.

"Whatever happens, wherever Surt appears, it'd be good to have as many Asgardians gathered to fight him as we can," he said. "Can we reach out to any of the others?"

Heimdall stirred where he'd been standing on the fringes. "I may have ideas for a couple. And I also—I was given to understand that through me we might bring the battle back to Surt instead of waiting around for him here. It seems like it's time I attempted to stretch my powers, perhaps in coordination with a few of you, the way Thor and the others have found their synchronicity around the valkyrie." He glanced at the thunder god rather than me. "If you could demonstrate—I haven't yet gotten to see how your powers merge in action."

Thor perked up at the prospect of getting to play out at least a fake battle and deflated a moment later. "We can't," he said. "Not without Hod. I don't think we should rouse him yet."

"Ah. Well... why don't you come along, then, and talk me through it, and—Skadi, your skills might be of use, and Njord, and Idunn."

The gods he'd called meandered away from the group with him. Loki had drifted away too, so stealthily I hadn't noticed him leaving.

Freya bent over the map again, and Odin moved to join her. Bragi turned back to his computer. Vidar dashed after Heimdall. "Before you get started—you mentioned there might be others you could point us too."

I rubbed my arms, my skin creeping with an uncomfortable sensation. Our group had gotten bigger, but it felt so scattered now. Not like a bunch of people with the same goal working together. How were we going to stop Surt if we were running off in every direction, arguing over every offer of help?

I didn't want to just stand here with those thoughts, and it was obvious no one out here had much use for me. I touched the phone in my pocket to confirm it was still there and turned toward the house. "I'll check on Hod."

17

Aria

Just past the school building's main entrance, I spotted a stack of bags in the room that had once been the front office. Someone had bought us a new stash of food. When Hod woke up, he'd probably need all the nourishment he could get.

I went over and crouched down to paw through the bags for whatever looked at least somewhat substantial. After a few minutes, I'd come up with a loaf of bread, a jar of peanut butter and a knife for spreading it, and a couple cartons of grape juice, which seemed like a safer bet for a god on the mend than the bottles of wine that had dominated the beverage selection. Doctors had people drink juice after they gave blood. Maybe the same principle would work for divine beings who'd given a whole bunch of their energy to saving the world.

I hadn't known for sure which room the gods had set

up Hod in, but I didn't need to spend much time searching. Voices traveled down the hall from a door standing ajar about halfway down. I knew before I reached it that I'd found my trickster too.

"So that's the long and the short of it," Loki was saying in his languid voice. "Since half of those dopes forget that anything exists beyond what they can see in front of them, I thought I'd better take it upon myself to see if you had any suggestions to make about our current activities."

"I can't say I'm thrilled about the raven going off to Surt, but if the others felt she was genuine..." Hod spoke with a faint rasp, his tone wary but not hostile. I couldn't remember if I'd ever seen the two of them talking one-on-one at all before. For most of the time I'd known the dark god and the trickster, their conversations had mainly consisted of sniping at each other. I guessed they were actually coming to terms with the horrors of their shared past and the revelations of the last few weeks.

"I'm not sure there's anything else I can offer," Hod went on. "Other than we'd better catch Surt quickly if he tries that tactic again. There was so much power in that blast." His voice trailed off again as I slipped past the door.

Sunlight was streaming from a single large window into the classroom-sized space on the other side. It left patches of brightness on the white walls and floor. The other gods had set Hod up on a real bed—well, maybe it was more of a cot—with a folded blanket as a pillow and another tucked over his trim frame. Loki was leaning against the empty bookcase near the door. He gave me a nod. He'd probably heard me coming from the moment I walked into the building.

From the looks of it, this room must have been the school nurse's office. Appropriate for its current use.

Hod had propped his shoulders up on the makeshift pillow at the head of the bed, positioning himself halfway between lying down and sitting. He turned his head toward me at the squeak of my sneakers on the old linoleum.

Had his face gotten thinner since yesterday? The shadows beneath his high cheekbones looked starker, or maybe that was just my imagination, seeing him laid up like that. His short black hair was sticking up at various angles exactly like it would on any normal person who'd just been sleeping for hours. My fingers itched to smooth over it, to touch his pale cheek.

"Ari?" he said, only slightly a question. I guessed any of the gods would have had significantly heavier footsteps.

"I thought you might be hungry," I said. "Or thirsty. I brought a few things... How are you feeling?"

"Better," Hod said, pushing himself higher on the bed. A small smile touched his face, softening the hollows that had worried me a moment ago. "I've already eaten—someone left a plate for me to find when I woke up."

I noticed the plate in question and a nearly drained water bottle on the little table at the side of the bed. My cargo felt suddenly awkward in my hands. I went over and set the bread and the rest on the floor beside the table. "Well, if you get hungry again later..."

"Thank you."

I stood there for a few seconds, torn between a longing to wrap him in a hug and nervousness that I might hurt him somehow if I so much as touched him. A furrow formed in Hod's brow. He reached out to me and slid his fingers lightly around my arm.

"Hey," he said. "I'm sorry I snapped at you last night. I wasn't angry at you or anything like that—it was just such an overwhelming situation—"

Was he worrying about that? A lump rose in my throat. I eased my arm up to take his hand and sat down carefully on the edge of the bed. "I know. Of course you were on edge. What you did was amazing. I'm just sorry if I made it at all harder."

He let out a dismissive snort. "Not possible. Come here, then, valkyrie. Shouldn't temporary invalid status earn me a little coddling?"

My heart swelled. I leaned into his embrace, tucking my head against his shoulder, hugging him as tightly as I dared. His body still held all the lean strength I was used to and that familiar salty smoky smell.

He was okay. He was really okay.

The lump in my throat rose even higher, and tears formed behind my closed eyelids. I willed them back. I'd done enough crying in front of Hod for a lifetime, and the last thing he needed right now was even more reasons to worry about me.

I wouldn't let myself think about what would happen if Surt struck again before Hod had fully recuperated. Wouldn't let myself think about how another blast might seep through his shadows and sear him away from me.

He was here now, solid and real. I had to focus on that fact.

"I'm glad you're all right," I murmured. "And I meant it—the way you stopped that blast and neutralized it was absolutely fucking amazing. We'd all have been fried if it wasn't for you. You can have all the coddling you want."

He chuckled, leaning in to kiss my temple. "I'm sure it won't go to my head. I should be back on my feet in an hour or two, and everyone can go back to not bothering to consult with me right in front of me instead of at a distance."

"I personally think most of the gods in that bunch have very bad taste in who they listen to," Loki said. "I supposed we should have expected as much, given that they gave up our excellent company for so long."

"We need them," Hod said. But even though his tone before had been wry, his muscles had tensed as he'd spoken. He'd told me before how the gods had treated him after Ragnarok: mostly avoiding him, only coming to him when they had a distasteful task he could handle that they barely wanted to acknowledge. And even before, everyone had always looked to Baldur the bright one over him.

Thinking back over the last few days, I couldn't remember anyone seeking out his opinions. He'd been sidelined almost as much as I had.

Hod's fingertips caressed down my back, warm through the thin silk of my tank top. An eager tingle ran through me at his touch. Suddenly I was remembering how Thor had reminded me how much I mattered to at least a few of the gods here when I'd been feeling out of sorts. That was exactly the sort of generosity I was more than happy to pass on.

I eased back and set my hand against Hod's face. "They need *you*," I said, "even if they're too stuck-up to admit it. *I* need you. Would you like me to demonstrate how much?"

He pushed himself forward as I leaned in, catching my mouth an instant before I'd meant my lips to brush his. My pulse skipped. His arm looped tighter around my waist and his other hand was teasing into my hair, and just like that, his kiss felt as necessary as air.

I cupped his jaw and kissed him harder. Hod pulled me onto his lap, parting my lips with his tongue. His thumb eased up my side to trace the underside of my breast, and a pleased murmur escaped me.

Loki cleared his throat. "Well, seeing as *I'm* hardly needed here any longer, I'll leave you to your recovery."

The amused lilt of his voice washed over me like a caress in itself. I couldn't suppress the shiver of longing that passed through me at the thought of that second pair of sly hands moving over my body in tandem with Hod's.

Hod stilled beneath me. He pulled back with one last brush of his lips against mine and said, "You don't have to leave."

My heart hiccupped. I glanced over my shoulder. Loki had frozen with his hand on the door, staring back at us.

"What are you saying?" he asked in a measured tone.

Hod's thumb stroked higher on my breast, just below the peak. I couldn't help pressing into his touch, encouraging it to continue its climb. His blind gaze was fixed on my face, but his expression was relaxed. Almost pleased.

"I'm saying our valkyrie could be enjoying this moment even more if you wanted to contribute."

"Hod," I said, choking up. Forgetting his hand and its tempting ascent, I bent my head so my forehead grazed his. "You're enough."

"I know," he said, so easily I believed him. "But why stop there? You think I don't want to hear how you could gasp a little sharper, feel how you could tremble a little harder?"

I did tremble then, with a wave of emotion that was a lot more than just lust.

"Fuck," Loki murmured, with a click as he kicked shut the door. He crossed the room like a blazing wind. Hod tugged my mouth back to his, palming my breast, and the trickster leaned over me, pressing a kiss to my spine through my top as his hand came to rest on my hip. Every nerve in my body lit up with the promise of what was to come.

All that emotion still pulsed in my chest, even as I whimpered at the swivel of Hod's fingers across my nipple. That was how much I meant to him—so much that he got more from my increased pleasure than he lost by sharing this interlude with a companion he'd only just made a tentative peace with after centuries of animosity.

That was how well he knew me, that he could read my desires in an instant.

Loki stroked my hip as he drew up my shirt, kissing bare skin now. Every press of his lips came with a flicker of fiery heat. A softly cool sensation I recognized as

Hod's shadows licked over my belly. Without breaking our kiss, I shifted my legs to straddle him. A different sort of need rose up inside me with a pinch of pain. He'd told me, shown me, over and over, how much I meant to him. But he might not realize he meant just as much to me.

In another minute, I'd be too lost in bliss to find the words. Or too lost for him to believe them. My throat tightened. I raised my head just slightly, my nose resting against Hod's, gazing into his dark green eyes that knew exactly where to find mine even if he couldn't have told me their color or their shape. My beautiful haunted dark god.

"I love you," I said. It came out in a whisper, buried under the rush of emotion that had propelled the words out, but he heard me. His lips parted with a startled breath.

Loki hesitated between kisses, his fingers halting with a jerk against my thigh. Did it bother him that I'd said it—that I'd said it to Hod? We'd made kind of a deal, the trickster and me, of no commitments and no grand declarations, and it wasn't as if he'd ever broken from that.

His reaction only lasted a second, and then he lowered his mouth to my back again as if nothing had changed. Hod trailed his fingers down the side of my face and skimmed my lips with his thumb.

"I love you too," he said hoarsely.

Our lips collided as if pulled together by an unstoppable force, and maybe that wasn't entirely untrue. A giddy tingling rushed through my chest, as if holding in that short statement had bottled up this huge anxious space inside me that was now opened up.

I loved him. I did. I loved all of them, didn't I? Loki and his quick humor covering the wounds that ran deep, Thor with his mix of gentleness and ferocity, Baldur and the harmony he could summon from just about anything. But right now I wanted to pour all that feeling into the god beneath me. He gave so much to all of us.

My mouth slipped to Hod's jaw. I kissed a path down his throat as I tugged the blanket away from between us. Loki unclasped my bra, Hod drew my top up over my head, and then the trickster was tracing my ribs with sizzles of flame while the dark god fondled my breasts. I almost forgot where I was going. But only almost.

I scooted farther down the bed and grasped the fly of Hod's jeans. He inhaled sharply. "Ari..."

"Lie back," I said, and licked up the trace of salt at the base of his belly. "Relax. You think I don't want to feel *you* enjoy the moment? I'm pretty sure you're still supposed to be resting. I can take care of you."

I swept my palm over the bulge of his erection, and he groaned. His body loosened, his hand coming to rest on my head. His fingers laced through the strands of my hair to caress my scalp as I yanked the zipper down.

His cock sprang free from his boxers with barely any encouragement needed from me. I nuzzled its silky firmness with a flick of my tongue, smiling at the way it twitched at my attentions. All Hod managed at that was a strangled sound. I swiped my tongue all up his pale length to the head and took him right into my mouth.

The sharp smokiness of him filled my mouth. His fingers tightened against my head. He bucked up with a ragged breath as I took him deeper. I worked him over carefully, gripping the base of his cock, applying the pressure of my tongue here, a teasing of teeth there, exploring. Discovering what I could do to make this man come completely undone in the most enjoyable possible way.

Loki had adjusted his position when I had. Now he leaned over me, gliding his hands up over my torso to cup the breasts Hod had relinquished. His thumbs darted over my nipples with flares of heat that sent a ripple of pleasure through me. He kissed my shoulder, the crook of my neck, and murmured with a scorching breath by my ear, "Oh, my valkyrie, you are glorious when you take control."

His voice provoked the same eager shiver it had before. I bobbed my head over Hod's cock, sucking hard, and he rocked to meet me, while the trickster sent his blissful flames licking down over my skin.

A whisper like cool velvet brushed my belly, and I knew Hod's shadows had rejoined Loki's flames. As I swiveled my tongue around what seemed to be the most sensitive spot on his cock, that shadowy sensation slipped lower. Under my jeans and my panties, tickling my clit with just enough pressure to make me whimper, and then nudging against my sex. All at once it felt like a solid thing probing my folds, as hard and taut as the cock in my mouth.

I couldn't hold back a gasp. Hod's hand stilled against my hair.

"Too much?" he rasped.

"No," I mumbled. "Fuck. Don't stop."

His next breath had the shape of a smile. That corded length of shadow pressed into me, stretching me, hitting every hungry place inside me. A needy sigh slipped from my lips. I arched to urge Hod's magic deeper and eased down over him again.

Loki chuckled with another wash of flickering heat. He ran his hands back down to my hips and tucked one between my thighs to massage the tingling bud at my core. Hod's shadowy instrument drove into me again and again, and Loki's flames laved over my clit.

With each plunge of that solid darkness inside me, it found new points of pleasure. I moaned over his cock, rocking instinctively with the rhythm he'd set. Bliss rang all through my body.

Hod's magic thrust harder. I started to shake. I was so close to that edge, but I meant to bring the dark god with me.

I pumped my hand over his now-slick cock, caressing my lips over the head in time with my movements. Hod's hips jerked. "Ari," he said, clenching my hair.

The salty spurt of his release flooded my mouth. His shadow bucked into me at a pace to match the stuttering of his breath. Loki bit down on my bare side, and I came with a lurch of my heart, feeling as if the rush of ecstasy would toss me head over heels. I clutched Hod's thighs as I cried out. My arms and legs gave, and I sagged down over him.

Hod tugged my shoulder and eased me up to cuddle against his still clothed but heated chest. I raised my head, and he met me with a kiss. It carried on and on until my heart ached with all the love I hadn't found more words for yet.

But I'd said the most important part. No matter what happened next, he knew.

Loki hunkered down next to the cot. My hand reached out of its own accord to trail over his neck and come to rest on his shoulder. He set his own hand over it.

"I never thought I'd be learning new tricks from you, Dark One," he said, sounding amused. "I'll have to put my own spin on that technique sometime."

I started to tense in anticipation of Hod's reaction, but the dark god just laughed. He kissed my forehead. "I have excellent inspiration to experiment. Perhaps sometime we should make a combined effort of it, if our valkyrie would like that. Our powers do seem to reach extra heights in combination."

"Mmmm," Loki hummed in what sounded like agreement, sending the ache in my chest straight to my core.

"Your valkyrie gives that plan two thumbs up," I said.

Hod laughed again and ducked his head next to mine. Loki's thumb traced a soft pattern over my knuckles. We relaxed there for a while, the last three any of the other gods would have bothered to come looking for, the three they didn't entirely want around. Right then, that antipathy didn't feel like an insult. It felt like its own little realm of freedom.

A shout of excitement filtered through the wall from outside. Loki sighed. "I suppose at some point we should see what the others have gotten themselves wrapped up in now."

He let go of my hand and started to stand. I eased myself up over Hod just in time to see the trickster freeze with one hand on the side of the bed, his back still bent. Hod's head snapped up.

"Surt?" he said.

"The bloody bastard," Loki muttered. "I don't think he's far this time. Let's see if we can melt *him* down first."

18

Hod

I'd jerked my clothes into place and was just swinging my legs over the side of the bed when Ari caught my arm. The trickster had already dashed out of the room.

"Are you sure you should come?" Ari said. "You already pushed yourself so hard last night—you weren't even planning on walking for a while yet."

If my sense of my body still felt a tad off-kilter, it was hard to say whether I could blame that on last night's efforts or the way Ari had just set me alight with pleasure. I touched her face, pulling her close enough that I could feel her breath.

"I know my limitations. The Trickster says it isn't far. And you were right. You—all of you—might need me again."

That, and there was no way in the nine realms I was letting her race off to battle Surt while I lounged around back here, especially not after the intimacy we'd just shared.

"Okay," she said quietly, in almost the same voice she'd used to tell me she loved me. The memory gave me a fresh thrill in spite of everything. It couldn't have been easy for her to say that, but she had, for me.

She slipped her fingers along my jaw to kiss me quickly, and then we hustled into the hall together.

"Let's go, let's go!" Thor was bellowing outside. I guessed Loki had passed on word first to his old adventuring companion. If there was anyone here the other gods were likely to rally around when it came to fighting giants, it was my older brother.

I'd used a strand of shadow to feel out any obstacles in the hall. The second we'd burst out the door, Ari unleashed her wings with a feathery hiss and I stretched my shadow into my usual ride. Up in the air, over this unfamiliar terrain, all I had to do was keep track of the others and assume they were going in the right direction.

It must have been around the middle of the afternoon. The sun beamed hot against the right side of my face as we set off in a direction I knew instinctively was south. The brisk wind raised by our flight cut through the worst of the summer heat. Some of the others were still shouting back and forth, debating strategy, but I tuned out everything except the rustling with each flap of Ari's wings and the faint murmur of Loki's enchanted shoes pushing off through the air.

He knew where we were going, and I knew there was only one strategy I'd need when we got there. If Surt was aiming to spark a second nuclear explosion, I'd just have to smother it with another wave of shadow.

Maybe if we got there earlier in the process this time, it wouldn't require every shred of strength I had in me.

It didn't exactly take a lot of physical effort to fly like this. All I had to do was stay balanced on the relatively wide strip of shadow. But within several minutes, a prickling sensation formed around my bent knees and my hips, the base of my neck, my hands braced against my conveyance.

All right, so I hadn't fully recovered my strength yet. It wouldn't matter if we reached Surt soon enough. Whatever he was doing now, I'd give everything I had to stop him.

I shifted my weight, adjusting my position by increments as new aches formed. The miles fell away beneath us.

"There," Loki said. The faint crackling of the flaming bridge reached my ears. The trickster sped forward even faster, and I pushed my shadow to follow with a thump of my pulse. Then Loki halted abruptly. The crackle vanished.

The Sly One let out a huff as I drew up nearby. "He's already gone. What in Hel's name was he doing *here*?"

I couldn't sense any explosive energy in the air, not even a hint of it on the verge of bursting. Our valkyrie glided over to join me. "It looks like a residential neighborhood," she said. "Some suburb—all wide streets lined with houses with big lawns. Nice place to live." Her tone was a bit dry. "No power plants. Nothing else destructive. Weird."

"We have to find exactly where he touched down," Loki was muttering. He edged forward again, one extended stride and then another. The rest of us moved after him.

"There's the mark!" Heimdall called, with more energy than I'd heard from him since he'd first arrived. Maybe he just liked that he'd beat the Trickster to our goal. "That yard is scorched from the bridge. He came down there."

I followed the others down to earth, noting the whispering leaves of a tree—birch, from the smell of it—and the sun-baked patio stones my feet landed on. Another impression, not quite a smell, not quite a feeling, quivered through my senses. It tugged at the deepest darkness inside me.

"Someone's died here," I said. "Recently. The body —" I gestured in the direction that quavering chill emanated from.

"I've found him," Freya said. Her voice was tight. "A dark elf. His throat's been burned through. But it looks like he was beat up plenty before the kill. He's got marks all over him—he's missing a couple of fingers—I think his knee is crushed."

"Surt tortured him," Thor said in a fierce rumble. "He must have needed the elf to tell him something or do something for him that he wasn't getting any other way. This house doesn't belong to the dirt-eaters, though, does it?"

We treaded cautiously around the building. A fresh quivering reached me from a different direction. I gritted my teeth. "The elf isn't the only one dead."

Broken glass crunched under our feet. We stepped through what I gathered was the shattered remains of a sliding door into the house. More glass rasped against the hardwood floor. My shadows helped me skirt a piano and an armchair. I stopped at an open door.

"That's the woman in the photos there," Baldur said softly. "This must be her home."

A few of the gods brushed past me to examine the body.

"She had a Ph.D. in nuclear engineering," Ari said. "Assuming that's her name on the certificate."

"Surt was trying to get an edge," Vidar muttered. "I wonder what information he got out of her."

I eased into the room, staying close to the walls. Whatever Surt had done to the woman, my powers were no use here. I could take life, but I couldn't offer it. There was nothing I could do for someone who'd already succumbed to the final darkness.

My hands encountered wooden shelves. Shelves full of books. I skimmed my fingers over the spines—most of them arced and creased, suggesting they'd been read fairly thoroughly.

I reached to pull one volume out and hesitated with my hand poised. That's exactly what the others would expect of me, wasn't it? Hod the dark loner, going straight to the books. I could remember the bemused murmurs as I'd added to my collection of texts in my hall with volumes gathered on earth. *Where does he think all that human rambling is going to get him?*

But it was human ramblings that had produced the inspirations to create the technology that had nearly destroyed *us* last night. It was human ramblings Surt had come here to learn about, presumably. Humans took the time to think about a lot of subjects the gods never bothered with, which did them credit.

What did I care what anyone here thought of me? No one that mattered to me would scoff. I wanted to know more about the woman Surt had killed, and what was on her shelves would tell me as clearly as anything.

I pulled out the book I'd already started to grasp and flipped it open to the first page. With a flick of my fingers, my magic darted across the paper, whispering the printed words into my ear.

It was a physics text, something about thermodynamics. Nothing very enlightening there. I picked another at random and another—a volume on organic chemistry and a memoir of a political figure I'd never heard of—and then I explored the shelves more thoughtfully. Which books here had held the most meaning for this woman?

"I can't get into her computer," Bragi was saying. "It's password protected."

"None of the papers on her desk look like anything Surt would have been interested in," Freyr said. "Just bills and ordinary things."

My fingers found a leather cover, stiff with age but solid and uncracked as though a lot of care had been taken with it. Hmm. I eased it out and opened it.

The first whisper that wound through my ear was an inscription. "To Dr. Carmen, Because you brightened our days and helped keep our boys safe. General Yancy & Sergeant Ramirez."

I stilled my fingers. "Are there any signs about the work she did?"

"Nuclear engineering, obviously," Freyr said.

"No, I mean who she worked *for*." I set down the book, cover open, on the desk. "I think she might have been a military scientist."

Someone snatched up the book less gently than I suspected Dr. Carmen would have approved of if she'd been alive to mind. Hinges squeaked, and the contents of desk drawers clinked. Ari came over to the shelves next to me.

"There's a plaque here," she said. "Some kind of commendation, it says. It looks like a military thing."

"We can't make too many assumptions from just those two things," Njord said, but he sounded doubtful of his own words.

"Oh, I don't know," Loki said, a thread of uneasiness running through his smooth voice. "I think we can put together a pretty convincing picture from what we've got. Surt wasn't content with the blast a power plant could offer. He's looking to get his hands on a bomb or two now."

My stomach flipped over. "Some of the bombs humans have developed—they have enough power to essentially end the world in one shot."

And there was no way I'd ever be able to contain that much fiery rage.

While the others gathered outside the building we'd

taken shelter in to concoct some sort of dinner, I lingered in the invalid room they'd given me before, paging through one of the books I'd borrowed from Dr. Carmen's study. I figured she wouldn't mind. She probably had friends and family still living who she'd have been happy to know her personal library had helped save.

If we were going to save them at all. So far what I was reading was only confirming my worst fears.

Weapons weren't exactly my topic of choice when it came to scientific treatises. I had enough death in my life as it was. So my standing knowledge of nuclear explosives was relatively limited. After I'd made my claim in Dr. Carmen's study, the other gods, even Thor, had laughed off the idea that humans could have constructed any weapon quite as destructive as I'd said. Loki's reminders not to underestimate humankind had been waved off as well.

It was true, though. The most powerful bombs humans had built could essentially wipe out all life on this realm. Maybe not all at once, but once the aftereffects spread...

I raised my fingers from the page and shut the book. I was already feeling queasy.

My renewed understanding had at least given me a shred of hope as well. I got up from the bed and headed down the hall, feeling for a familiar presence that was bright even to me. I'd always been able to pick my twin out of a crowd.

To my surprise, I didn't find him with the crowd this time. He'd wandered off a short ways into the field behind the building. It was a cool night coming on, and his innate warmth bled out into the air as if he were a miniature sun himself.

"Hod," he said, moving toward me before I'd reached him. "What is it? Did you find something?"

He'd helped me carry some of those books.

"Nothing that gives us any less reason to worry," I said. "If Surt manages to get his hands on those missiles or bombs, even one of them... Humanity may very well be doomed."

I didn't think my twin could help himself from looking at the bright side. "We don't know for sure that Surt even knew about the scientist's military connections. It could just be a coincidence, and he was looking for information on more effectively using the plants for his purposes."

Which would hardly be a good thing either, but I didn't think either of us wanted to count on it.

"Maybe," I said. "But without knowing, we have to be prepared for the worst. And I think... I think you'd be the key to stopping him, if it comes to that."

I felt the movement of air as Baldur's head jerked up. "*Me*?" he said. "You're the one who tamped down on that energy with your darkness before."

"I know," I said. "But it was hard enough at the power plant. With an actual bomb... I wouldn't stand a chance, Baldur. I can admit that."

"And you think I would?"

My mouth twisted as I said the only thing I could that was true. "I think if Surt detonates one of those bombs, we're all cinders. But their impact relies on a chain reaction that requires all the parts to be in just the right state. You could use your powers to melt down the elements inside—slowly—fusing them together. Even if you only managed to get to a small portion in time, it might be enough to stop the reaction and the deadliest part of the explosion completely."

"I don't know," Baldur said. "If it's not— Let me think about it."

He turned away from me. His voice had gone short. He was clamming up—maybe not into the dreamy haze he'd spent so much time in since we'd been reborn, but retreating from me all the same.

My instinct was to retreat in turn. There'd been a long time when I'd backed away from any uncomfortable topic between us. Whatever I could do to keep the darkness away from his light.

But he'd had darkness in him all along anyway. Darkness I could have helped him grapple with sooner if I'd let those conversations happen. I dragged in a breath and stood my ground.

"What's wrong, brother?" I said. "Tell me about it even if you don't want to talk to them." I tipped my head toward the gods gathered near the parking lot.

Baldur was silent a moment longer. He rubbed his smooth jaw. "I... Last night. When we reached the power station. I felt the explosion about to happen, and I tried to interfere, but my light—it only made the effect stronger. It *fed* the explosion. My power, the brightness in me, it was almost the same as that... that energy that almost killed us all. The energy you're talking about that could bring the entire realm to ruin in a matter of minutes."

"Light has always been able to burn," I said. "We'd enjoy the sun a lot less if we were standing right next to it."

"I know," Baldur said. "I just never thought I had that side of it in me." A brief laugh hitched out of him. "I was so worried about the darkness I'd absorbed, when really it's the affinity that's most a part of me that the rest of you should be frightened of."

"Hey." I clapped my twin on the shoulder, my gut clenching at the horror in his words. Horror at *himself* of all people. "No one's going to be frightened of you, because we know you control that power. You use it to bring life, not to take it away. You accidentally encouraged the explosion because you didn't know what to expect. Now you do know."

"And you want me to meddle with any bombs Surt collects."

Ah. I could see now why he'd balked. "Before the explosion is set off," I said. "To fuse them, under your control. Using your energy to act on the components before Surt can use them for his ends."

"If it really is that simple," Baldur said.

"I think it is," I said. "I think it's the best chance we'd have if we're faced with that situation. Better to take that risk than to know for sure he's going to annihilate us, right?"

Baldur's shoulders rose and fell with a long breath. His posture started to straighten. "How do you do it?" he asked, his voice a little less strained now. "Keep going, knowing there's something deadly inside you? Something that's what makes you *you*."

"I haven't had much choice," I said frankly. "I... I serve a purpose. I bring balance. As much as I can, I use my power to take away pain rather than to deal it out. We all have to make choices like that."

"I suppose that's what makes us gods," Baldur said. He let out another laugh, looser this time. "Thank you—for listening. And for the plan. I'll be prepared, if it comes to that."

He moved to amble over to the others, slowly enough that I could tell he expected—and wanted—me to join him. I fell into step beside him.

With our home stolen and Surt posing threats we'd never had to consider, maybe all of us Asgardians had been feeling a little adrift. A little apart from our comrades. But the darkness in those gaps between us didn't need to be empty. I could fill it with something more.

19

Aria

The ring of the phone brought me flailing out of my sleeping bag, my heart thudding and my eyes bleary from a night that had involved more waiting in tensed anticipation for a call to arms than actual rest. It took my panicking body a second to remember that if Loki had sensed Surt's arrival in this world, he wouldn't have been telling me over the phone.

I'd only given this number to one person. My pulse started to thump all over again as I fumbled for the answer button.

"Harrison?" I said, blinking myself into sharper alertness.

"There you are, Ari," the gang commander replied. "I was starting to think you'd gone and ascended to the heavens or something."

I made a face. "I answered as fast as I could. What's the news?"

"We got it."

I sat up straighter, my fingers tightening around the phone. "All of it?"

"Everything your people said they wanted. The cash was more than enough to cover the equipment. Maybe I should consider switching bosses." His tone was dryly amused.

"I don't think 'my people' are going to be hiring after the whole saving the world thing is over with," I said. "But that's great. Can you get the whole arsenal out here, along with enough people to handle it, ASAP?"

"I figured that'd be the next step," Harrison said. "I'm just rounding up our little army right now. Unless we run into an unexpected hiccup, we'll be seeing you in a few hours."

"Perfect," I said. "Same spot as before. And thank you."

"Hey, I'm raking in dough and saving my own hide at the same time. Generosity didn't even figure into the equation. Hang tight or whatever valkyries do until I get there."

From the light streaming through the narrow window, my restless sleep had ended with me sleeping in. I'd kept my regular clothes on in case of a late-night emergency, so I jogged straight into the hall, running my fingers through the tangled waves of my hair as I went. The rooms I passed where the other gods had been sleeping were empty.

Heimdall was in the front office where we'd been

stashing our food, poking at the offerings with a dissatisfied expression. No, I wasn't telling him the news first. Better to start with the gods who'd actually be happy about it. They could discuss it with the others. It wasn't as if most of the other gods gave me the time of day in the first place.

Thor and Baldur were standing not far from each other in a cluster of gods talking together in the yard outside. I caught Thor's eye and jerked my chin to the side. He tipped his head and grasped his brother's shoulder. I spotted Hod sitting with his back against the worn bricks down near the back of the school, his fingers skimming over the pages of a book he was vaguely staring at. Thor and Baldur followed me over there.

"Hey," I said as I reached Hod and the other two caught up. "Has anyone seen Loki?" It made me edgy all over again not seeing him around. I couldn't imagine him going far when he was our only way of tracking Surt's movements, though. Last night we'd had a brief scare when he'd sensed Surt's fiery magic, but we'd only just set off when the impression had vanished again.

The giant couldn't have gotten much done in the ten or so minutes he'd been in Midgard, but he'd been doing *something*, and the fact that we didn't know what gnawed at me.

Before anyone had a chance to answer, the trickster himself slipped into view from behind the building. "You called?" he said with his sly grin, but the good humor in it didn't quite reach his amber eyes. He was wound tight too. "Good to see you're finally out of bed, pixie."

"Not that you can really call it a 'bed'," I muttered. "I

had a call from Harrison. He's gotten the weapons together, and now he's just rounding up his people. They're aiming to get out here in a few hours."

Thor's face brightened. "Rocket launchers and machine guns?"

Loki chuckled. "Are you considering trading in Mjolnir, old friend?"

"Of course not." The thunder god patted his ever-present hammer affectionately. "But I can't say I'm not curious what it'd be like to give some of this human technology a whirl."

"I think we'd better all stick to our strengths," I said. "At least those of us whose strengths already work against Surt. Maybe I should get a few lessons in machine gun usage, if there's time for that. It'd stop you from having to worry so much about me, anyway."

Hod had stood up. He reached to tug a lock of my hair, grazing my cheek with his knuckles as he did. "I don't expect there's anything you could be armed with that'd stop us worrying, valkyrie. Unless you're going to tell me you don't worry about us too."

I elbowed him lightly. "Somehow I think there's a *little* more worry going one way than the other. But never mind that. We're going to need to come up with a plan for what we do with these guys—and girls, maybe—when they get here." I glanced at Loki. "You haven't gotten any closer to figuring out what Surt was up to last night?"

The trickster shook his head. "I haven't gotten a hint of him since then. It might have been nothing more than a feint, intended to confuse us. I'm not sure he realizes that I can't trace the point where the bridge came down after he's removed it. He may not even have worked out how we're finding him at all. He might be reasonably clever as giants go, but with giants, that isn't saying a whole lot. With myself being the obvious exception."

"Obviously," Hod said with an arch of his eyebrow, but he sounded more amused than anything else.

"He's appeared in North America three times in succession, as far as we can tell, hasn't he?" Baldur said in his soothingly serene way. "We can probably—"

He stopped, his gaze sliding to something beyond my shoulder. Some*one* beyond my shoulder, I determined from the scrap of boots over the dusty earth. I turned to see the other gods who'd been conversing together heading our way, Vidar in the lead.

"What's this private conference you've got going on over here?" the muscular god asked. His tone wasn't quite accusing yet, but his eyes had a hard glint to them. "If you're making plans, shouldn't we all be involved? I believe that's what we agreed on yesterday."

By which he meant, he and some of the others had agreed, and they'd assumed I had to follow whatever they told me.

"Brother," Thor said, giving the side of Vidar's arm a playful cuff. "We were just determining whether we had a plan to present to the rest of you before we got to the presenting part."

"That tends to be the most productive order," Loki added helpfully.

"They've got their own little clique here," Skadi said, coming up beside Vidar with her arms folded over her chest. "Around their little valkyrie."

I managed not to bristle other than the terse smile that sprang to my face. Baldur set a reassuring hand on the small of my back.

"The four of us had a lot of time with just each other over the last few centuries," he said. "I think it's normal that we gravitate toward each other even with so many of you here now. And Ari knows us far better than she knows anyone else here. It was only a conversation."

"We're seeing a lot of these separate conversations happening between the bunch of you," Freyr put in. "After all the work you put into gathering us, you give off an awfully strong impression that you don't feel you really need our input."

"Now, hold on," Thor said, still trying to keep his voice warm. "We weren't making any decisions, and we certainly don't consider ourselves in charge. That's the Allfather's role, and I wouldn't want it if he offered it to me. You're here now. Let's talk. Unless you'd rather fight with us than with the draugr."

Vidar glowered at him. "I say you should—"

A shout went up farther across the yard. A glimmering white figure glided down by the side of the road, with two companions flanking her: an elderly man and a young woman who didn't look like she could have been older than me. It was Idunn, the goddess of regeneration who'd joined us in the last wave of newcomers, and two more gods she'd managed to find, I guessed with Heimdall's directions.

Thor sucked in his breath, a sound that wasn't all that pleased. "What?" I said, peering at him.

"That girl," he said, nodding to the young woman,

who was winding a lock of her golden hair around one finger as she made her cautious approach. "That's Hnoss. Freya's daughter."

Knowing the family connection, it was impossible not to see the echo of Freya's face and frame in Hnoss's—even when they were at opposite ends of the yard.

I fiddled with my switchblade in my pocket as I looked from one to the other. Hnoss was talking with several of the other newer gods, her stance still tensed after a couple hours in our presence. She'd angled herself away from her mother. Freya had drawn closer to Odin, who seemed to be consulting with Njord about something right now, but her gaze kept darting toward the younger goddess.

After all the anguish I'd seen Freya express over her separation from her daughter, their reunion had been a flop. Maybe the reasons for that anguish were why it'd been a flop. The goddess of love and war had come dashing out of the old school building when someone must have passed on word to her. Hnoss had looked up at the squeal of the door. Their eyes had met, Hnoss's jaw had clenched as she'd turned away, and Freya had stopped in her tracks, her arms sagging at her sides.

"But that's the thing," Bragi was saying over on Hnoss's side of the yard now. "We can't be sure what understanding Surt is working with, so we can't predict his next moves, not even with a pattern in the past."

We'd spent most of the time since the two new

arrivals had reached us catching them up and then discussing the dilemma of what to do next. Thor had managed to break the news that Harrison's men and their weapons were on the way, but most of the others had looked uncomfortable even starting to discuss that. I guessed we'd get down to that part of our strategy when there were a few dozen living breathing human beings here in front of them that they'd find much harder to ignore.

"We can still make a reasonable guess," Vidar said, motioning to the map. Before he could continue, the Allfather strode over to that larger group, Freya and Njord trailing behind him.

"I feel we are moving swiftly toward the critical junction," Odin said in his low but resonant voice. It sent an uneasy shiver down my back. "The visions I brought back may hold the key. We should do our best to decipher them before we proceed."

"I'd imagine your insights about those visions would be the most accurate, father," Baldur said. "You have the full context."

"But perhaps I don't." The Allfather trailed the end of his spear across the packed earth. "The context is Surt and these battles and all of you."

"'The light of day can burn before a fire, but only the highest water can put out all the flames'," Loki intoned. "That was it, wasn't it?"

Baldur glanced toward his twin. "The first part—the light of day—that could refer to my powers. I'll be on watch for chances to use them to hold off Surt's fire."

Which the bright god would have been doing

anyway. I wasn't sure how Odin's ramblings had helped us there. The other gods stirred, a restless energy moving through the group.

"The highest water could mean some sort of mountain spring," Idunn ventured. "What is the highest peak in Midgard?"

Freya stepped to the map, and Heimdall let out a sharp sound. "Is this really what we're going to do?" he said. "Run all around the world looking for mountain water instead of focusing on the next battle?"

Odin swept his arm. "The water of my visions, if found, could end the entire—"

"Enough!" Heimdall interrupted. "You're the Allfather and you led us well for a long while, but we need a real leader right now, not an old man's dreaming. Do you even listen to yourself anymore? 'Light of day' and 'highest water'—this isn't one of Bragi's poems, it's an actual *war*, and it's happening right now."

"Not that you'd know," Vidar tossed out. "Since you haven't been here."

I shifted my weight, hugging myself instinctively. The shift in the tone of this conversation left my nerves prickling. I wasn't Odin's biggest fan, but this didn't seem like a good time to hash out all the gods' personal complaints about his past leadership.

"Now, hold on," Freya said, holding up her hand. "Odin's words, even when vague, have often set us on the right course—"

"Have they?" Hnoss's clear voice, as sweet as her mother's even when there was an edge to it, rang out. She stepped closer to the front, looking at Freya rather than

Odin. "They led us straight into Ragnarok, didn't they? Not that he'd ever admit any fault there. What does he care about the rest of us over preserving his high position?"

Thor's eyes flashed. "Whatever else you can say about my father, he's always done his best for all of Asgard."

Hnoss glared at the thunder god. "Then his best fell far short of what we were owed."

"Hnoss," Freya started.

Her daughter's head snapped back around. "Don't even start. You know how I feel. It obviously never changed anything for you."

Loki clapped his hands with a fiery crackle. For a second, even the uneasy murmurs in the crowd fell silent.

"My good people," the trickster said jauntily, "you all know I am never one to shy from offering criticism. But even if there may be elements of Odin's methods I've disagreed with, I believe his visions were always accurate, once the meaning became clear. I don't say we should dash off in search of mountain springs, but we could spend a few minutes discussing the possibilities before moving on?"

"Why would we follow *your* advice, Trickster?" Freyr sneered. "You've led us into more ruin than anyone."

I winced on Loki's behalf. The trickster simply gazed back at Freya's brother balefully.

"Exactly," Hnoss said. "If the Sly One says we

should listen to Odin, that's all the more reason we shouldn't. He's never been anything but treachery."

A protest rose in my throat, but I wasn't sure if I'd be helping the situation or only adding more fuel to the fire by saying what I knew. If even Loki didn't seem to think it was wise to get into the full accounting of blame—

"No!" The single syllable rolled across the yard like a thunderclap, in time with the smack of Odin's spear against the ground. His knuckles had whitened where he was gripping the staff. His single eye glowed with a fierceness nearly as bright as Baldur's magic.

"You want an admission of fault?" the Allfather said to Hnoss. "I will make it. The Trickster has been the most loyal of any of Asgard's citizens. He carried out my instructions as I expected him to, often against his own wishes, in deference to the blood oath we'd taken. Ragnarok was looming over us. I needed everything in order, to take us through it in the smoothest possible way. We required chaos to come through to peace; we required a villain; I put that responsibility on his shoulders."

He paused, and his voice turned a little ragged. His gaze swept over all the assembled gods. "I may not have judged everything correctly. I may have caused you more pain than was necessary. And perhaps I could have spared some of the pain that had to come by revealing more. I regret that, and I regret that it has taken me so long to say as much to you."

For a few seconds, no one seemed to know how to respond. The angry vibe that had been swelling amid the gods had petered out. I guessed it was hard to stay furious with someone who'd just accepted all that anger and acknowledged it was fair.

Loki was staring at Odin. From the shock on his face, he'd never had the slightest expectation that the Allfather would ever volunteer the truth about their association. He wet his lips and raised his chin.

"Our king may overstate the case," he said, managing to keep his usual light tone. "I'm sure I took more than a few digs on my own behalf. You're welcome to continue hating me if you'll rest easier that way."

"Odin," Njord said, his eyes wide. He didn't seem to know how to continue.

The Allfather bowed his head. "We can speak on this matter more if you wish. But I will defer to Vidar and Heimdall now. We have a battle that must be fought. My visions will clarify themselves when the time comes. All I ask is you remember them and act if you see your chance."

"Well," Vidar said. He looked at the map and back up at his father, his jaw working. "I suppose..."

Engines rumbled in the distance. My heart leapt. A familiar SUV, a small transport truck, and a few vans were making their way along the road toward us. Harrison and his reinforcements had arrived.

20

Aria

The gang's vehicles pulled into the parking lot one after the other. A shiver of energy raced through the air as several of the gods must have willed themselves visible to mortal eyes. I did the same with a fresh gust of the hot summer breeze over my skin.

The engines cut out, and people started hopping out. Harrison headed over to us first while his team hung back. He nodded to me and considered the gods, his eyes sharp as ever behind those rectangular glasses. I wondered if he could pick up on the fact that they'd just been arguing.

"I brought all the weapons you asked for and the people to wield them," he said. "Do you want to look them all over?"

Thor strode forward before anyone had a chance to express hesitation. I jogged to catch up with him, and a bunch of the others trailed along behind us. Harrison gestured to the guy who'd gone to stand at the rear of the truck, and the younger man opened the back with a jerk. We peered into the dark space. A cloying metallic smell filled my nose.

Harrison hopped in along with the young guy and shoved some of the crates closer to the sunlight. He snapped the lid open on one to show us a pretty impressive bazooka, and then another to display a few machine guns. "We're well-stocked for ammo too," he said. "If bullets and missiles can take this giant down, he's going down, absolutely."

Vidar had come up beside us. His back stiffened as he eyed the truck's contents. "This is not how gods fight," he muttered.

Harrison gave the warrior god a puzzled look. "That's why my people are here too. I understood we'd be handling the guns."

"That's the idea," I said quickly. I turned to Vidar. Maybe he'd be less critical if I made him feel like he was more in charge of the situation. Odin had pretty much offered that role to him anyway. "We could have groups of them stationed at each of the most likely targets, just so we'll have back-up on hand right away wherever Surt shows up. Which did you think were the key places? Should we stick to this region, since he's mostly appeared here?"

Vidar's expression was still wary, but he stepped back from the truck and glanced toward the map still spread on the ground. "That would be my suggestion, at least for local allies." He touched the side of the truck. "How quickly could these get into place?"

"We drive fast," Harrison said with a smile. "You tell us where to go, and we'll be on it."

"Don't take off with all of these," Loki said, leaning in to run his fingers over the bazooka. "Lovely. Let's see how Surt feels about *this* kind of fire." He turned and beckoned the rest of the gods closer. "Come on, who here isn't much of a fighter? With fancy contraptions like these, you'll be out-blasting even Thor!"

Thor grumbled quietly in protest, but a grin stretched across his face as a few of his fellow gods made their way over to consider the weapons on offer.

"Wait," Vidar said. "We battle with our own powers and the weapons we know. That was what we decided."

"I don't think we came to any final decisions, brother," Thor said. He hefted a machine gun and offered it to Bragi, who cradled it as if he were afraid it might explode in his hands if he jostled it. "Why shouldn't we all fight to our fullest, even those of us whose powers don't lean that way?"

"I can't see anything good coming of this," Freyr muttered. "How much can we trust these human inventions anyway? They might blast us instead."

"I can assure you that we're careful in picking our suppliers," Harrison said. "It's *our* world we're trying to keep in one piece, remember. We're not going to cut any corners."

"To the best of their judgment," Skadi said from where she was pacing near the back of the bunch. "However much that's worth."

My teeth set on edge. "Hey," I said. "We've got one more way to take down Surt. As long as you all have good enough judgment not to aim the guns the wrong way around, you should manage not to blow yourselves up with them."

Bragi adjusted the gun in his grip, testing his hold with growing confidence. Vidar watched him, and his jaw clenched. He shook his head.

"I know what we discussed before," the warrior god said. "But Thor, you bowled the rest of us over insisting on it. This isn't what we need. Not humans, and not human weapons. I know you've got a soft spot for your valkyrie, but look at this. We need the best of our own weapons, not... that." He made a dismissive gesture toward Bragi's machine gun.

Oh, for fuck's sake, couldn't we get through any situation without an argument? I was starting to see why the gods had gone their separate ways before. But they'd rallied against all kinds of threats, before Ragnarok, hadn't they? If they'd worked together then, they should be able to now.

"Any weapons you don't have on you are back in Asgard," Loki said dryly. "Which I shouldn't have to remind you is under the control of the giant we are looking to blow up. Unless you have some grand plan for retrieving them that for some reason you've failed to share up until now..."

"Then we go to the dark elves and *insist* they craft us something suitable."

Hod tensed where he was standing near the edge of the crowd. "Our peace with them is fragile enough as it is," he said. "Try to bully them, and they'll take Surt's side all over again."

"Not while Surt is searing their throats through," Heimdall remarked.

Harrison raised his hands. "Maybe I got my wires crossed here. What I heard was that you wanted these weapons and my people to fight for you. It was your money I spent to get them. No skin off my back if you don't use them. But I know my guys. We'll keep up with you. You can't say we didn't come through."

"'Keep up'," Vidar said under his breath. "'Come through.' You barely even comprehend what we're up against. This is just..." He spun to face the largest part of the crowd, the gods still hesitating, and snatched the wrist of Harrison's young lackey who was standing nearby. "Look at them? Is this what we want to throw at Surt—mortals? *Humans*? We'll be tripping over them. He'll take one look at this 'army' and laugh, and then—"

He waggled the guy's arm, making the guy's whole body shudder. I wasn't sure what exactly Vidar had hoped to demonstrate, but I could already see this wasn't going to end well. I pushed toward him. "Let him—"

The crack of a breaking bone cut through the air. The guy cried out and muffled a curse with his free hand. Vidar blinked, staring down at the figure he'd been shaking with his godly strength, at the arm now bent where it shouldn't have, and then dropped the guy's wrist as if it had burned him.

Whatever he'd been going for, it obviously hadn't been *that*.

"What the hell?" Harrison demanded, rushing to the

guy's side. He wrenched off his checkered shirt to tie it into a makeshift sling as his lackey braced himself with a hiss through his teeth. The gang commander swiveled toward Vidar, his eyes blazing with anger but his stance defensive.

My stomach flipped over. I'd used fear to get Harrison involved—fear of what would happen to all of us if we didn't stop Surt. Now he was afraid of the gods too.

"You don't want us here," the gang commander bit out. "We can take a hint. I think we'll take these weapons too, since you don't seem to want them either, and we'll keep our own eyes out. Maybe we'll take down this giant without any help from you."

Vidar's horror fell away as he bristled at the suggestion. "Now look here—"

"Stop." Thor grasped his brother's shoulder. "If anyone can right this, it's not you, not now." He turned to Harrison. "I am so sorry for my brother's reckless behavior. Baldur can heal your man's arm—which doesn't make up for the injury caused, but at least it'll fix the injury?"

The bright god had already moved to the lackey's side. He offered a small smile. Harrison looked from him to Thor and then to me, familiar compared to the divine beings around us even with all the supernatural features I'd gained since we'd known each other.

"Baldur's healed me from worse than that," I said. "Better than any of our doctors could." I didn't know what to say about Vidar's actions.

The young guy's body went rigid when Baldur offered his hand, but after a moment he nodded. A glow seeped from the bright god's palm through the makeshift sling, and the lines of pain in the guy's face fell away almost immediately. Harrison wavered on his feet, his shoulders up and movements tight, like a wild animal unsure whether it could simply flee without having to claw its way free.

Freya tugged Vidar to the side to snap something at him under her breath.

"You'd better put that back where it came from," Skadi said to Bragi, and the poet god's grip tightened on the machine gun.

Odin eased into the middle of the crowd. "If we could all take a step back to give our human allies some space, perhaps there is still room for a calm discussion."

Whether that was true and how that discussion would have gone, I never got to find out. Because an instant later, a black shape dove out of the sky like a streak of lightning.

Muninn hit the ground so hard she stumbled as she transformed. Odin caught her arm to steady her. She swept her hair from her eyes and spun to take us all in with a panicked expression. A burn that hadn't been visible in her raven form formed a dark streak across her cheek.

"We have to go," she said. "Now. Surt's settled on his next destination. He's organizing his army and giving them their instructions. We might be able to get there before him—"

"Where?" Thor broke in, his voice rough. "Where is he going?"

"Albuquerque," she said. "New Mexico. He was

talking about some kind of weapons storage facility there—he grabbed a human, and he's been torturing the man for information, I think that's how he settled on it—but I didn't hear any details until just now. One of the guards in Valhalla almost sliced my head off as I was leaving. Surt might know by now that I was there."

Weapons storage. Thor caught my eye, his expression as anguished as I felt. "They must be nuclear weapons. He's going for the bombs."

Loki swore. He started to speak and then looked to Odin. "Allfather?" he said, like a request.

Would the gods gathered here even listen to their king? Odin cleared his throat and motioned to the crowd. "We must go, quickly, every one of us with all the power we can summon. The survival of this realm may depend on reaching this facility before Surt."

"What about—" My gaze slid to Harrison. The gang commander was standing there stunned. He stared as several of the gods dashed for their weapons or leapt into the air to start their flight.

But some of those gods still didn't have weapons. We couldn't know if the powers we had would be enough to stop Surt and his army even if we did make it there first.

I stepped up to Harrison and waited until his eyes met mine. "Please," I said. "This monster is aiming to get his hands on a crapload of nuclear weapons. We're all goners if he does. I know some of the gods are assholes, but a broken arm vs. total annihilation..."

Harrison swiped his hand over his mouth. He glanced toward his lackey, who was flexing his once-broken arm with an awed expression. "How do we know we won't all end up killed by one side or the other?" he said.

I swallowed hard. "I guess you don't," I said. "But if Surt wins, you know for sure we're all dead. You came out here ready to do this. Don't let one jerk on a power trip cancel out all the reasons you signed on in the first place."

He drew in a ragged breath and turned toward his people standing around the vehicles. "I'm not going to order you," he said. "I told you from the beginning this was a special job and a risky one. If anyone wants out..."

"If you say we're good, then we're good, boss," said a woman who was leaning her arm out the window of one of the vans. The others nodded.

"Yeah," a guy said. "Let's show that motherfucker what we're made off."

Given how these gangs worked, I would have been surprised if none of them had ever been roughed up by their own comrades or superiors before. The broken arm might have shocked the other gods more than it had them.

Harrison faced me again. "I might not trust your colleagues, but I'm going to trust you, Ari. Now how the hell are we getting us and our equipment all the way to New Mexico as fast as you need us there?"

I hadn't even thought that far yet. No way could any vehicle drive that far that fast. I hesitated, and Loki swooped in with a hand on my shoulder.

"We can take care of that," he said with a tight smile, and motioned to Hod, who'd lifted into the air on his shadowy flying carpet but waited for me. "Dark One, I think we'd better work together sooner than anticipated."

Hod's mouth twisted, but all he said was, "What do you need, Sly One?"

"Conjure me up a chariot out of those shadows of yours—like Thor's old one, but larger?"

"Large enough to carry the humans and their weapons," Hod filled in. "I don't think I can manage to drag all that as fast as we need to go."

Loki's smile widened and tightened at the same time. "You won't need to pull it," he said. "I'll take care of that."

With a loose shrug, he hunched over. His body rippled and expanded in an instant. One second I was looking at the god, and the next an enormous stallion stood in his place, mane and body a pale roan almost the same shade as the trickster's hair.

"Fuck me," one of the gang lackeys muttered. Several of Harrison's people were gaping. If they hadn't been totally convinced this wasn't all some elaborate prank before, they knew for sure it was real now.

Hod was already whipping up a structure of solid darkness. It lashed around Loki's stallion body and stretched out behind him, half was wide as the parking lot.

"You can handle that?" the dark god called down, and Loki tossed his head as if to say, *Don't you dare doubt me.*

Harrison sprang into action. "All right, all right, everybody grab a crate and get on there. Hang back if this has gotten too crazy—but if you're not coming, you don't get a share of the cash."

Five minutes later, the chariot was packed. Loki tossed his head again and hurtled forward, his hooves striking the ground and then rising off it, his shoes of flight speeding him on even in this unusual form. I took off after him, Hod right beside me, and we bolted for the south.

Oh, please, I prayed to I didn't know whom, *let us get there in time.*

21

Loki

Even hauling our little human army and their weapons supply, I'd outpaced the rest of the gods by the time our destination came into view. For a place that could lead to the end of all Midgard, the site looked rather drab and unimpressive. At the southern edge of the sprawling city, just before shrub-dotted red-brown plains rose into a ridge of hills, several rows of low buildings squatted in a yard cut through with a few narrow roads.

A car was puttering along one of those roads. A few human figures crossed the paved ground from one of the smaller buildings to a larger one with a pale spotted roof. I hadn't had time to think while I'd been conveying our mortal allies here about the mortals who would already be on hand. They didn't look ready to fend off a sudden invasion of draugr.

I cantered in a circle over the base as the other gods caught up. The mad dash in horse form had actually been invigorating. Now I was itching to set down to earth and grab one of those very tempting-looking rocket launchers for myself. Let Surt bring on his army and his flames. We were ready for him now, no more chasing at his heels.

"Stay above until the bridge appears," Thor was yelling. "Humans, get your weapons ready. We'll tackle him here above."

Well, I supposed that was a reasonable strategy too, even if it left me as nothing more than a carthorse for the battle. I let out a snort and kicked my heels a little faster for good measure. Ari soared past me, exchanging a few words with the leader of her former colleagues. She veered close enough to me to brush her fingers against my neck. I turned toward her—

And the sky split with a streak of fire that raced toward the ground like a bolt of lightning.

Surt had upped his game. The gods shouted and sprang forward, and the rattle of machine gun fire sounded behind me, but the flaming bridge had shot Surt past us in the blink of an eye. He leapt off its base into the yard and charged toward the nearest building.

So much for an ambush. I dove down at a gallop. The second Hod's chariot of shadows touched the ground, I shook off my animal form and leapt toward the weaponry. With a wave of my hand, I cast a swath of concealing magic over the humans there. The soldiers from the base were already yelling to each other. We hardly needed them shooting at our allies.

All they'd see was the results of the chaos, not the cause.

The bridge had brought a surge of draugr with it too. Dozens spilled across the asphalt yard as more poured down from above.

Thor's hammer slammed through the nearest contingent. Vidar, Heimdall, Freya, and Freyr raced in with their swords. Blazing light and burning shadows seared past me. A missile whined through the air and blew apart at least twenty of those undead bodies just as they barged off the bridge.

I snatched up one of the bazookas and swung around to where I'd last seen Surt. He was just bashing through the doorway of the building he'd run for. Thor and Vidar raced after him with matching roars.

I couldn't get a clear shot without blasting straight through the gods. Damn it. I swung around and let loose one of my missiles into the swarm of draugr instead.

The undead figures swung out with their fire-enhanced swords and hid behind their shields, but taking on this many gods and our human allies was a far more balanced fight than when they'd descended on the six of us and our valkyrie in Asgard a few days ago. Even our raven was diving into the fray now, clawing at the face of a draug that had been barreling toward Odin. The putrid forms tumbled left and right, sliced through, shattered, or burnt to a crisp.

I set aside the human gun to whip a blaze over a line of draugr. They shrieked as if in pain, but it was all part of the horrific magic that had animated their bodies. We were putting those poor bodies out of the misery of their slavery.

"Where's Surt?" Ari called out where she was wheeling just above our heads. She'd grabbed a machine gun of her own, looking like some kind of unholy avenging angel with her silvery wings outstretched and that cold black shape in her hands. I could have sat back and simply admired her all day if we hadn't had more draugr—and that bloody giant—still to deal with.

Thor stumbled toward us. Blood seeped down his shirt from a wound across his belly that was burnt black along the edges but raw red through the middle. Surt had caught him with his damned fiery sword.

Ari's face paled. "Baldur!" she cried, searching the crowd.

"I'll survive," the Thunderer said raggedly. "Surt's gone below. Vidar chased after him. We have to follow. If the weapons are down there..."

"The destruction will spread farther if he ignites them aboveground," Hod said grimly. "He'll come back up to us. Let's be ready for him."

We converged on the building. My pulse thrummed in my veins. It hadn't felt fully real before, being on this side of the battle. The right side, Asgard's side—the side I wanted to be on. There might have been gods around me I'd sooner piss on than do a favor for, but I still liked them far better than the brute who'd instigated this conflict.

Maybe no one would remember this battle over that first one, but being here, fighting where I wanted to be, was enough in itself.

"Where do you need us now?" the leader of our

human allies hollered.

Thor waved Ari's former colleagues out of the chariot and around our blockade. Despite the Thunderer's protests, Baldur had already reached his side, sealing the wound with the glow of his magic.

Near me, Hod toppled another few draugr with a slash of his dark magic. Between the gods and the human guns, we'd slaughtered most of them. The base's soldiers were picking them off too even as they gaped, bewildered, at the scene they could only see part of.

"Should we try to break through the ground to go after Surt?" Ari asked, landing between Hod and me. "If we used our combined powers, like we did at his fortress, we might be able to break straight through."

"We knew exactly where to strike there," Hod said. "I'm not sure—we don't know exactly where the weapons are, or how our magic might affect them. The last thing we want is to help Surt's plan along."

"He's not getting away from us," Thor rumbled. "We really have destroyed his army now, and—"

A chorus of battle cries resonated through the air. We spun around to face a horde of giants that had appeared over the crest of the bridge.

I had battled innumerable giants in my time, most often with the Thunderer by my side as he was now. I'd lived among them for the first sorry span of my life. Nevertheless, seeing that swarm of them careening down toward us over the flames of Surt's bridge made the bottom of my stomach drop out.

While we'd been accumulating allies, Surt had been gathering more of his own as well.

Ari's former colleagues opened fire. A missile struck one giant in the shoulder as he leapt off the bridge, sending him crashing to the ground, but two more heaved themselves into the midst of the humans at the same time. The slam of their arms and the slash of the blades they carried cracked skulls and splattered blood.

Ari let out a pained sound and lunged forward as if she meant to challenge a hundred giants all on her own. My pulse stuttered. I dashed faster than she could, catching her by the elbow.

"We fight them together, pixie," I said. "We need you with us."

"They're all going to die," she mumbled. "I asked them to come, and now they're going to be slaughtered."

"Not on our watch," I said firmly, catching Thor's and Baldur's eyes. Hod was already skimming toward us on one of his shadows. I swept my arm toward the giants, and we charged. The other gods barrelled forward around us.

Unfortunately, a fair number of our human allies were beyond saving. The giants flung their lifeless bodies toward us and crushed this gun and that rocket launcher with heaves of their bulging arms. Flecks of blood and what might have been bits of brain matter dabbled my cheek. I grimaced and thrust my arms forward with all the searing magic I could summon.

The other four of our quintet moved at the same time. That bizarre cohesion we'd developed between us around our valkyrie crackled through my nerves. My fire blazed over Thor's hammer and tangled with Hod's shadows and Baldur's knife-edged wave of light.

We'd mainly used our combined powers against dark elves and draugr before now. Several of the giants toppled with the onslaught, but a few of them immediately started shoving back to their feet, burnt and bleeding but not conquered. More of their kin streamed around us.

Blades flashed, and teeth gnashed. Even as we whirled to try to push back another lot of them, I saw a giant catching Njord with a sword through his back. The old sea god collapsed with a gush of blood. Somewhere in the fray, a voice I knew must be Skadi's shrieked.

Even as our next attack left a dozen giants sprawling, another wave charged in to fill the gap. The asphalt around the base of the bridge was melting, sticking to my shoes and filling the air with a tarry tang. Bragi aimed the machine gun he'd retrieved at our foes, but as the bullets tore through two of their chests, another giant hurled himself at the poet. Bragi's skull collapsed under the bash of the brute's spiked club.

I wrenched my eyes away from the sight and dragged in a painful breath. We could still do this. The giants were battering us, but we were battering them in turn. Maybe we'd lose a few more of our number before the battle was done, but they couldn't overcome all of us. I was certain of that much.

Then a bellow of victory reached my ears, and I realized overcoming the giants eventually might not be enough.

Across the yard, Surt had emerged from the building he'd vanished into. He had a sort of metal net slung against his back with a haul of at least ten shiny white missiles, each nearly as tall as he was and as thick as his thigh. His leg arm and his side were stained with blood, but he stood steadily enough, brandishing his sword. His loot clattered as he dropped it on the ground. He reached for the nearest nuclear warhead with a fiery gleam in his eyes.

"Look at what he's doing!" Ari shouted at the other giants as they closed in around us, barricading us gods from the giant who meant to end this world. "If he sets off that bomb, it's going to kill all of you too! Don't you care? Don't *you* want to live?"

Oh, my darling valkyrie. My dearest Ari, who'd once expressed so much fear at the darkness inside her, was trying to get through to the damned giants as if they might listen to reason and save themselves. She never gave up on anyone, did she?

The thought brought a strange tightness to my throat. Ahead of me, Thor shoved toward Surt, but the giant's comrades had managed to surround us completely. Thor's hammer shattered a raised shield without displacing the giant behind it and flew back into his hand.

Baldur's blazing light tossed a few giants back into the wall of bodies behind them, and their fellows shoved them back upright. Freya's and her brother's swords clanged against blazing blades raised to meet theirs.

We'd break our way through eventually, yes, with many more of them falling than of us, but it might not be in time to stop Surt's intended wave of destruction. If we were going to blast a quick path through his allies to him, we'd need both speed and distraction.

Two elements no one here was better equipped to supply than me.

I saw how it would play out in a flash, perhaps the same way Odin's visions came to him. I saw every move I could make; I saw the way the crowd would sway; I glimpsed the inevitable end. And even though my stomach clenched, a larger part of me felt suddenly freed, light as a breeze.

This was my moment, as surely as if it'd been laid out for me. I'd be a villain if I didn't take it.

I wasn't quite so selfless to spring into that opening without a second thought. My gaze snagged on Ari's face, so beautiful in its frantic fierceness, and my heart squeezed in that way I was only just starting to get used to.

I couldn't give her a chance to interfere, but after all the ways she'd trusted me, after all the pain I might bring no matter how much I'd have liked to spare her, I could make one small offering of truth for her to hold on to when I was gone.

Bodies pushed and swiveled around me. I caught my valkyrie's hand and tugged her close enough that my lips brushed her cheek.

"I love you," I said, quiet but clear. Not really a proclamation, just a simple statement of fact.

She sucked in a startled breath, and I was already propelling myself away from her, toward the wall of giants around us.

My shoes of flight launched me through the air so swiftly that I raced between the swings of swords and over the swipe of a spear. Flames blazed from my palms.

I threw fire out on every side, lighting up the space around me in stark relief, so bright no giant could fail to see me.

I didn't run toward Surt. That direction contained so much glory if I succeeded, but too much risk if I didn't. I slammed my heels into the heads of several giants at that end of their ring, and grasping hands nearly snagged my ankles. Spinning away with a mocking jeer, I dashed in the opposite direction.

The crowd surged around me as the giants started to give chase. I could have darted higher, but they wouldn't follow if they knew there was no chance of catching me. Besides, this way I could batter a few more giant heads along the way. I kicked a forehead here, hurled fire into a face there. Let them fall, let them fall, let them—

Not one of the gods could have run fast or nimbly enough to outpace the horde like this forever. I darted on for as long as any of us could have. Too many hands snatched after me at once, and one closed around my foot with a yank that nearly dislocated my knee. I whipped around, slicing out with lashes of flame. Giants stumbled back with groans and grunts, the grip on my foot loosened—and a club slammed into my ribs with a piercing *crack*.

I jerked my head up for one last look. Most of the giants had rushed after me, and the other gods were shoving past the few left behind toward Surt. A smile crossed my face.

Then a fist pummeled my skull. One last gush of fire exploded from my hands just before a searing pain gouged into my chest. I fell away into darkness.

22

Aria

It happened so quickly I barely had time to think: Loki's whisper by my ear, his blazing dash across the giants' heads, the sea of them parting as they took up chase, and the gods around me surging forward toward the one giant we had to stop more than any other.

My heart tugged after Loki, but I threw myself forward with the other gods. Surt's head snapped up where he was bent over his haul of warheads. His teeth gritted, and his hand shot toward his sword.

Thor tore through the last few giants between us and Surt, his hammer splitting flesh and shattering bones. He hurled Mjolnir ahead of him. Surt managed to deflect the hammer with a smack of his sword, dodging twin blasts of light and shadow at the same time. He braced himself to fling a wave of his own fire toward us.

Before he had a chance to, a *boom* rattled my

eardrums right beside me. A bazooka missile screamed through the air and ripped straight through the giant's shoulder.

Harrison let out a hoarse breath where he'd planted his feet to make the shot. The missile launcher wobbled in his grasp. His hair was damp with sweat and blood, and the side of his face was scraped raw, but he'd survived the slaughter.

Surt let out a roar that sounded as much like agony as rage. His sword arm dangled uselessly at his side. Thor and the others barreled on toward him. With a snarled curse, the giant wrenched his netted heap of warheads off the ground with his good arm and threw himself toward his bridge.

The flaming arch licked up to catch his leap. With a hiss of heat, he vanished into the sky with his bounty —alone.

Some of the giant companions he'd abandoned on the ground were hurtling toward us from behind. We spun around, Thor's hammer flying, Odin's spear slashing, swords flashing as they sliced open our enemies' bodies. I'd lost the gun I'd grabbed somewhere in the fray. I launched myself off the ground and at the giants with the most innate weapon I had.

My fingers grazed the top of one giant's head. The void of darkness inside me opened at my beckoning, and I yanked his life into that hollow place. The waft of energy came, stickier and thicker than the dark elf lives I'd wrenched away before.

As he collapsed, I barely heaved myself out of the way before another giant swung her dagger right where my neck had been. I whirled around—and my gaze caught on a tall slim form sprawled amid the other bodies with so little grace that my mind jarred against recognition.

But it *was* Loki. It was my slyly defiant trickster, trampled and bludgeoned, a ragged gash in his chest where it looked as if the giants had torn his heart right out.

My own heart flipped over. Vomit seared the base of my throat. I choked, sputtered, and pushed myself forward, willing my eyes to be wrong.

I could hardly see by the time I reached the trickster's body, my vision was so blurred with tears. I sucked back a sob and raised a shaking hand to his pale red hair, streaked scarlet now with his blood. His jaw slanted at an unnatural angle. One of his perfect sharp cheekbones had been pummeled flat. Another surge of nausea rolled over me.

Loki had known what he was doing. He'd known he'd have to give the giants a chance to catch him if he was going to draw enough of them away. Why else would he have said those three words to me before he'd taken off?

He hadn't thought he'd get another chance.

And he wouldn't. He was lying here without a hint of life in his body. As much as I wanted to believe he'd suddenly drag in a breath, sit up, and smirk at me as if my tears were ridiculous, every moment I crouched there beside his prone form confirmed what we'd learned with Tyr, what the maimed bodies of the other gods who'd fallen today proved. They'd already gotten their second chance. They wouldn't rise again.

Unless...

My chest clenched. I stared at my hand hovering over the trickster's face. My small trembling *valkyrie* hand.

That hand had stolen the life out of a giant just a minute ago. It was supposed to be able to restore lives too—to summon them up to Valhalla. I'd never tried—I didn't know if I could—

Every second I hesitated, Loki's spirit might be slipping farther away from me.

My pulse rattled in my ears as I leaned over him, setting both of my hands on his chest while avoiding the bloody wound at its center. My eyes slipped shut. I reached down into the depths of my being to the place where that killing darkness lurked. At the same time, I drew up every memory of why this spirit was deserving.

The weight of responsibility Loki had carried leading up to Ragnarok. The insults and sneers he'd so often shrugged off with a simple glib remark. The way he'd been able to see worth even in me, and the lengths he'd gone to in order to convince me of it—so many words of admiration my heart swelled thinking of them. The passion with which he'd leapt into every battle I'd fought with him. His haste to track down Surt no matter the time or situation.

Just now, hurling insults and flinging flames as he raced to his doom to clear the way for us to save my realm.

He'd told me not that long ago that while he wasn't a

villain, he wasn't much of a hero either. I couldn't imagine many people meeting his definition if it didn't include him.

Beneath the coiled darkness in my gut, a spark flared. Its heat spread through my torso and out into my limbs, raising the hairs on my arms and the back of my neck. The air in my lungs shimmered. I focused all my strength into that sensation.

Him. Him. Let him rise.

"Let me claim him for Valhalla," I said, the last plea slipping from my throat.

The spark cracked open with a blaze of light that blinded me from the inside out.

In that searing white, I tasted the spicy sweet flavor that always lingered on Loki's skin. My hands clasped around a quiver of an even brighter light. It thrummed in my grasp with an energy that felt almost like a sly grin. Gasping, I tossed it upward with all my power, up to the vast hall of Valhalla with its walls of glinting blades, away from this mortal realm.

The spirit flitted up toward Asgard away from me, and my stomach cramped with a pang of loss. My awareness was tumbling back to earth.

No. I had to be there—I had to make sure my gambit worked, that Surt's guards didn't sever Loki's life all over again.

I heaved myself off the asphalt with my mind trained on that image of Valhalla. The smell of stale mead trickled through my senses. I willed myself there with all my being.

The air shuddered, and I stumbled amid the long oak

tables beneath the high vaulted ceiling.

There was a rasp and a grunt somewhere near me. The giants poised near the hearth and Odin's throne at the far end of the hall were already spinning around.

A strange exhilaration raced through me. My hand snatched my switchblade from my pocket faster than I'd ever moved before. I whipped it straight and hard between one guard's eyes while I hurtled toward another with a swift flap of my wings.

My hand brushed the guard's forehead as he swung at me, yanking out his life by the roots. I wheeled out of reach of a third giant's sword—

And that one erupted into flames.

My gaze snapped down the hall in time to see a tall slim figure with hair like a lick of flame hurling another fiery bolt at the guards. Loki snatched two daggers off the wall, one in each hand, and flung them simultaneously at the two giants still standing. The blades slammed into the guards' hearts. They collapsed together with a resounding thud.

Loki swiped his palms together with a sharp satisfied smile. "Well, that takes care of our most immediate problem." He glanced around the hall and then down at himself.

He'd appeared in the same clothes he'd been wearing moments ago in Midgard, a typical green tunic and gray slacks, but the cloth was whole and unbloodied, not at all like it had looked those few moments ago. A hint of confusion crossed his face. "Maybe you can enlighten me on how exactly we ended up here, pixie, because I seem to have a disturbing blank in my memory."

Seeing him so vibrant and real and *alive* knocked the breath out of me. I'd done it. I'd actually done it. With a thrill that shot straight through my wings, I dove to meet him. I caught him, my arms wrapping tight around his waist, my face pressed to his chest, drinking in his spicy sweet scent.

"You got yourself *killed*," I said. "That's what happened."

His arms settled around my shoulders. He ducked his head, his lips brushing my hair. "I remember that part," he said, quietly but lightly. "Apparently it didn't play out quite as I expected it to."

"Because you're lucky enough to have a valkyrie on your side," I grumbled into his shirt.

"So, you—" He let out a laugh, all amused awe. "You resurrected me to the hall of warriors."

"I had to try." I clutched him harder, revelling in how warm and whole his body was against mine, and then pulled back to look him in the eyes. My throat closed up for an instant, but this second time was easier. The words still tumbled together as they rushed out. "I love you too. You didn't have to pull a stunt like that to get me to say it back, you lunatic."

Loki laughed again, short and breathless, and then he was kissing me with so much heat my nerves ignited. I wanted to melt right into him, to lose myself in the joy of his survival, but this wasn't the best time or place for that.

As Loki knew as well. He kissed me once more, tenderly, with a graze of his fingertips down the side of my face. Then he eased back and glanced around.

"What happened on Midgard after my untimely end?" he asked. "Did Surt..."

"We reached him before he could detonate any of the warheads," I said. "But he got away with them, back up here. One of my guys took a good shot at him with a bazooka. He's hurt. Not sure how much that'll slow him down."

"I suppose we're in an ideal position to find that out." The trickster glanced toward the main door with a grin. "We can gather some of those weapons Vidar was moaning about missing while we're at it. Let's see if my powers of concealment survived my second resurrection, shall we?"

"Hold on." I strode over to the first giant I'd killed and wrenched my switchblade from his skull. I wiped it on his shirt before jamming it back into my pocket. Then I tugged a short sword I liked the look of off the wall. Its narrow blade gleamed menacingly. "Okay, now I'm ready."

Loki's grin widened. "My valkyrie."

I waggled the sword at him, my own lips twitching upward. "Oh, no, I'm not your valkyrie anymore. You're *my* raised hero."

Loki blinked at me. The smile that crossed his face next was nothing but light, beaming bright as the sun outside.

"So I am," he said, the same brilliance sparkling through his voice. "Come along then, and we'll discover what heroics lie ahead of me."

He tucked his hand around mine, and we stepped together toward the door.

23

Aria

As the trickster and I reached Valhalla's entrance, my earlier sense of exhilaration kept tingling through my veins.

I'd used the greatest power a valkyrie had. I'd brought back a life instead of just taking them.

I wanted to do it all over again.

We could have had a much larger army if Valhalla were full again. Did Odin need to be in the hall if he wanted to summon more valkyries? I guessed that possibility might have gone off the table as soon as Surt had conquered Asgard. But if there'd been more of us, and we'd all summoned heroes from Midgard...

Loki made a sweeping motion with his hand around us, and the light shimmered for a second before settling down. "We won't be noticeable as long as we steer clear of any direct interaction with Surt and his minions," he said. "Don't go stabbing anyone, and we should get past them just fine."

"I think I can manage that," I said.

He raised an eyebrow. "I know you must be looking forward to trying out that sword."

When he eased open the door, I realized that avoiding any kind of interaction with our enemies might be a little more difficult than I'd assumed. Surt clearly hadn't brought his whole army down to the weapons facility. At least a hundred draugr were shuffling around the courtyard and along the divine city's streets—between the halls now blackened and in places bashed right open.

A couple of giants appeared to be delighting in smashing the statue in the middle of the courtyard's fountain. Several other of their kind stood clustered not far from Valhalla, muttering to themselves. It was a good thing we'd dispatched the guards in the hall before they'd had time to raise the alarm, or we'd have been toast.

The sight of the wandering undead dampened my giddiness. All those haggard vacant human faces... What Surt had done wasn't at all like what I'd done for Loki. I'd brought the trickster back fully to life, with all his thoughts and free will. But at the same time, the idea of raising an army of fallen human warriors to do our bidding suddenly turned my stomach.

Maybe it was better that we hadn't had the option. Using that tactic would have been like stooping to Surt's level. I'd known Loki—known he would want to live on if he could—and it wasn't as if I really had any power over him. To resurrect strangers and send them off to battle giants and draugr without them having any real say in it... In some ways, that might be even worse. These zombies, at least, were mindless. Risen warriors would know they were being used.

I remembered too well how I'd felt when my gods had told me how they'd summoned me. They'd given me a choice, but dying all over again hadn't felt like much of an alternative. I was happy with the hand I'd been dealt now, but, no, I didn't think I'd be calling up a host of formerly dead human beings any time soon.

Loki slunk out into the city, and I followed just behind him. "Thor has quite a stash of weapons, many of them dark-elf made," the trickster said under his breath. "That seems like a reasonable place to start our collection."

We crossed the courtyard and started up the tiled road, veering around giants and draugr alike. They ambled on by without so much as a glance at us. My skin prickled passing so close to our enemies. I might not have planned on stabbing anyone, but I kept my hand tight around the hilt of the sword I'd grabbed and my wings unfurled over my back.

More giants were standing around Thor's hall. A few seconds later, I understood why. Surt's ragged voice bellowed through the walls.

"You will tell me how to work these weapons. Don't tell me you can't."

A yelp pierced the air—one that sounded distinctly human. My shoulders tensed.

"Muninn said Surt had grabbed another human from Midgard," I said. "That must be what he was doing that brief visit we couldn't track. Another nuclear scientist, maybe?"

"He's trying to fill in the blanks in his knowledge," Loki said. "I might allow myself to be slightly impressed by his resourcefulness if it wasn't leading toward the destruction of everything we hold dear. It sounds as though he hasn't gotten very far, as a consolation."

It also sounded as if he was torturing the man trying to get what he wanted. My muscles itched to fly at the door, to rush in and haul the poor guy away from the giant, but that would blow our cover completely. If I even made it far enough to help the man. Coming closer, I could see that giant guards surrounded the whole hall, swords and axes gleaming in their hands. Surt was keeping himself well-protected.

"It figures he'd set himself up in the Thunderer's home," Loki muttered. "He wishes he were even half the warrior Thor is. But perhaps we'd best give that stash a miss. I know other treasures we can lay our hands on more easily."

He stalked on up the road. I dodged splatters of blood that darkened the pale gray tiles. Surt had still been bleeding from that missile wound when he'd made it back up here. Had Harrison managed to ruin his sword arm for good?

Not that his sword was what we really needed to worry about right now while the giant was carting around a dozen or so nuclear warheads.

Loki's hall had taken an especially brutal beating. One whole side of the building was charred all the way across the roof. Several chunks of the thatching had fallen in.

We ducked inside to sunlight streaming through the holes in the ceiling. The trickster sighed and kicked aside fallen cinders as he headed down the front hall. "I have to say I don't much care for Surt's interior decorating tastes."

His death and resurrection obviously hadn't affected his sense of humor. I jogged to keep up. He stopped at a locked door, applied his finger to the keyhole, and pushed it open.

The room on the other side smelled like machine oil. Crates and sacks were heaped along the walls. Loki tugged open one and then another while I stood there looking around.

"What is all this stuff?" I asked.

"I'm in the habit of collecting a few things here and there myself," the trickster said. "Not around quite as combat-focused a theme as the Thunderer's loot, naturally, but I should have a few things that could be of use... Ah." He tucked something small into his slacks pocket. A few moments later, he slung an entire sack over his shoulder. He stuffed a box about the size of a textbook in to join whatever contents the sack already held. Finally, from a box in the corner, he retrieved a sleek dagger with a leather-wrapped hilt that shone like a moonbeam when he offered it to me.

"I think you'll find this serves you even better than that lovely piece you picked up, pixie," he said. "The magic on the blade will allow it to cut through any material you have the will to pierce."

Oh, I had the will to slash up quite a few things. I took the dagger carefully, my fingers closing around the grip as if it'd been made for them. I gave the air an experimental slash, and a shiver of power ran up my arm.

I smiled. Now *this* was a real weapon. I just hoped I had the chance to apply it to Surt sooner rather than later.

After leaving Loki's hall, we slipped into Freya's. Loki turned up his nose at most of her weapons collection—"functional but not exceptional," he remarked—but he did scoop up the polished sword in its scabbard near the doorway.

"She didn't have time to go back for her favorite blade when Surt attacked," he said. "I think she'll appreciate having this the next time we do battle."

Farther down the road, the trickster inclined his head toward a tall building with bronzed thatching that had been lightly scorched. "Vidar's hall," he said. "I noticed he isn't wearing his famous shoes. If they were good enough to break my son's jaws, they should be good enough for tackling Surt."

"Famous shoes?" I repeated, hurrying after him. "Like yours?"

"Does Vidar seem like the type to have similar interests to mine?" Loki asked. "Swiftness and flight weren't important to him. He found himself the strongest and sturdiest shoes in existence. That really is how he killed Fenrir. They kept his toes intact when he kicked my son's mouth open to shove a sword down his throat."

He found the shoes in question in the back of a cabinet and tossed them into his sack too. When we returned to the road, he set off straight toward the forest beyond the city's main buildings, not even glancing at any of the other halls.

"Where are we going now?" I asked.

Another bellow echoed through the air from behind us. Surt sounded even angrier than before. "That isn't enough! I don't care about your people's 'policies'!"

"We're almost done," Loki said. "There's one last thing—I'm not even entirely sure it'll be there. But I've heard rumors, and the Norns aren't around anymore to dissuade a little prying."

"Rumors about what?"

We passed into the woods, Loki's steps speeding up to a supernatural pace. I lifted off the ground and flew after him so he didn't leave me behind.

"Have you ever heard the story of Freyr's sword?" he said.

I shook my head. "I don't know anything about Freyr except he's Freya's brother."

"I suppose it doesn't make the most exciting telling," the trickster said. "My and Thor's exploits are much more entertaining. Well. One of Freyr's prized possessions was a sword that could fight on its own, with barely any guidance from its owner. It'd guide your hand, know exactly how to hit the mark... Some say that if Freyr had kept it for Ragnarok, he might have defeated Surt then. So it stands to reason it'd be helpful to have it against the brute now in place of the lesser one he's been using."

"He didn't have that sword for Ragnarok?" I said. "Why not?"

"Oh, that ridiculous affliction called love." Loki shot

me a crooked smile over his shoulder. "An emotion that can provoke wondrous acts, to be sure, but also rather idiotic ones at times. Freyr got it into his head that he absolutely had to marry a particular giantess. My former people demanded his sword before they'd allow her to consider it. He was smitten enough that he agreed. So, if you look at it from a certain angle, *he's* really the one who caused Asgard's fall, not me."

I made a face. "Somehow I have a feeling Odin had a hand in that story somewhere too."

"I wouldn't be surprised, but the Allfather never mentioned it to me. In any case, the rumor I heard was that one of the giant kings brought the sword to the Norns while they were still sharing their visions of past and future. He had some important matter he wanted them to weigh in on, and that was the most valuable item he could offer in payment. It seems likely they would have accepted it. The only questions are whether that story is true at all, and if it is, where they'd have hidden it."

He drew to a stop in a clearing I recognized from my travels through the warped version of Asgard we'd explored in Muninn's prison. The arc of a huge tree root jutted from the ground—part of Yggdrasil, the great tree that connected the realms, from what Freya had told me then. A stone well stood next to it. Otherwise the clearing was empty, no sign anyone had been through here in ages.

"What happened to the Norns?" I asked as Loki prowled around the well.

"None of us are entirely sure," Loki said. "They

became rather faded over the years since Ragnarok. I think perhaps as the gods turned to them less and less, and other realms began to forget they even existed, their ties to the present faded. They never were quite beings of a concrete nature the way we are. I wouldn't be surprised if they reappear someday just for the pleasure of keeping us on our toes."

We searched all around the clearing, testing the stones on the sides of the well, the ground all around it, and the trunks on the trees edging the open space. Finally, Loki stopped and crossed his arms with a defeated huff.

"Perhaps they took the damned thing with them. I supposed the one sword can't matter that much. If it'd been the key to defeating Surt, I'd have expected something to have turned up in Odin's visions about blades or steel or..."

He trailed off, his eyes narrowing as he considered the well.

"What?" I said.

"I'm thinking about what Odin visions *did* offer us. 'The highest water.' Asgard is the highest of the realms. The Norns' well was held up as sacred. You might say it could burn through the haze of what was and what has yet to be. It could be his visions meant this."

I gave the well a skeptical look. "You really think that water could stop Surt?"

Loki shrugged. "We're here now. It can't hurt to take some."

He dropped the bucket down to a distant splash. As he hauled it back up with one arm, he drew a couple of small pouches from his sack with his other hand.

The water in the bucket glinted with an unearthly energy that made my skin prickle. Maybe it did have the power to make a difference. Loki dipped in one pouch, slipped it into his pocket, and then offered the other he filled to me.

"Just in case," he said, his crooked grin coming back. "I have managed to get myself killed once."

I jabbed him in the chest with my finger as I took the pouch. "It'd better be the last time you do that. Now what?"

Loki frowned. "We don't want to give Surt a chance to detonate those bombs back on Midgard. Let's take a look at how heavily he has Bifrost's gate guarded right now. You can find your way to Odin quickly through Valhalla's doors. If we can clear the way, you could bring our findings down and tell them to get up here and fight."

I suspected Surt would have the place where the rainbow bridge could form nearly as heavily guarded as his chosen hall. Maybe we could draw some of his allies away with Loki's trickery if we couldn't brute force the issue?

We hustled back through the woods and into the city. We'd just passed the first of the halls when a cry rang out from up ahead that wasn't furious or pained at all, which somehow made it even more awful.

"Yes! I can feel it. That's the key. Come on, come on, we have to move. Midgard will belong to me before the end of the hour."

Surt burst from Thor's hall with a stream of giants

behind him. His shout brought the wandering draugr hustling his way. His sword arm still dangling limp at his side, his shoulder packed with a thick bandage that was already mottled with blood, but his other arm moved without a hitch as he swept it through the air. The flames of his bridge arced off the ground. He sprang onto it, his net of warheads slung against his broad back.

My heart stuttered. "He's going now. Down to Midgard somewhere with the bombs." And from the sound of that joyful cry, he was sure he knew how to set them off now. "We have to follow him—we have to stop him."

Dozens of giants and draugr were rushing onto the flaming surface after their leader. Loki's mouth twisted. "Even I'm not arrogant enough to think the two of us can take down his whole army alone."

Inspiration hit me like a smack to the face. "We won't have to be alone," I said. I sprang off the ground, soaring as quickly as I could toward Valhalla.

24

Baldur

"They'll find their way back," I said to Hod as he paced the stretch of New Mexico desert we'd retreated to. "You know Loki can find his way out of anything. And Aria—"

And Aria fell out of the sky.

She hit the dry ground in a crouch, her wings spread to slow her fall and soften the impact. We'd barely turned when she was springing upright. She dashed not to us but to Odin.

"You have to open the bridge to Asgard," she said, grabbing the edge of his cloak. "*Now*. Surt is about to detonate the bombs—it's the only way we can get to him in time—"

"Wait a moment, valkyrie," the Allfather said in his distant way.

Aria let out a noise of frustration before he could say

anything else. "No. There's no time to wait. This is what we have to do. I've just been up there in Asgard—I know what's happening. Can you just trust me?"

All of us gathered there—all the gods we'd found except the three who'd fallen in that last battle, as well as Aria's human colleague and a handful of his underlings—fell silent as we watched Odin. He stared at Aria for a second. Then, to my surprised relief, he raised his hands.

"I think perhaps this is where we must part ways," he said to the leader of the humans. "We must go quickly, and the one who carried you before is no longer with us."

The man who'd shot Surt stared at the expanse of shimmering color rising up into the sky and let out a choked laugh. "I'll have to trust your judgment. Take that asshole down for us, all right?"

Thor hurried up beside our valkyrie as we started up the bridge. He brushed his broad hand over her hair. "Loki?" he asked.

"I summoned him up to Valhalla," she said with a little smile, managing to look just a shade pleased despite the tension still tightening her face. "He's distracting the guards who were watching for the bridge. There aren't that many. Surt was getting low on lackeys. He brought most of them with him—to wherever he's going." She touched his side gently. "Are you okay?"

He patted the spot where I'd sealed up his wound as well as I could. I could tell from the slight hitch in his steps that he was still hurt. I'd stretched my energy thin as it was, healing all of us I could heal. And I might need more power yet before the end of the hour. I gazed up toward Asgard as I loped faster over Bifrost's gleaming surface, my stomach knotting.

I couldn't deny what Hod had said about my affinity for light. I'd been shaken by the burning energy in the nuclear plant that had harmonized with mine before nearly wiping us out, but if I found the right way to use it, to control it...

The words were right there in the vision Odin had related to us. *The light of day can burn before a fire.* Burn up all the explosive power those bombs might have unleashed?

The streaks of color flew by beneath my feet. Muninn soared over our heads, and the other gods raced on alongside me. Some of their breaths had already turned ragged. Surt was injured from that last battle, but we'd taken plenty of hits too, and we were tired. The allies he'd brought with him were those he'd left stationed in Asgard, fresh for this fight.

We'd lost a lot. Njord. Bragi. Vidar, somewhere in the depths of the facility where he'd tried to chase after Surt. So many of those human allies Aria had brought to us. Nearly Loki. How many more would be gone, beyond my or her ability to save, before we ended this war? Would any of us survive?

I pushed my strides faster, speeding my feet along with bolts of light. Hod glided along beside me, relying on his shadows, his expression taut with determination. Thor barrelled on at the front of our charge despite his small limp. Mjolnir flashed in his hand.

No matter what might lie ahead, we were not backing down.

We burst out through the clouds. My heart ached at the sight of Asgard before me, so welcome and yet so horrifying with the halls blackened and the fountain smashed.

A few giants were standing at the edge of the realm, braced as they watched the bridge. Thor leapt forward to hurl his hammer, and I moved at the same time instinctively, whipping a spear of light. Aria slashed her glowing dagger through the air, Hod threw a surge of shadow—and our trickster dashed into view around the side of the nearest hall, tossing a ball of fire as if he'd known this was the time to meet us. Which perhaps he had.

Our powers whirled around the giants and slammed them together with a shower of sparks. Mjolnir bashed right through all three of their skulls before flying back to Thor's hand. He nodded to Loki with a wide grin.

"Sly One. You managed to slip even death."

"Only Ari can take the credit there," the trickster said. "I thought it had me through and through this time. And it may yet if you don't all light a fire under your feet. Literally. Let's go!"

He waved his arm, and my gaze followed his gesture. Surt's bridge of flames seared up across the realm from the road beyond the courtyard.

Aria darted forward, her wings flapping with a whisper of feathers. The rest of us ran on alongside her. The heat of the bridge prickled over my face as we drew close. A black patch was spreading across the marble tiles it had sprung up from.

But the giants and the draugr had survived walking on that surface. I braced myself and rushed onward.

"Freya," Loki said. "I thought you might appreciate this." He tossed a sword to the goddess, who threw her lesser blade aside and snatched the new one up with a smile. The trickster glanced around as we ran on. His expression darkened. "Did Vidar fall?"

"We lost him somewhere in those tunnels beneath the buildings," Thor said. "We called for him, tried to reach him, but he didn't answer, and the human army was pouring in to secure the base as well as they could... He may make it still." The thunder god couldn't summon much hope into his tone. He might not want to admit what he knew, but I'd felt our brother's passing like a slice across my gut as the same wrenching crossed Hod's face.

Loki passed a few more items from the sack he carried to the other gods. The flames of the bridge hissed as our feet trampled over them. A thicker heat washed over my body. My skin felt as if it were baking, but I could survive that.

Much like Bifrost's shape, Surt's bridge arched up and then plummeted down toward Midgard. Sparks sizzled through the clouds it had parted. A smell like hot iron clogged my lungs.

As we half-raced, half-tumbled down the bridge's steep slope, the fiery giant and his remaining army came into view on the ground below. He'd set down on the top of a grassy hill. Nothing stirred there except for him and his minions, but just a few miles away, the suburbs of a massive city sprawled toward the glinting skyscrapers of its downtown.

Surt wanted to make sure he destroyed as many humans as possible with that first blast.

Not now. Not ever, if we had any say in it.

We hurtled downward, Thor splitting the air with his battle cry. Surt was waving his working hand toward us, urging his army into motion.

"Whatever it takes, whatever we have to do," Aria called out to us. "If he ignites even one of those warheads, we've lost everything."

She pointed her dagger toward Surt, diving faster. Heimdall brought his battle horn to his lips and blared it like a warning and a call to arms all at once.

"All of us together," I shouted, determination blazing through me. Every god still with us threw themselves forward with their magic and their weapons, but only five of us moved in perfect unison.

Many times now, I'd felt a connection with my brothers and Loki around our valkyrie while we fought. In that moment, the sensation hummed through me more potent than ever before. I could feel Hod's sharp inhalation, the twinge in Thor's abdomen, the gritting of the trickster's teeth as we launched our attacks together.

We weren't just ourselves in that moment but part of a larger whole, a larger harmony.

Our mingling wave of magic laced around Mjolnir and toppled the first row of attackers careening toward us. Freya swooped by, slashing with her sword. Odin sprang from the flaming bridge with an agility I hadn't known my father still possessed and stabbed his spear through the chest of a giant. Freyr dove in with his own sword singing through the air.

Surt's army swarmed to meet us, to blockade us off from the giant we needed to stop as they had before. Our greatest enemy was hunched over his stack of cylindrical bombs, his good hand braced against the metal surface. From the clenching of his jaw, he was exerting some sort of magical energy on it to bend it to his will. To force it to explode.

My pulse hiccupped. In that instant, focusing on him and the weapon beneath his palm, an impression of all the caustic energy that shell contained radiated through me like a thousand searing needles. A thousand searing needles that quivered in tune with the glow of power inside me. Nausea swelled in my gut.

I didn't want to touch those weapons, not even from this far away with only my magic. I wanted to put all the distance I could between my being and that awful devastating potential.

But I couldn't outrun the destruction. My absence wouldn't prevent it. It wasn't a question of whether I made those devices explode or not. It was only a matter of whether I could stop the explosion or whether I didn't risk trying.

I glanced over at my twin. Hod was braced behind a shield of shadow, hurling lashes of darkness into the fray. I couldn't imagine how he must experience a battle like this with no vision to orient him, only the shouts and grunts and clangs, the smells of metal and blood. He didn't hold back. He took the darkness inside him and shaped it to his will to save as many as he could. He'd carried so much responsibility on his shoulders for so very long.

If he could stand up under all that weight, Asgard help me if I didn't too.

I sucked in a breath and sent another draugr crumpling with a bolt of magic. Then I backed up to the foot of the bridge, climbing a few paces so I could see Surt and his stockpile clearly.

Training all my attention on his weapons, I sent out a stream of light, so thin he shouldn't notice it with the sun beaming down over him. My magic licked over the bomb he was working on and through the metal shell.

There. This was the substance tremoring and ready to cascade into the chain reaction Hod had talked about.

I closed my fingers toward my palms, willing more heat into my stream of light. Slowly, carefully, I fused particle by particle, easing back when they started to quiver harder. I melded this one to this one to this one, on and on, until I could feel the material settling like a massive weight condensed in the casing—inert and unshakeable.

Sweat trickled down my back. I shifted my feet to steady my weight and focused on the next of the bombs. Confidence started to ripple through me, but I didn't let it hurry me. What I'd done had only worked because I'd kept such a tight leash on my powers.

Another clump of matter hardened inside the metal shell, large enough to block the reaction. Swallowing thickly, I started on the next, and then the next. The heat of the bridge thickened around me, searing into my lungs, but I tuned it out. If I could just reach them all—if I could disable every one of those missiles...

I'd made it to the sixth when Surt slammed his hands

against the one he'd been working on with a curse. He heaved it off the stack and reached for the one underneath, which I hadn't targeted yet. I snapped my attention to that one as swiftly as I dared. Melt it down, fuse it solid, before he could spark the sharper flame.

Whatever technique he'd been using to feel out the weapon, the giant was getting more confident too. After just a minute, he frowned and shoved that bomb away too. The next one I'd already tackled. I started on the eighth, but this time it was only a few seconds before Surt leapt to his feet with a roar.

I wasn't looking directly at him, but my skin still flared when his gaze found me. I clenched my hands, willing more energy into the bomb. Just a few more left. Just a few more and at least this one crisis would have been averted.

"The bright one," Surt hollered with a jab of his hand. "On the bridge. He's interfering somehow. Get him!"

Giants and draugr charged around the cluster of gods to challenge me. I shifted my stream of energy to the ninth bomb and whipped a scorching line of light around me toward my attackers at the same time.

A few fell back, but the others converged around me. I tried to dodge, my exhausted legs wobbled, and a giant barrelled straight into me, tackling me to the ground. He slammed his club down on my head at the same time as my skull smacked the dirt, and my focus snapped.

25

Aria

A cry caught in my throat as the giant crashed into Baldur. I heaved my wings even faster and jabbed my dagger into the back of the brute's head.

The giant's club struck Baldur across the forehead, and they both sprawled in the grass. Baldur's face was pale, blood streaking from the gash the club had opened. I couldn't tell if he was breathing.

"Idunn!" I shouted. My chest was clenching achingly tight around my lungs, but I didn't have time to make sure the light god was okay—that he was even alive. The rest of the gods hadn't managed to break through Surt's forces to get to him yet. It might take every one of us to make sure any of us survived.

With a wisp of relief, I caught sight of the skinny shimmering goddess slipping through the fray to Baldur. I threw myself back to the fringes of the battle.

As long as I wasn't in any of my gods' eyeline, I didn't have to worry they'd hesitate in their fighting to protect me. I'd been skirting the crowd, picking off draugr and the occasional giant that tried to come at the gods from behind. I just hadn't been quite fast enough to dispatch the bunch of attackers that had all run at Baldur at once.

Surt had ordered that charge—the light god must have been doing something to foil his plans. It hadn't looked like he'd finished yet. Panic had flashed across his face right before he'd fallen. The giant was still grappling with his warheads.

Surt hadn't paid much attention to me during this battle, either because I'd kept out of view or because he was too occupied with his new arsenal. I bashed my heel into a draug's skull, slashed the dagger Loki had given me through a giant's throat as if her flesh were butter, and peered at Surt through the milling bodies. He'd already tossed a couple of the warheads aside. Because Baldur had ruined them somehow?

As I watched, the fiery giant cursed and heaved another one out of the way. Muninn flung herself over the heads of his minions toward him, raven claws outstretched, and he paused just long enough to swipe his sword in her direction. She dodged, but the stream of fire veered after her. It smacked her head over heels, sending her tumbling to the ground. I winced. Let Idunn get to her in time too.

The swarm of attackers between our forces and the fiery giant pressed harder with sweeps of their own flaming blades, as if they meant to herd us right back up the bridge. Not a chance. I knocked two more draugr aside and found myself next to Heimdall.

The watchful god was breathing hard, his muscles rippling through his arms as he slammed his sword right through a draug's chest. "Wouldn't this be a good time for you and your devotees to work some of that valkyrie-merged magic?" he hollered at me.

I propelled myself up to smack my palm against a nearby giant's head and ripped the life energy from his body. "We can't," I snapped as the giant fell. "Baldur's down. The connection needs all five of us together. So, unless you want to finally give it a try with *your* magic..."

Heimdall's jaw clenched. He dispatched another draug. I was scanning the fray again, looking to see where I was needed and not really expecting him to answer, when he exhaled in a rush.

"Maybe I should."

Even as my gaze jerked to him with a startled stare, he was tapping Freyr's shoulder next to him, calling out to all the other gods around us. "We started to see some effect when we worked together before," he said. "Push forward on my word, moving at the same time, and I'll connect our efforts as well as I can. Ready? Now!"

He whipped his sword and swept his other arm through the air to signal their attack. The gods hurtled forward around him. A hum of energy rippled through the air, and Freya's bright magic leapt from blade to blade to Odin's spear. A streak of Hod's searing darkness caught around one of Skadi's arrows.

The effect wasn't quite as explosive as what my four gods had managed to produce before, but it added an extra punch that sent several of the giants stumbling backward. More draugr fell with their eerie groans. The gods pressed the momentary advantage they'd gained, slicing and blazing a path through our attackers toward the crest of the hill where Surt still held the highest ground.

My gaze found the giant, and my stomach flipped. He'd cast aside several of the warheads, but he was gripping a new one now, and a pleased smile was stretching across his gnarled bearded face. He leaned closer, sliding his hands over the metal casing, and bellowed at his army. "Hold them, slaughter them, make them pay!"

The words seemed to rally the draugr. They flung themselves at us even more ferociously, with no concern for themselves at all, as far as I could see. They existed for nothing except to serve the master who'd raised them.

The giants in the swarm roared, launching themselves at the nearest gods. I flapped my wings to lift out of reach of a stabbing sword and saw Loki leaping from the ground too—but four giants barged at him from all around, yanking him back. One of them burst into flames, and he slashed out at another.

The casing beneath Surt's hands started to glow.

The fiery giant's chuckle carried over the cries and clatter of the battle. My pulse hiccupped. In that instant, my awareness narrowed down to one simple fact: I had a straight line to the giant, and no one else did.

My throat closed up, and my fingers tightened around the handle of my dagger, but at the same time, Odin's words about acting if we saw our chance rose up in the back of my mind.

Maybe I was only a valkyrie and not a god, maybe this body could break much easier than any of those below me, but this was my realm. I would defend it with every ounce of my being, whether that was enough or not.

I threw myself forward, dagger raised, my other hand shooting to the pouch of well water Loki had given me. *Only the highest water can put out all the flames.* This had better be that water.

The wind shrieked in my ears. Surt's head jerked up, his lips parting in a triumphant snarl. His arm swung up to heave me back, but I wasn't aiming at him.

I slammed the dagger into the warhead's casing with all the strength and will in my body. The blade drove straight down through the metal. I splashed the contents of my pouch over the opening.

The glow that had infused the shell crackled away. Surt made a strangled sound and swung his fist at me. The first bash clocked me across the temple and sent me sprawling on the grass, my ears ringing. The giant lunged at me, a ball of hissing fire forming around his clenched hand—

—and the gods burst through his army.

The flames had only just seared my cheek when Thor hauled Surt back. A blast of shadow smacked into the giant's face. Surt fumbled for his sword, swiping at the darkness clinging to his eyes, but he couldn't get his bearings fast enough.

Odin loomed over the giant. With a bellow, the Allfather plunged the tip of his spear right through Surt's throat.

The giant's body went slack and crumpled to the ground between the useless shells of his warheads. His flaming bridge sizzled and snuffed out, leaving only the taint of smoke in the air. I stared at Surt's prone body, my own body tensed, half-expecting him to stir and rise.

Freya strode up to him, her eyes glinting fiercely and her golden hair flowing out behind her. She lifted her sword and swung it down to sever the giant's neck. His head rolled to the side, thumping into one of his missiles, eyes glazed and beard soaked through with blood.

My heart thudded for several beats before the reality of the moment hit me. He was done. Gone. We'd finally beaten him.

A slightly hysterical giggle bubbled in my chest. Loki dropped down from the sky next to me, touching the battered side of my head with a grimace. As I struggled to my feet through a wave of dizziness, the rest of the gods spun to take on the remains of Surt's army.

The draugr had frozen in place as their master died. They sagged as if as one, their bodies folding in on themselves, some of them—the older ones, I guessed—crumbling into dust. The couple dozen giants still standing gaped at the fallen draugr and their slain leader. They took in the flash of the gods' blades and the flare of their magic. And then they scattered, fleeing down the hill.

"Baldur?" I croaked. "Where is he? Is he all right?" If Surt's minions had killed him, I had to get to him in time to work my valkyrie magic. Even if my own head felt about ready to pop off my shoulders, the way it was throbbing.

Loki tucked a gentle arm around my waist and

walked me over to the place where the bright god had fallen. Baldur was sitting up, his forehead bruised but his blue eyes alert as Idunn straightened up over him. She'd managed to heal him. The air rushed from my lungs in relief.

"I think this one could use a little of your magic," Loki said, ruffling my hair gingerly. I grasped the side of his tunic as my relief merged into another rush of dizziness.

"Muninn needs healing too," I said raggedly.

A hoarse voice carried across the field. "I can wait. See to the valkyrie first." The raven woman was sitting up on the grass in her human form, hunched with one seared arm cradled in front of her but in good enough spirits to manage a tight smile.

Idunn nodded and moved to me. I sank down next to Baldur and let the goddess attend to my head.

"The warheads," I said to the bright god. "You did something to them so they wouldn't explode?"

"Most of them," Baldur said. "I couldn't quite— I used my light to melt the cores so they couldn't... shatter apart."

"You got enough of them to slow Surt down until we could reach him," I said, and paused. "Your light. The light of day?" The giggle I'd been suppressing broke from my throat. "Odin's visions came true."

Hod had come up behind us. He set a gentle hand on my head. "They always seem to," he said. "Like a light in the darkness, giving direction if not certainty. There's a reason he's led Asgard for so long, regardless of the complaints any of us might raise."

The other gods gathered around. When Idunn had healed me well enough that my skull didn't feel ready to crack open, she moved to Muninn.

Skadi meandered closer to us, her elbow pressed to her side where I'd seen her take a heavy blow. Baldur pushed himself to his feet to offer his own healing powers. The goddess of the hunt glanced down at me, her eyes gleaming sharp as ever. But her voice was hesitantly warm.

"You did all right out there, valkyrie. My respects."

A grin tugged at my lips. "Thank you."

Freya turned to her daughter, who had a raw scrape across her cheek. Hnoss stiffened, but she didn't back away when her mother set a cautious hand on her shoulder. No one seemed to know quite what else to say.

"What do we do now?" I said finally, to break the silence. "We're safe now, aren't we?"

"The giant of flames is felled," Odin said. "Midgard is saved, and Asgard belongs to the gods again."

"And he's left us with quite the reconstruction job up there," Loki said. "I foresee a great deal of scrubbing and stone-laying in our future."

"All of our futures?" Thor said. He glanced around at his fellow gods. "Will you come back to Asgard with us?"

The gods we'd gathered for our fight hesitated. Freyr swiped his hand across his mouth.

"I suppose now that we've reclaimed it, we might as well revisit the old realm," he said. "It was probably about time I stopped by and reinvigorated my powers."

"I don't expect I'll stay very long," Skadi put in.

"We wouldn't put demands on anyone," Freya said.

"But you *are* all welcome. It's your home as much as it is ours. We can return and make what repairs we need to, and then we'll see how we all feel. None of us could have planned for this... but perhaps the one good thing that's come of Surt's uprising is that it's given us a chance to find each other again." She gave her daughter a tentative smile. "To make long-needed amends."

"Then let us ascend," Odin said. With a thump of his spear and a sweep of his arm, he ushered forth the arc of his rainbow bridge.

26

Aria

The glittering ground shimmered brighter as Baldur poured more of his magic into it. The hollow patches that had formed in the crystal-like surface filled back in. The stretch of trees to our left seemed to shudder, their leaves glinting a richer green.

The god of light leaned back on his heels with a pleased smile. A week after our final battle with Surt, a faint pink mark still showed on his forehead where the one giant had bashed him. He'd told me he'd rather let it heal the rest of the way on its own. *Some things are better solved without rushing.*

"That's all there is to it," he said now, motioning to the shining landscape around us.

Alfheim, the realm of the light elves, lived up to its people's name, especially once Baldur had worked his restorative power. Everything glinted or gleamed, from the grass poking through the soil to the tops of the distant mountains.

"I'll come once every few days, like Hod has been doing for the dark elves, until the realm is stable again," Baldur went on. "And after that we'll have to make sure to come by and touch base with the light elves regularly, so that things don't start to run down again."

"They've been welcoming?" I asked.

He nodded. "Distant but appreciative. As the light elves tend to be." The corner of his mouth curled up. "I expect Thor's reception in Jotunheim will be much less friendly."

The thunder god was planning on dropping in on the land of giants after a little more time had passed. Approaching them too soon after the battles seemed more likely to stir up new conflicts than heal old wounds.

"They'd better appreciate him," I muttered. "They should be begging our forgiveness."

"The giants are as they are," Baldur said. "For all the troubles we've had with them, we've also mingled with them enough. Maybe if we hadn't neglected them so long as we did the other realms, Surt wouldn't have riled them up against us so easily."

And no one really wanted any of the nine realms to fall apart. Freya and Freyr had gone together to check in on their original home, Vanaheim, and to bring the news of their father's death. Skadi had offered to help as much as she could in Niflheim, the realm of constant winter, and Loki was lending some fire to Muspelheim, as much as it already seemed to have. *There's always a balance to be kept, pixie,* he'd told me with a smirk when I'd commented on that.

Odin himself had traveled at least once to the lowest realm, the land of the dead, where Loki's daughter, Hel, apparently still ruled. The Allfather hadn't said much on his return, but at least he *had* returned, so I guessed the visit couldn't have gone too horribly wrong.

There wasn't much I could contribute to healing the realms, but I'd been curious to see at least one of the gods at work. Maybe in part because it was about time I healed something that felt much more fragile.

Baldur glanced at me as he ambled closer to the trees. "Aren't you supposed to be taking that trip to Midgard soon?"

I dragged in a breath. "Yeah. I should probably be getting back. I told Hod I'd find him after he finished with the dark elves today."

I should have been relieved that this day had arrived, even excited, but instead my nerves were jumping, poking at my gut. Baldur stopped and touched the side of my face. "Whatever you decide to say, it'll be right. You know him better than anyone."

"I know," I said. "I just... He matters to me more than anyone."

"And you'll be there for him, just like you were meant to be." The god of light stroked his thumb over my cheek, and I bobbed up for a kiss. A little of his brightness flared through me, settling my nerves.

"Okay," I said. "I'm doing this. I'll see you tonight."

I slipped away through the trees to the gate that would lead me back to Asgard. The jolt through blackness that came with passing through was starting to feel familiar. I emerged onto Yggdrasil's branch and hurried along its trunk to the hearth entrance into Valhalla.

It wasn't hard to find Hod, because the dark god was already in the hall waiting for me. He turned at the sound of my steps over the hardwood floor. A smile crossed his face, so much more relaxed than the ones he'd been able to offer most of the time I'd known him. That fond expression made him so handsome my heart still skipped a beat, even though I'd been surrounded by divinely attractive gods for weeks now.

I'd talked to Baldur as if I were ready for what Hod and I had planned, but seeing him there, prepared to go, made my chest clench up all over again. I walked to him and wrapped my arms around him, escaping for a moment into his solid embrace.

"Hey," the dark god said, leaning his head next to mine. "You can take more time. We don't have to do this now."

"We do," I said. "I wish I hadn't left it as long as I already have. I just—what if it goes wrong?"

Memories from Muninn's prison flitted through my head—false ones of events she'd invented, but horrible all the same.

"That's why I'm coming," Hod said. "My magic can help smooth things over."

"Right." I breathed in his faintly smoky smell and found the determination to step back. "Odin didn't have any objections?"

"He seemed to like the idea, actually," Hod said. "He should be waiting for us at the edge of the courtyard now.

I think you've managed to win him over with all that tough love, valkyrie."

I elbowed him in mock-offense, and he chuckled as we headed out of the hall of warriors.

The Allfather was indeed already standing at the far end of the main courtyard. At the sight of us, he swept out his arm, and the rainbow bridge leapt from the land's edge toward the realm below. His ability to direct Bifrost to any end point he wanted was going to make this a much shorter trip than if we'd had to find our way from Yggdrasil's gate.

"Go well and return at peace," Odin intoned as if delivering a prophecy. I'd be happy to take those words as one.

"Thank you," I said, and he tipped his broad-brimmed hat to us—a new one that was no longer burnt but somehow just as rumpled as the old one had been.

I extended my wings so I could take the trip over the bridge faster. Now that we were going, I didn't want to drag out the journey. Hod glided along beside me on a patch of shadow, and we followed the curve of the rainbow bridge down into the clouds.

We came out over a residential neighborhood, all pastels and steepled roofs, quiet in the early hours of the morning. My heart thumped faster as we made our way toward the house I'd stared at for so long in the past and in my memories.

"Take your time, and let me know if you need anything else from me," Hod said. "I'll stay out of the way and follow the plan we discussed."

We came to a stop by the bedroom window at the

back of the house. The light was still on, a pale yellow glow filling the room. My little brother sat cross-legged on his foster home's bed, a chapter book open on his lap, a dragon-shaped pillow tucked under one of his skinny arms. Not quite as skinny as it had been a few weeks ago when we'd whisked him away from my mother's house. That sight gave me a little burst of confidence.

Leaving him had been hard and had caused us both some pain, but it'd been better than the alternatives. And now I could make amends.

I came to rest on the window ledge and readied myself. Then I willed myself visible and knocked lightly on the wooden frame.

Petey glanced up. His blue-gray eyes widened when he saw me—all of me, wings included. He blinked as if he thought I might disappear if he cleared his gaze.

"Hey," I said softly through the screen. "Petey. May I come in?"

Petey's mouth opened and closed and opened again. He didn't look frightened so much as startled and uncertain. I could handle that.

"Who are you?" he said. "How do you know my name?"

"Don't you remember me?" I said with a quick glance toward Hod, who was hovering beside me invisibly. "It's Ari. Your imaginary friend."

Hod made a delicate motion with his hand. He was the one who'd shadowed most of Petey's memories in the first place. Now he was lifting that veil just a little, just enough for some of my brother's memories of me to seep through, without the full context of who I was or where we'd known each other.

"Ari," Petey murmured, and recognition lit in his eyes. The smile that sprang to his face was so bright it brought tears to my eyes. I swiped them away quickly as he darted over to the window.

"So, can I come in, buddy?" I asked.

"Of course," he said, still staring at me. I detached the screen carefully with a nudge of my valkyrie strength and set it on the floor inside next to the window. Then I climbed in, keeping my wings close to my back.

I hadn't been sure how much my brother would trust me, coming to him like this, with his memories still so fractured. I hadn't wanted to push for more than he was comfortable with. But the second my feet hit the floor, Petey flung his arms around my waist, squeezing me tight. He pressed his face to my chest.

"I was scared," he said in a ragged voice. "I thought—I couldn't remember anything from before. I didn't know anything. Why haven't you come in so long? What happened?"

I knelt down in front of him, blinking hard to hold back any further tears, and set my hands on his shoulders as I held his gaze.

"You were in danger," I said. I'd practiced my explanation so many times the words came automatically. "There were people who wanted to hurt you. Now they're gone, but they—they wanted you to forget everything."

It was easier to blame his clouded mind on our enemies than to try to explain why I'd needed to do it. I wouldn't have needed to take that step if it hadn't been for Surt and his minions anyway—and I still needed to protect Petey from our mother and the men she'd let shove him around.

"I had to make sure they were completely beaten before I came to see you again," I added. "But now they are. You're totally safe. You're happy here, aren't you?"

"Yeah," Petey said. "Brenda and Stuart—they say I can call them Mom and Dad if I feel like it, but I don't know yet—they're really nice. But I knew there was someone I was missing. I knew there had to be." His hands closed around my arms. "You don't feel imaginary."

"Well, I'll tell you a little secret." I dropped my voice. "I'm only imaginary to everyone else. To you, I'm totally real. You're the only one I want to let see me, because you're special."

He looked up at my wings, open down above my back, and knit his brow. "Did you always have wings?"

I swallowed a laugh. Those wouldn't have figured into any of his memories. "I did. I just wasn't sure if you'd think they were too strange. But you don't mind them, do you?"

"No," he said with an awed expression. "I think they're awesome. Can I grow wings too?"

I did laugh out loud then. "No, kiddo. But you don't need them. They come with the whole imaginary friend thing." I brushed my fingers down the side of his pale face, my heart aching. I wanted to just hold him for an hour, but there were certain boundaries I had to keep. He needed to stay focused on his real life. I needed to accept that I was never going to be as much a part of that real life as I'd used to be.

But I could still be a part of it, even if only a small one.

"I can't stay much longer," I told him. "I just wanted to let you know that I'm still here. I've looked out for you since the day you were born, Petey, and I'll be here for you all through the rest of your life. I'll come talk to you now and then, but if you ever need me right away, stick something red over your windowsill, okay? I'll come as soon as I see it."

Petey nodded. "Okay. You don't have to leave *right* now, do you?"

I swallowed the lump in my throat. "No. Not quite yet. Come here?"

He nestled into my arms again, and I did hold him, even if it was only for five minutes instead of the hour I'd have preferred. Then I kissed his forehead and stood up.

"I'll see you soon," I said. "You'd better get to bed. Remember, no matter what happens, you'll always have me."

"Thank you, Ari," he said, beaming.

It took all my self-control to walk back to the window and clamber out. Hod pulled me straight into a hug. I ducked my head into the crook of his neck and let out a sob Petey could no longer hear.

"That was perfect," the dark god said, stroking his hand over my hair. "You gave him everything he needed."

I wanted to protest. If I'd led the life I'd meant to before I died, I'd have given Petey a home myself, been everything he needed in a parent. But he did have everything he needed here too. And the fact was that if I hadn't died and gotten swept up into this godly mess, maybe Surt would have conquered Midgard after all.

It was hard to have any real regrets, knowing that.

"Time to head back?" Hod asked when I'd gotten a grip on my emotions.

"Actually," I said, "there was one other thing I wanted to do first. It'll just be a little detour."

We arrived back in Asgard with both of us laden down with bulging takeout bags. The smells wafting out of them already had my mouth watering. Hod grinned at me as we carted our loads over to the hall that was now mine.

Loki was standing outside his own hall with a few of the other gods who'd lingered on in Asgard at least for a little while. Freyr was laughing at something the trickster had said, clapping him on the shoulder with amusement that looked genuine. Hnoss made a wild gesture that got Idunn giggling too, and Loki waved her off with mock-horror that quickly broke with a chuckle. His eyes gleamed so eagerly I almost choked up all over again.

They were treating him like an equal. Like a friend—like someone who belonged here in Asgard. I could tell from the tension that lingered in his posture that the trickster wasn't quite sure whether to relax into their acceptance yet. After all that time when they'd shunned him, it'd probably take a while before he could completely believe they weren't going to change their minds all over again. But those last few battles, the truths Odin had shared, and the sacrifice Loki had made to save the rest of us had shifted the balance between him and the gods in a way I suspected would last.

He caught sight of us and left the others after giving Freyr a playful nudge. His eyebrows arched with curiosity as he sauntered over. "You've brought back quite the haul."

"I brought back dinner," I said. "A real Midgard dinner, not a bunch of convenience store junk. Can you find Thor and Baldur and remind them we were supposed to eat together?"

"I doubt the Thunderer will have forgotten where he's getting his next meal," Loki said with a wink, and sped off on his enchanted shoes.

By the time the trickster returned with the other two gods in tow, I'd spread out our feast along with bottles of mead on the hall's ridiculously large dining table. I could have seated all the current inhabitants of Asgard around it, but I wanted to share tonight just with my four.

Thor strode in and immediately caught me by the waist with an epic hug. "What do we have here?" he asked, bending over me.

"Chinese takeout," I announced. "From my favorite restaurant in Philly. I got three roast ducks just for you."

Thor let out a rumble of a laugh and tipped my chin up for a kiss. "A woman after my own heart."

My pulse leapt at the brush of his lips against mine and the thought of things I'd meant to say tonight. But maybe I'd save that until after we'd eaten. "I thought this heart was already mine," I teased, poking his chest when he released me.

"You know it is, Ari," he murmured, his voice so low my knees wobbled.

"Was the rest of your trip a success?" Loki asked as we grabbed plastic forks and dug in. He kept his usual light tone, but he was watching me carefully. He knew how much my visit to Petey had meant to me.

"I think so," I said. "He accepted the story once he had whatever memories Hod brought back. He's got that reassurance now—that someone from his past life is still around and looking after him. I think it's the best way I could have stayed in his life given..." I waved to my wings before pulling them into my back.

"Here's to you and your brother, then," the trickster said, lifting his glass of mead. "And to Hod, for his deft magic. Ah, why not to his brothers too? I'm sure you two are good for something or other." He smirked good-naturedly.

Hod shook his head with a wry smile and jostled Loki on purpose as he moved past him to grab the chow mein.

Baldur swallowed a mouthful of lemon chicken with a blissful expression and gazed around the table at us. "I think this is really it," he said. "We've found our peace. No more attacks, no more enemies known or unknown."

"You never know," Loki said, waggling a finger. "The raven may change her mind and challenge Odin for rule of Asgard yet."

I laughed. "I think ruling anywhere is the last thing Muninn wants." The raven woman had looked about as content as I'd ever seen her the few times she'd dropped in on us in human form in the past week, but mostly she seemed to be reveling in her freedom, out from under every thumb that had ever pinned her down.

"It is good," Thor said, slinging his arm around the bright god. "We deserve a little peace after all that strife. And I mean it when I say there's no one other than the four of you I'd rather enjoy that peace with."

"Although we do have another couple guests arriving," Hod remarked, his head coming up at a sound from down the hall. He turned to me. "I hope you don't mind. We told Odin he could stop by—he wanted to speak with you after you returned from Midgard. I don't think he expects any of the dinner."

"Oh," I said. "Okay." I *had* wanted this to be just the five of us, but if Odin wasn't going to stay long, I guessed it didn't matter.

What did the Allfather want with me now? I might not have been as irritated with him as I had been during the first period in which I'd known him, but we weren't exactly chummy.

I set down my fork as Odin and Freya appeared in the dining room doorway. The Allfather's singular gaze settled on me at once. "Aria," he said. "Thank you for receiving us. I was hoping we could have a word." He motioned me over to him.

My legs balked for a second. I made myself walk over. What could be wrong? Freya wouldn't be smiling like that if they'd come with bad news, I didn't think.

I stopped in front of Odin, feeling suddenly awkward, aware of the four gazes behind me directed my way, including the blind one. Odin peered down at me, his deep brown eye as penetrating as always.

"The patchwork valkyrie," he said, leaning a little of his weight onto his spear. "I've given the matter of your existence a lot of thought in the time since we ended Surt's rebellion. The truth of it is, there's a reason I dismissed those who lived in Valhalla quite some time ago. Well, several reasons. But the most relevant one at this moment is, I don't have much need for a valkyrie. There is no one in Valhalla to serve, and I have no interest in beginning a new collection of risen warriors."

"All right," I said. My spine had stiffened. Why was he saying all this? He wasn't going to send me off to make my own way through the realms, was he?

"Dear one," Freya said, squeezing her husband's arm. "Less rambling, more getting to the important part? You're worrying her."

Odin made a face that looked almost apologetic. "My point is that I'm hoping you can contribute more than the valkyries of old used to. You already intend to return to Midgard regularly to check in on your brother. I would like, if you would accept the responsibility—and the honor—to name you the official overseer of that realm."

I stared at him. "I—what?"

"It would be your duty to check in on all the areas of Midgard as you have time to," Odin said. "Seeing as you can come and go as you please via Valhalla, there is no one better suited. And you understand that realm in its current state better than any of us, even the gods who've been living there but at a distance from humans for ages. You would simply watch over humanity and let us know if you saw any trouble with which you felt we should intervene."

An eager shiver ran through me. I wouldn't just be a hanger-on in Asgard, living among the gods but without any real role. I'd be working alongside them to oversee the realms like an equal. For the second time in as many hours, tears started to prickle at the backs of my eyes.

"Of course I'll take that responsibility," I said. "And the honor. It is one. Overseer of Midgard." I couldn't help grinning. "It's perfect."

Odin brushed his fingertips over my forehead. "Then consider it done. I expect you will do Asgard credit. Now I will leave the five of you to your feasting."

He swept back down the hall. Freya blew me a kiss and followed. I turned, a little dazed, and found all four of my gods beaming at me in kind of a knowing way. A suspicion wriggled through my mind.

"This was your idea," I said. "You suggested it to him."

Loki shrugged. "I will neither confirm nor deny. Whoever's idea it may have been, it was an excellent one, don't you agree?"

"We wouldn't want you getting bored of Asgard—and of us," Hod said.

"As if *that* could ever happen," I said, rolling my eyes. "I just never thought..."

"Never thought what?" Baldur asked gently.

My voice snagged in my throat for a moment before I could force the words out. "I never thought I'd ever do anything that would really make a difference."

A wave of the emotion I'd been trying to hold in

rushed over me. I dropped my face into my hands. My gods were around me in an instant, their arms encircling me, their heads bowed together toward mine.

"You've already made a difference," Hod said, rubbing my arm. "A huge one. You know that, don't you, Ari?"

All I could do was nod. I twined my arms with theirs, leaning into Thor's brawny chest, absorbing their mingling scents. Right then, I could have believed almost anything.

The words I thought I might struggle with tumbled out of me as if I'd said them a dozen times already. Which maybe I had, silently, in my head. "I love you. All of you. *You* know that, don't you?"

I looked up at Thor, gripped his hand. "I love you." I met Baldur's eyes next, cupped his jaw. "I love you." I let my hand come to rest on Loki's tunic over the heart that still beat because of my powers. "I love you." I turned to Hod, leaning close enough to brush a kiss against his cheek. "I love you."

"I think the bond between all of us runs deep enough that I can say without a doubt that we all love you," Baldur said. "Our valkyrie."

My smile came back. "My gods."

Thor dipped his head to nip the crook of my neck. "Worth saying all the same. I love you."

Loki teased a flicker of flame along my waist with his lithe hand. "I love you."

Hod trailed his fingers across my shoulder, nudging the strap of my tank top down my arm. "I love you."

Baldur eased a step closer. "I love you," he

murmured, his mouth grazing mine. Then he was kissing me, his light washing over all of us, twining with Thor's sparks and Loki's fire and Hod's shadows. All the elements that had made me who I was now.

I tugged them all closer, wanting to feel them around me in every possible way.

I'd found my freedom too. The freedom to shed all the scars of the past that had held me back so long. The freedom to enjoy love given and to offer it back in return. The freedom to construct a new life out of the gifts I'd been given, one that could change the very course of the world toward something better.

I would do myself proud—myself and the gods I loved.

ABOUT THE AUTHOR

Eva Chase lives in Canada with her family. She loves stories both swoony and supernatural, and strong women and the men who appreciate them. Along with the Their Dark Valkyrie series, she is the author of the Witch's Consorts series, the Dragon Shifter's Mates series, the Demons of Fame Romance series, the Legends Reborn trilogy, and the Alpha Project Psychic Romance series.

Connect with Eva online:
www.evachase.com
eva@evachase.com